Comes The Retribution

James R. Elstad

Book Cover designed by Ronnell Porter and Mary D. Scott
www.SpiritDrivenEvents.com

Library of Congress Cataloging-in-Publication Data available upon request.

ISBN-13: 978-1499798647
ISBN-10: 1499798644

Printed in the United States of America

June 2014

DEDICATION

To: My wife, Bonniejean, who was my best friend and supporter; my children (the lights of my life): Amber, Shannon, Peter, and Chris; my grandchildren (the shining stars in my life): Laura, Emily, Victoria, Juliet, and Liam; and to the family I grew up with: Linda, Rita, David, and Donna, and most of all, to my Mom and Dad, who made me what I am.

ACKNOWLEDGMENTS

Editor: Mike Foley; **Critique Group:** Suzanne and Willard Brumbaugh, Robert Foster, Loralie Kay, Marilyn Ramirez, Amanda Smith, Mary Thompson, and Richard Zone; **Research Support:** Alex Delannoy, Mike Douglas, and Lochlain Seabrook; **Website and Book Publishing:** Mary D. Scott

First Book in the series by James R. Elstad:
Comes The Southern Revolution

"Very imaginative treatment of Civil War in modern times"
- William Creed, Author

Comes The Retribution

James R. Elstad

TABLE OF CONTENTS

PROLOGUE – Comes The Retribution

In "Comes The Southern Revolution," General Robert E. Lee wanted his grandson to get an education on how to handle his finances. Contrary to Lee's instructions, the twelve men he chose to educate the boy manipulated him to believe that "He really wants us to resume 'Mr. Lincoln's War.'

Several times during the ensuing decades, succeeding "Councils" planned to follow through with their supposed mandate. But events on the world stage, The Spanish-American War, World War I, The Great Depression, World War II, The Korean War, and The Vietnam War, forced the postponement of their plans to drive the Federal Occupation Forces from Dixie.

In 1972, upon graduation from West Point, Second Lieutenant Jefferson Hampton Lee was called to his grandfather's mansion and was informed of his legacy. Reluctant at first, Lee worked relentlessly to fulfill his destiny.

Over the next forty-four years, using his military connections, he organized a vast conspiracy of interest groups into small cells. Some were aware of the true goal. Others thought and believed their benefactor was a true believer in their cause who wanted to remain anonymous.

During the 2016 Primary Election Campaign, speculation had it that General Lee would run for President against Vice President Larry Gressette. In reality, he became the first President of "The Republic Of America."

The Saturday after the "Super South Primary," in which Lee and Gressette were the front-runners in every state, Lee sponsored a Conference (at four different locations throughout the South). Most Federal military members, above the rank of Colonel, were required to attend. As the officers arrived and registered, they were informed they had a message from their office. They were taken to a room where they could talk in "private." After a member of the Federal brass was captured, the Rebels had one of their own to take

i

his place.

While all this was happening, Lee launched a two pronged attack. The first was when three US Navy Carrier groups were supposedly having a war game. The premise was that a lone nuclear sub was to attempt to sink as many of each task force's ships as possible. The second was when the Rebels attempted to over-power seven nuclear submarines.

Everything went extremely well. In the end, with the help of the "Knights Of The Golden Circle," the Rebels removed sixty-five cargo truck-loads of gold bullion from Ft. Knox, disabled the three carrier groups as planned, and apprehended six of the seven submarines they tried to capture.

In the next several months, combatants on both sides fought for their God and their country.

Toward the end, it appeared the Federals had the upper hand. They had recovered from the initial shock, and launched an attack with stealth gliders that caught the Rebel leaders off-guard. Then, when they overran General Lee's Headquarters in Rock Hill, SC, it appeared that with General Lee dead of an apparent heart attack, and the rest of the Council dead or fleeing for their lives, that the ROA was finished.

Things weren't what they seemed. Bobby Lee, General Lee's last surviving grandson, and the new heir-apparent, had escaped in a small aircraft from an underground hanger.

ALPHA – The Blockade
(Late September)

Art rotated the periscope on the Rebel Submarine Dallas. He listened to the sounds of his crew, and the chatter over the intercom. *Everything's running smoothly. This operation should clinch it. Soon we'll have the Federals on their knees.* He heard footsteps. Without taking his eyes off the scope, he said, "Lieutenant, You're late, I need answers, what do you have?"

Guzman stammered, "Sir, my team is working on the details as we speak."

The periscope handles clanked as Art collapsed them against the stem. He turned, and then pointed over his shoulder and demanded. "I need answers now! Your target is out there, waiting for you."

Just because he did well last time, doesn't mean he can do it again. I have to keep the pressure on. He jabbed a finger at the young Marine officer and continued, "The surface fleet will sink two captured civilian vessels under the span. Hopefully the ships will hit bottom in such a way as to obstruct traffic. Prior to that, your divers need to place their charges on the base of each tower. They are to set their explosives for the prescribed time and return. When you perform your mission, the bridge will blow up thirty minutes later. If the two sunken vessels don't block shipping, the bridge wreckage will."

A Rebel Coast Guard officer stood next to the Marine, and ruffled papers on his clipboard. Art turned and said, "Lieutenant what does your commander plan to do?"

The six-foot-five-inch Rebel officer leaned over the chart and pointed to a grid square. "My Captain will bring our cutter, disguised as a Federal ship, close to the oil tanker. He paused and referred to a list, "The Exxon Fairbanks,' at approximately 1800 hours tomorrow night, I'll lead the boarding party. We'll use the recent Singapore Flu outbreak as a ruse to get aboard. The other ship will be led by. . ." Again he referred to his notes, "Ensign Watkins. She will use the same ploy on the Maersk Amsterdam containership.

"Once aboard I'll have the Captain assemble the crew. We'll give them an injection. In reality it's a sedative that will knock them out. My team will transport them to our ship. I'll pilot the craft to the designated coordinates and scuttle it. Watkins' crew should be right behind. We expect to complete our task at low tide, approximately 0333. The depth of the channel under the bridge varies from 45-100 feet." He pointed to Guzman. "Lieutenant, if your charges go off, at 0600, you might catch some Federal rescue ships in your explosion."

Art smiled at the image in his mind *that'll be sweet, two ships blowing up in the channel*. "Excellent, tell your Commander that's what I wanted. Review everything with my XO, and then go back to your ship." Then he focused on the Marine Officer, "Who's going to replace your Gunny after his appendicitis attack?"

"Staff Sergeant Jessica Haines is next in line."

Art scowled as he turned, "Why her? Just because she did well in the Lexington attack, doesn't mean that she can handle this critical mission. You know how I feel about women in combat." He pointed over his shoulder and outside the boat at the bridge three miles away. Then, at a chart, "I need your teams here, here, and here, by 2100. I need the charges set by 0100. Can you guarantee it? It's risky using someone as green as Haines."

Guzman gulped and choked as he swallowed his chaw of tobacco. "Sir, she's the best Marine I have. How close can you get us?"

Several officers nearby stared, wide-eyed, while Guzman confronted the Captain.

Guzman continued, "Last April you got us two hundred yards closer than we trained for. That enabled us to succeed." He tapped on the paper in front of him. "This operations order doesn't state how close you plan get us. We'll fail if the Federal Coast Guard gets to us before we complete the mission."

Art pushed his glasses back up the bridge of his nose and scratched his chin; *he pulled it off last time. I'll give him what he wants, but he's gonna have to work for it.* "How much time do you need?"

Guzman sighed and looked at his watch, "Like I said, my team's going over your draft operations order as we speak. I'll have an answer for you by 1400. I'm thinking, two teams, and two divers." He stared into the Captain's eyes. "With all due respect Sir, last time, we got away with it because they weren't looking for us. Now," he took a deep breath, "we don't know if they're expecting us or not. I need as much as you can give me."

Art surveyed the conning tower. When his eyes came back to Guzman, he said, "We've stretched the Federals' resources to the limit. Our plan to blockade the entire Federal coastline will break their resolve. President Gressette plans on getting their surrender in a matter of weeks, if not days."

Art put his hands on the table, "Tell me, how the new hi-tech face masks are working out. What was causing all the headaches?"

Apparently relieved that he wasn't in the hot seat anymore, Guzman relaxed and set his notes on the counter. "Sir, it seems the headaches are a normal reaction. If a diver focuses on the data layer at the bottom of their mask, it causes headaches. We had to train everyone to only glance, not stare at the data they need. The factory rep told us the migraines are normal when divers focus on the numbers for more than ten seconds."

Art rolled up several charts, and said, "Good, we're counting on those masks to help your teams get to your targets."

He put the charts on a shelf and turned his head back to the Marine. "After I review all aspects of your plan I'll let you know." He stood. "Dismissed."

#####

Attention on the Boat. Attention on the Boat. Turn your attention to the nearest monitor. We have a video you need to see before we start our next mission.

A picture of Bobby appeared on screens throughout the vessel. Although he tried to hide the fact, it was apparent that he was in a hurry.

I'd like to take this time to address all members of our naval fleet as you embark on this important mission. In the next few hours we need you to focus on completing all tasks your commanders have given you. This is a crucial time for us. The Federals think they have us on the ropes. I admit it's not over, we haven't won yet. But if you successfully blockade all Yankee seaports it will definitely mark the beginning of the end. You have the fate of our nation, the fate of our struggle in your hands. Don't fail me now."

Bobby stood at attention and gave a Rebel salute. "I salute each and every one of you for the sacrifices you've made and what you're about to accomplish. I wish you God speed and good luck."

#####

Guzman smiled as he scanned the water around him. He heard static over his headset. He adjusted a dial with his tongue. *This is cool. I like these new under water radios. I can do everything inside my mask.* As his power scooter headed north, he listened to his team's chatter.

"This is going to be easy."

"Don't get cocky Corporal. Just 'cause we have the upper hand so far, doesn't mean we are. . . ."

Guzman, cut into their conversation, "Knock off the chatter. You know the drill, no unnecessary communications."

The wayward Rebels meekly responded, "Yes, Sir."

As they headed toward their target, the sound of his breathing and the purring of the Mark-25 power scooter was the only thing he heard. Both teams sped in opposite directions toward their assignment. He viewed Rebel Staff Sergeant Haines' scooter heading south. As team two moved out of his line of sight, he glanced at her course through the data line on his mask, and noticed they had drifted. "Team 2, you're drifting, get back on course."

Jessica's calm voice came over his headset, "Got it, Sir."

"Pay attention young lady, we have a lot riding on this." Then Guzman focused on his partner.

#####

Monica and her radio operator ran to their up-armored Hummer. She jumped into the passenger seat and quickly buckled her seatbelt. "Tell me Lieutenant, how did you get assigned to this mission? I thought they'd send an enlisted soldier."

"Until last year, when all this started, I was a radio operator, in the middle of Officer Candidate School." He turned the ignition switch on and while he waited for the glow plug to warm up, he fastened his safety harness. As soon as the engine turned over he stepped on the accelerator and the vehicle lurched across the parking lot.

Ma'am, I understand you want to stop off at the north side of the bridge. Any particular spot?"

Monica focused her binos on the bridge span five miles away *why couldn't I have met this guy at a party? Oh well, duty calls.* "Yes, go past the visitor's center, and down by the maintenance shed. I want to get to the lighthouse that's at the base of the north tower."

The young officer maneuvered their vehicle through the early evening traffic. "You got it Boss. I've never been to the lighthouse. Do you know the way?"

She took her eyes away from her glasses and glanced at her fellow officer, and gave him a *What do you think I am, stupid? Look.* She resumed her search of the bridge. "A good officer evaluates every aspect of the mission before she moves out. Of course I know the way, and I have the gate keys."

As they pulled onto the bridge both looked out for anything unusual. "Her driver rambled on, "Yep, I graduated first in my class. For generations my family has had an officer in the Army. It all started with the Civil War."

Monica listened to her radio operator ramble on.

". . . I was the lead Exercise Team Member into the compound. I carried ninety-five pounds of gear and then my rifle. . . ."

Her mind drifted as he continued to brag. Now he asked a direct question.

"Listen, Gorgeous, how come we never dated before? I know we can make beautiful music together."

Oh brother, we're on a mission. How did you come up with that line? The next thing you'll do is put your hand on my knee and move on up my thigh.

No sooner did she complete the thought, when he followed through.

She shoved his hand aside, "Buddy, you have no idea who you're dealing with. I'm warning you. Keep your hands to yourself."

The tall man appeared to be taken aback at her response. "What did you expect? We have plenty of time." He leaned over, and stroked her cheek.

Monica grabbed his finger and bent it.

He screamed. Their vehicle drifted over a lane as he reacted to the pain.

Through her clenched teeth she said, "I told you, you don't know who you're dealing with." Then she released his digit and he yanked his hand away. "Now pull in front of the gate. I'll open it."

Tires slid on the gravel. Monica jumped out and ran to the entrance. She unlocked the chain and pushed the frame away from her. As the Hummer moved alongside, she jumped back in, the door bounced away from the body of the truck. She grabbed it and secured the latch.

"Park outside the next gate. Then bring your radio to the west side of the lighthouse. Check in with headquarters. Let them know we're onsite."

Still rubbing his finger, a subdued Lieutenant nodded, "Roger that."

As she fumbled with her rucksack, she checked the area out. "Aha, here it is." She pulled a pair of small night vision goggles out of a multi-colored bag, and opened the case. She put the headset on, and scanned the base of the north tower.

"For your information, *Lover Boy,* I'm the Coast Guard equivalent of a Navy Seal. You're here because my partner got sick on our way over. I stopped in at your headquarters and requested a radio operator. Now sit back, stay out of my way, and do your job."

The officer's jaw dropped, he sat, wounded, speechless, rubbed his dislocated finger, and then setup his equipment.

She turned and checked the base of both towers for activity. "We got a tip the Rebels might try to destroy the Golden Gate Bridge, I've been tasked to be on the lookout." Suddenly she turned her goggles back to a section she'd passed over. "Hello, that power scooter wasn't there before."

She half-stood, and then crawled to a better vantage point. "Gotcha, you Rebels, looks like two divers on the north tower, one's used a rope to get onto some girders. The other's at the base. She turned her attention to the south tower. "Aha, I see a wet suit climbing up the tower, and another at the base. Her eyes flared with anger. "Too bad my sister's not with you. I'd give her what for." She turned and said to her radioman. "My twin sister Jessica's been entangled with the Rebels for years. Even though some of our ancestors belonged to *The Knights of The Golden Compass,* nobody in the family knew about her activity. Daddy was furious that a farm girl from Michigan would be a Rebel." *If I ever meet up with her, I'll show her a thing or two.*

She pointed to the pistol in his holster. "I hope you know how to use that. If anyone but me comes back, shoot them in the legs. I want them alive."

She took the microphone from the radioman's hand and spoke. "Fox 1, this is Searchlight 4. Spotted activity, going to investigate, send reinforcements, I'm at the lighthouse by the north tower." She peered at the other tower. "Looks like another scooter on the other base. Suggest you send a chopper to check it out. Gotta go. The noise from waves should muffle my activity." She unslung her carbine and handed it to the young man. Then started off.

8

#####

She crawled onto the base of the north tower. *There's a diver on the west side, and one moving up on this side. I'll go after the guy above first.* She pulled a pair of gloves from a cargo pocket. After putting them on she jumped up and grabbed the rope that was swaying in the breeze. When she reached the top of a girder, she paused to catch her breath. *He's six sections above. Hopefully he will stop before I run out of gas.*

She twisted the rope around a leg and hoisted herself up. *Focus now, the wind should cover the sound of me coming up.*

Twenty minutes later the Rebel diver hoisted his bag of mines and tied it to a girder. He climbed inside the tower. As he placed his third mine, Monica came from behind. Startled, he flinched.

As he fell, her dagger pierced the Yankee's side. He slipped through her grasp and his head caught between two beams, breaking his neck.

As she watched his body thrash in the throes of death, she wiped his blood off her dagger. *One down, one to go.* Then started back down.

#####

Guzman pulled his scooter onto the shore as his teammate moved toward his assignment. He placed his fifth charge then heard a footstep behind him, turned and saw Monica, crouched with one knee on the ground, her head sticking out from around a corner of the tower.

"Hold it right there. Don't move. I just caught one of your friends by surprise."

Guzman appeared to be shocked. "What?"
"I suggest you stop what you're doing and back away."

9

As he stared down the barrel of Monica's pistol, Guzman, for the first time in his life, faced death.

Shouts came from the lighthouse. Ten minutes later, the Federal troops Monica had sent for led Guzman away. She approached the petty-officer-in-charge, "I need you to wrap everything up. Headquarters is sending a team to the other tower. I'm taking the traitor's wet suit, tanks, and their scooter. There's a rebel sub out there somewhere, I'll use their GPS to find it. Tell Chief I'm going locate that boat. I'll radio when I have information."

"Yes, Ma'am. Will do." He saluted, and called out to his crew, "We're pulling out as soon as the body is loaded. EOD's going to take care of the charges on this tower." He turned and said, "Ma'am, are you sure you want to do this? What're you going to do? You're one woman against a submarine full of rebels."

Monica looked out to sea, "It's the least I can do. I have to make up for all the damage my sister's done." With that she reached down, picked up Guzman's sack of charges, zipped up the borrowed wetsuit, dipped the mask in the water, and put it on. She pushed the scooter into the bay.

Hello, what's this? There's a data line of some sort at the base of the mask. Wow! Compass heading, remaining oxygen, depth, and water temp. When she reached fifty feet, Monica let go of one of the scooter's hand grips and pressed it against the mask. *Where's this headache coming from?* She shook her head as if that would eliminate the pain.

She felt a little better as she focused on the direction the scooter was going. She felt the hum of the motor through her hands, and gazed at the GPS. *That's not too far. The homing feature should take me straight to it. I can make it in no time. What have we here?* She glanced at the stenciling on the side of the underwater vehicle. *This scooter belongs to the Dallas. That's Jessica's boat.*

As the craft scurried toward its home, Monica secured a bag of charges to an empty hand-hold and opened it. She pulled out a charge; *I've used this model before. I'll set the timer on these for twenty minutes. I should be at the sub in ten, that'll give me time to get away.*

#####

Jessica checked her watch and called out to her partner, "Five minutes, hurry it up."

Her companion shouted out from above, "Comin' Sarge just setting the last one, there that's it."

Soon Jessica's team slid into the water, and headed back to their vessel.

Twenty minutes later the second squad's scooter approached the bow of their boat. Jessica called out over the radio. "Check it out. Is that Guzman I see under the hull? What's he. . ."

The other diver interrupted. "Unless he's had a sex change operation since we left, it's not Guzman. That's a girl."

Jessica did a double-take, "Good eyes, Corporal." *Let's see, female diver, Monica's stationed nearby.* "Listen up." Her voice grew firmer, "She's mine." She tapped the other diver and motioned for him to get in place.

"Sergeant, I need you to watch the Federal and myself. Give me room to maneuver."

Monica's voice crackled over everyone's headset. "You're too late dear sister. You don't have enough time to disarm the mines I set. Now, if you don't mind I think I'll leave."

While she talked Monica had swum toward her power scooter. Jessica resumed control of her vessel and was upon her sister before she could get hers to full power.

11

Jessica's partner flanked Monica as the two women divers prepared for battle. Both unsheathed their weapons. Jessica called out, "Hey, Mon. I wondered if we'd ever meet."

"Well, I've been praying for the opportunity to regain our family honor."

The two combatants parried, "You always were the spiritual one. Weren't you?"

Ignoring her sister's taunts, Monica blinked and shook her head. *Why's this headache coming back?*

Immediately they were engulfed in a battle for their lives. The other Rebel diver kept his distance, apparently not because he didn't want to get involved, he couldn't tell which diver was friend or foe.

Sensing her chance, Jessica lunged forward, sliced her sister's airline and put a knife to Monica's side. "Sergeant, give me a hand." Then she focused on her sibling, "Fight me and I'll make you suffer. We're close to an airlock, hold your breath, you can make it. Daddy wouldn't like it if I killed you."

To ensure her cooperation, the male diver put a hand on Monica's shoulder. Jessica led both to the open airlock. "Steady now, Yankee, don't fight me. We'll get you some air real soon."

As soon as her team was on board, Jessica leaned on a bulkhead and composed herself as her body trembled.

A corpsman ran to her side. "Jessie? Are you okay?"

"Yeah, I'm fine. Get her to the Brig." She turned toward her partner. Go back out there. I'll have the Chief send as many other divers as he can to help you. See if she placed any mines on our hull. I'm going to report to the Captain."

She grabbed a towel from a shelf, ran it through her short hair, tossed it into a hamper, and hurried off. *What a coup! How was Monica able to overpower Guzman? He was the best hand-to-hand fighter we had.* She grabbed another towel from a shelf and headed toward the conning tower. Five minutes later she stood in front of Art.

"Staff Sergeant, I heard about Guzman. Do you think he was killed? Or is he a prisoner?"

"Sir, XO is interrogating my sister as we speak. Monica's a good fighter. My guess is she got the drop on him." Tears welled up in her eyes.

When she'd regained her composure, she glanced up at Art and resumed her report. "I sent my partner to remove all the charges she set."

Art patted her on the shoulder. "Staff Sergeant, you've lived up to the high expectations he had of you. I know it was hard for you, tell me about your mission and then get some down-time. You've earned it."

"Thank you Sir. I appreciate the complement." She relaxed, pulled a map out, and spread it in front of them.

Jessica pointed toward the south Tower. "As planned we set forty charges around the base, and fifteen more sixty feet up. We were undetected and left on-time." She paused as Art made notes on the chart. When he looked back up, she resumed. "Since Monica was wearing his diving suit, I think we should assume his team was discovered and/or captured."

Art frowned. "You're probably right." He checked his watch and shook his head. "It's risky, but we have to proceed."

At that moment the Chief of the Boat rushed up. "Sir, our divers have removed all the mines the Federal diver had placed on our hull. I sent additional divers out to double-check the entire boat. They should be reporting in soon."

"Good call Chief. Keep me informed."

Art raised his head and called out, "Battle Stations!" He removed his glasses and rubbed his eyes. *The red glow from the battle lights always gives me a sinking feeling.* He turned to Jessica, and called out to the senior enlisted crewman on the boat. "Chief, how many divers did you send out?"

"Four, Captain. All who were suited up."

"Send out four more. We gotta make sure there aren't any more mines on our hull!"

No sooner did the last diver exit the airlock when the boat shuddered.

The sound of watertight doors slamming shut and klaxons blaring echoed through the Dallas. Art calmly called out, "Damage report!" Then listened to the speaker over his head as he scribbled on his tablet. After the last department head reported in, he reached up and keyed the microphone over his head. "Engineering, how much power can you give me?"

"Right now, all I can guarantee is forty percent, Cap'n, I wouldn't try for more until I check the rest of the systems."

Art picked up the hand mic, "Well, when can you give me a hundred percent?"

The exasperated ensign responded, "Sir, I need at least another hour to make sure the reactor's safe. Those mines were awfully close to the power plant."

Still aggravated, Art keyed the mic again. "Alright, get me forty percent. Automatically give me more power as you get the capability. Call me as soon as you get full power." Aggravated, he tossed the microphone onto the counter top.

He stared at the clock on the bulkhead. *0330. Almost time.* He yanked at the periscope handles and spun it around to view the Golden Gate. He called out to the crew in the conning tower, "I see both ships headed into the bay. Good the container ship's ahead of schedule. Both are on course."

Right on time, the tanker shuddered, appeared to slow and in ten minutes sank with its bow sticking up and a large oil slick spewing across the water. The container ship veered off course and struck the sunken tanker's mid-section.

Art yelled, "Hallelujah! We did it. Now we need the towers to fall."

The speaker over his head squawked, "Sir, Sparks here, we're monitoring local radio stations. They're reporting a Rebel was captured, and that all explosives were disarmed on both towers."

Art slammed his fist on the table top. He quickly raised the scope and checked the bridge. "Go..." At that moment there was an explosion from the south tower.

"Woo hoo! Those Feds didn't get all the charges we set." The structure started to lean and then steadied. At that moment, the boat started to sway.

Five minutes later, Sparks' voice came back over the box. Art looked up at the speaker. "Sir, that radio station says they just had a 7.5 quake. He quickly peered through the scope and watched as the north tower fell into the bay. Shortly after, the bridge surface collapsed onto the sunken vessels. "Wow, talk about timing. That quake did what we couldn't. They won't be using this waterway anytime soon."

BRAVO – Cleaning Up New York
(Last August)

Major David Torkelson sat at his desk and stared at the computer. *Lord it's been five months since I re-dedicated my life to you. How come I'm not doing better? I've been tithing, and trying to be a better father. What else am I supposed to achieve?*

A secretary walking by brought him back to reality. He noticed the hustle and bustle as aides carried out the President's bidding. He turned his head when the door to the oval office opened and Lyle came over.

"Major, President Barnes would like you to come in."

Startled, David logged off, and pulled his ID card from the computer. *Why does he want me? I've got all the nuclear codes. I hope we're not going to nuke the Rebels.* "Yes, Sir." He picked up the briefcase shackled to his left wrist. He followed Lyle through the door and moved around several men and women who were seated around the table to where he was directed.

Barnes looked up when the two of them walked in. He nodded for David to stand before him.

David marched twenty feet, stood at attention, and saluted. "Major Torkelson reporting as ordered, Sir."

Barnes returned the salute, "Major, take a seat." David sat where directed, between two men who scooted over, a third slid a chair up to the table for Torkelson.

Lyle slid a tablet of paper across the table at the Major. David pulled a pen from a pocket and put the current date on the top of the page.

President Barnes paced back and forth. He pointed a finger at a woman seated at the end of the conference table. "Ms. Smith, you're telling me New York won't be a radioactive desert for thousands of years? That goes against everything I've understood about nuclear fallout."

The senior bio-chemist from Missouri stood in front of the room. "Mr. President, all those projections were made by liberal scientists who used junk science to further their agenda. I'm not saying that you'll be able to farm on the land around New York. All I'm saying is that we shouldn't give up and expect to be at the mercy of this disaster."

David dropped his pen and wiped his forehead. *What in the world have you gotten me into Lord?*

Lyle jumped from his seat. "Now wait a minute! I know many of those men and women. They're good people."

The scientist glared back at him. "They may be good people, but their priorities are with their liberal agenda." She looked around the room, stroked her chin and snapped her fingers. "Mr. President, when you visited Japan last year, didn't you visit Hiroshima and Nagasaki?"

Barnes sat in the nearest chair. "Yes, I did. What does that have to do with anything?" He glanced down at her biographical sheet. "Wait a minute! Ms. Maria McClellan-Smith, I see here that you're from the south. How did you get through security?"

"Sir, I take umbrage with your characterization that all southerners are Rebels. You know my credentials. My father is General McClellan. I was born at Ft. Leonard Wood. While my father was on active duty we lived in every Army base in the South. That doesn't mean I'm a security risk. There were many southerners who sided with you in the original conflict, just as there are many of us who support you now." She stood erect and directly faced Barnes. "I don't believe the issue of slavery caused the Civil War. I don't believe the South, then or now, had the legal right to secede from the Union. I believe the Union will fail unless we stay united."

She put her hands on the table in front of her. If you're satisfied with my allegiance, can we get back to the subject at hand? While in Japan, did you notice the flowers in the parks? I know you did. Did you have to wear any protective clothing? I know you didn't. Even though the Taliban Bomb was bigger than we used on Japan, I predict that we'll be able to have New York cleaned up in less than ten years."

Her fellow scientists turned toward Maria. Several exclaimed, "WHAT?"

She chuckled. "Be that as it may, we can't do anything about the fallout in the atmosphere. It's going to go where wind currents take it. The issue is how to deal with the radioactivity that contaminates the buildings and land in the Big Apple as we speak." She walked over to her briefcase and pulled out several folders. As she passed them out she continued, "We need. . . ."

Lyle looked over at the President. Barnes nodded back. The Chief of Staff rose and pointed a finger and interrupted. "Ma'am, you're going against everything we've ever been told."

David scribbled on his note pad, set his pen down and took a deep breath. *Lord, I'm in the middle of an argument and I don't know what side to take. What do I do?*

The Scientist took a breath and slowly let it out. She glanced around the room. "Mr. President, ladies, and gentlemen, you don't have to agree with me. But we do need to get decon teams into the contaminated area. The first step is to send the teams in. Each team has decon trailers, and are self-contained. These trailers are different from the ones we first sent in right after the bomb went off back in June. This time, instead of decontaminating citizens, they contain the equipment needed to decon buildings, land, and equipment." She looked around the room as she drank from a water bottle.

"Each team will cover a city block. They'll remain on that block until the task is completed. We're not putting a time limit on how long it should take to remove the radiation in any given section. We'll start at the perimeter," she paused and glanced out a window, "I'm recommending a hundred mile radius. As teams complete a section, we'll move them closer in. We may not get the job done in ten years. It may take a hundred, but definitely not thousands."

Barnes interrupted. "What about sections that have taller buildings?"

"Larger teams, multiple teams, or the first team assigned will be allowed to take longer to finish the task."

Everyone kept silent while Barnes seemed to ponder his choices. After a few moments he pointed to David. "Major I want you to work with the Army Corps of Engineers. I'm promoting you to Lieutenant Colonel, and giving you the temporary rank of Colonel. I need you to have the necessary rank to pull this off. Get in touch with the Pentagon. They'll give you the support you need to supervise the civilian contractors to get the job done." He turned to the Maria, "work out the details with him."

David stood, started to gather his papers and files; and then moved toward Maria's side of the room. *Well Lord, I'll have to do what Pastor said in this week's sermon:* "How do you eat an elephant? One bite at a time."

#####

Jennifer Eagleton hung up the phone as Staff Sergeant Wilkins entered her office. *This guy sure has changed. I hope he continues to do the right thing. Let's see how he does on this mission.* "Wilkins, good, you came before I had to send a runner to find you. Have a seat. I have a job for you."

Apparently, startled at the pleasant tone of her voice, he sat where she directed. "U, uh, yes First Sergeant. Did you say a job for me?"

Jennifer smiled and pulled papers from the printer next to her desk. "Yes, when I first met you, you had a chip on your shoulder about how the system had treated you. In the past few months you've set all that aside. When LTC Van Ruiten asked for a Sergeant First Class for a mission, I recommended you."

Wilkins looked down at the rank on his uniform. He raised an eyebrow at Jennifer.

She winked, opened a drawer and retrieved the proper rank insignia. "The Battalion Commander agreed with me. You deserve the promotion. We don't have time for a regular ceremony. They're sending a car for you, you leave immediately. You're going to be detailed to work with the Army Corps of Engineers. When the driver drops you off at the airport, he'll give you a packet with all the information you need." She paused and handed him his orders, promotion paperwork, and new chevrons. "Your civilian experience with drones and robots will come in handy."

He took the papers as Jennifer came from behind her desk and shook his hand. "Washington has a plan for cleaning up New York. They want to use drones and robots to survey the city. You need to be there in two days. Other than that, I don't have any information.

Colonel David Torkelson and Maria McClellan-Smith stood on an auditorium stage in Wilkes-Barre, Pennsylvania. David walked in front of the podium and spoke to several hundred soldiers and contractors.

"Ladies and Gentlemen, we have an enormous task in front of us. In a few moments Ms. Smith will explain the decontamination process she's developed. Each team has one military service member as the government's representative. Consider all instructions given by them as coming from me." He turned and nodded to Maria. "Ma'am, you're on."

Maria, her long hair draping her shoulders, stepped forward wearing boots, khaki pants and long-sleeved shirt, glasses, and carried her broad-brimmed hat. "You service members have been chosen because of your skills. You Contractors have been selected to fulfill the commitment your companies have made with the Federal government. As you came in, you were handed the operations manual for our decontamination procedure. I can't emphasize enough that you need to follow them to the letter. Starting this afternoon your teams will begin their hands-on training. In one week we'll start approximately one-hundred miles from the epicenter of the blast. The Army Corps of Engineers has placed markers around the perimeter as a starting point."

She referred to a map she pulled from a cargo pocket and then continued. "Sample pictures of these markers are in your manuals. They've been placed around the initial perimeter five miles apart. I've assigned two teams to start at each marker. Team A will be on the left and Team B on the right. At the end of the first week I'm projecting each team will have covered a section of land one mile long and one hundred yards wide. After they've completed all buildings in a sector a helicopter will spray the entire area. " She paused and acknowledged a hand that had been raised. "You sir, what question do you have?"

A lanky man stood, "Ma'am, Sergeant First Class Wilkins here. I hate to be a spoil sport, but what about the wilderness sections? If my team is in those cumbersome suits I saw displayed in the lobby, I can't picture them crawling through dense brush."

She smiled, "Good question. When a team gets to a gold-painted, as opposed to the silver-painted marker, or if they determine the terrain is more than they can safely handle, they'll stop and redirect their efforts. The aerial teams will take over from there." She put a hand up. "I know what you're going to say, I didn't tell you how we'll decon the wilderness areas. Easy, we have crop dusters for that. Then you won't have to walk through the wilderness until after the bacteria have had almost a month to do their job."

She paused, leaned on a podium and continued, "At the end of a week, or a mile from their initial marker, (whichever comes first) the team will turn right or left depending on whether they were Team A or B. After the bacteria have had a week to propagate, we'll give them a week to digest all the radioactivity they can. At the beginning of the third week, a crew will come in with Geiger counters. If necessary a section will get a second treatment. That's why it's important that you put a heavy coat of the gel throughout your area of responsibility."

She put her hands on her hips and then pointed a finger at the audience. "I need to caution you about the gel we use to encapsulate the bacteria. It is very slippery and it is impossible walk on or through. Be sure you back out of whatever area you're treating. One step on it and you won't be able to stand."

She straightened and glanced around the auditorium. "I'll be working with each Team Leader and explain issues that might come up as you work on different types of buildings. For example, a residential home, as opposed to a skyscraper." She turned to David. "Colonel, I'm finished until this afternoon."

David took the hand mic from her and glanced at his watch. "It is eleven-hundred hours. Let's break for lunch. Check your agenda for which class you're scheduled for this afternoon." He came to attention and called out: "Dismissed."

#####

Wilkins called out over the engine noise. "Driver, pull over there next to your assigned marker. I want to start my survey." *Let's see, it's 1100 hours. We should be done by 1800 hours. That'll be enough time for me to hit a few bars.*

"No problem." The pickup's tires screeched as Seaman Jeremiah Benton pulled up alongside a disabled semi-trailer. The rest of their convoy pulled up behind.

The Sergeant set a crate on the ground in front of a tree. After opening it he set a drone VTOL helicopter on top of a rock. In minutes the chopper rose as he maneuvered his hands over the control panel.

Several team members shielded their eyes from the sun as they watched the drone head toward their first assignment.

The sailor lowered the tailgate on his pick-up truck, for the Team Leader, and then trotted over to Wilkins' side.

She jumped up into the truck-bed and called out. "Let's go. Let's not take all day. The Army Corps of Engineers is paying our company good money for this job." She put her arms behind her back. "You have twenty minutes to get your suits on. All tanks were pressurized last night, so all you have to do is check your gauges."

She pulled up her shirt sleeve and checked her watch, then called out to Wilkins. "We're ready."

Wilkins handed the drone's controls to his driver, walked over, and stood in the middle of the twenty members of the Decon Crew. He pointed to the map he'd laid on the tailgate. "Today's objective is these buildings just a mile north. Remember, I need a thick coat of the bacteria on everything in order for it to do any good. Don't rush your spray and be sure to overlap each pass. Remember, work your way backwards, and don't step on this stuff."

He looked around, "Team Leader, let's get this show on the road."

Immediately everyone hurried off to follow their instructions.

Wilkins shouted to his driver who was twenty yards away. "Put your earphones on." After the young man complied, he walked over and peered over his shoulder. "Do you hear anything on the Geiger-counter?"

"No, I don't." He adjusted a few dials. "Now I've got it. It registers 150 roentgens."

"That's about what I expected."

"Sergeant what I don't understand is how the bacteria are going to do the job? Whoever heard of reducing radiation with a system like this?"

Wilkins swallowed water from his camelback drinking system. He pointed at the building in the distance. "Some scientist in Missouri found out that in a closed environment, such as an old salt mine; the bacteria ate all radiation in sight. The problem was when we tried to use it in open spaces the bacteria died within minutes. This woman must've been a genius. She came up with the idea of encapsulating the germ in a gel. It's worked well in the lab, and then we tried it on a smaller scale at one of the old atomic testing sites. Now, it's time for the big leagues."

Wilkins pointed to the decontamination crew standing a few yards away. They'll be awhile. Tell me young man, how did you get this assignment?"

Seaman Benton's eyes welled up.

Wilkins looked over at the young man. "Is everything alright son?"

"Sarge, I was remembering when I fought for my life last April. I was a naïve boy when I enlisted in the navy two years ago. I joined to see the world. Little did I know that I would be involved in the first battle. I was stabbed in the leg. They gave me a forty-percent disability. I don't qualify for a pension. But they let me continue to serve where I can."

The Team Leader called out, "Sergeant First Class, my crew's headed in. Any special instructions?"

He responded without taking his eyes off the monitor. "I've told you before, it's Sergeant or Sarge."

The middle-aged man winked. "Sorry Sarge. I'm a former Marine. I'm used to showing respect by saying your entire rank."

"Well, I'm not a Marine. You can call me Sarge. Now have them move out according to the original plan." His hands flew across the keyboard and the twenty-inch screen divided into ten different pictures. The last picture came from the drone. *These new drones are so nimble they can fly inside by themselves as long as there's an open door.*

"Team 1 to Base."

Wilkins responded, "Base to Team 1. Go ahead."

"Suggest you record this. The counter shows over two-hundred-fifty roentgens. This is the highest reading we've had since we started."

The Sergeant's baritone voice came across everyone's headset. "Base to Team 1, Got it. Listen up everyone; put an extra thick dose on any area with more than one-hundred-fifty."

A two-man team walked up the steps of a small two story home. "Hey Boss," said the first man to reach the front door.

His partner paused, and with an aggravated tone said, "What do you want now?"

"Don't get an attitude. It was her choice to marry me and not you."

"Let's focus on the job on hand. Remember this is an open mic. Keep the personal comments to a minimum."

"Yeah, right." His helmet shook sideways. "All I wanted to say was I'll go in first."

The boss raised a hand and said, "Yeah, right, suit yourself."

His partner opened the door and headed up the stairway to the second floor. Then went back to the kitchen and started spraying the ceiling and walls.

Both men worked backwards toward the front of the house.

"Hey Boss, you there? I hear nothing but static." The worker, his finger on the sprayer control, continued moving the nozzle back and forth as he walked backward down the stairs.

Down below, his partner glanced up at the man who stole his girl years ago. "Yeah, I'm here, right below you." Then he pointed the tip of his sprayer at his rival's feet. Immediately the man above slipped and fell backward.

"Man down! Get me a medic!"

#####

Jeremiah jumped up and shouted, "SARGE, you're not going to believe what I just recorded on camera five."

Apparently sensing the tension in the young man's voice, the Soldier and his Team Leader dropped their papers and ran across the staging area.

"We need a medic at site four. We have two men down." He

26

glanced between his superiors and his video screen. The young employee pulled up the beginning of the file he'd just saved. "Sirs, I just heard a call for a medic. I immediately called for one. It'll take a while for them to get here."

His hands shook as he punched on the keyboard. "As you directed, I've been checking all the saved files. The time-stamp says that this happened on camera five just minutes ago. Tell me what you think?"

The two older men looked in horror as they watched the picture their drone had just taken.

The Team Leader shook his head. "That Supervisor's new. He joined my team last week. The look on his face is complete hatred." He leaned over and examined the still picture on the screen. "He requested to be on the same team with that guy. I had no idea he had any issues with him."

Wilkins nodded for his driver to resume showing the video file. *And I thought my life was a mess? If I don't get my life straight this could be me. Listening to the audio tells it all.* "This was no accident. Even if we didn't have the audio the look on his face as he backed out of the kitchen and glared at his partner coming down the stairs above him tells the entire story. He deliberately pointed his sprayer at his partner's feet. That, my friend is murder."

The Team Leader nodded. "Look at what happens next!"

All three Federals looked on in astonishment as one of their workers fell through the bannister and landed on top of his boss.

#####

Maria and David sat across the conference table from Lyle and Barnes. David took the lead from Maria. "Sir, as with any new procedure we've had some ups and downs. In the past three weeks we've deployed one-hundred-fifty-five decon teams. This includes the fixed and rotary wing spraying operations." He paused and took a deep breath. "Our initial findings are that we need to give the bacteria another week to produce the results we want. With that in mind it'll be another week or so before we have a definitive answer as to how effective our method has been."

Barnes frowned. "Why can't you get me the results you promised? I promoted you to Colonel to give you the power to make this happen. You get me results by our next meeting or I'll get someone else to do both your jobs."

He slammed his organizer shut, rose, and started to leave the room.

David realized the meeting was over, put his pen away and considered his options. *I've seen this before, I'm sure of it. He has all the symptoms of PTSD. What do I do? Who can I trust? Maria? No, she doesn't have the experience.*

Maria, seemingly aggravated at Barnes' rude treatment of them, jumped from her seat. "I beg your pardon Sir. You're being unrealistic. Initially we gave you estimates. We told you they were estimates. You've been in the field. You know that especially with a new procedure anything could happen. It's the same as a unit going into combat. The battle plan's only good until the first shot's fired. Then you have to adjust."

Her temper flared and she stood at a corner of the table. "Sir, you've already threatened to fire me. Go ahead if you want. But if I do say so I am the best expert on radiation decon in the world." She pointed to David standing beside her, "and this man has worked night and day to help me implement my plan. We've gone three weeks averaging three-to-four hours of sleep per night. You might cut us some slack."

Lyle stepped between Maria and Barnes. "Listen up you two. Calm down." He pointed at Maria. "You young lady, heard him say you have the time you requested." He turned to the President,

"And you Sir have not been well. I know you've had headaches, you've told me about your nightmares. You shouldn't make such a drastic decision when you're not at your best."

Barnes ran a hand over his bald head. "Aarggh! I don't need this. I need something good to happen."

Lyle winked at David and Maria. "Mr. President you gave them time, let them use it and brief you in three weeks."

The Commander-In-Chief scrunched his face and nodded.

CHARLIE – Response To The Blockade
(Mid-October)

As a sunbeam flooded the floor, Garfield picked up a highlighter and thumbed through his Bible, "Chaplain, we've been at this for an hour. I think I see what you mean about…"

There was a knock at the door. Garfield glanced at Chaplain Charlie. "Excuse me Chaplain." He raised his head and called out, "Enter."

A Sergeant came in and set a stack of messages in front of his commander. "Sir, we're getting these from all over. It appears the Rebels are setting up a blockade on both coasts, every port is closed."

Garfield squinted as he skimmed each page. *You would think that when I became a Christian that The Lord would make it easier on me.* "Can they make the font any smaller?" At that moment Sergeant Major Hart rushed in.

"Sir, there's been a 7.6 magnitude earthquake in San Francisco, and divers from a Rebel Sub placed mines on both towers to the Golden Gate Bridge. The north tower was weakened by the blast. The charges on the south tower were disabled prior to detonation. The quake sent the bridge into the channel."

Garfield jerked his head as his enlisted aide spoke, and turned toward the Chaplain, sat down hard in his seat and slammed a fist on the tabletop. "Why's God doing this to me?"

Hart appeared frustrated as he shuffled the papers. "It gets worse. Before the Rebel mines exploded, they sank a tanker and a container ship under the Golden Gate. Minutes after the charges went off, the earthquake toppled the bridge on top of the vessels."

He placed his hands on the table between Garfield and him. "Sir, there's more." Tears welled up. "The list of ports they've blockaded is long. Most not as serious as San Francisco, but they've effectively cut our international supply lines."

As Hart talked the young sergeant standing next to him gasped, "Oh my God!"

At the junior soldier's comment, Garfield stood, and turned. "Sergeant, I've given strict orders that nobody's to take The Lord's name in vain."

"Sir, may I speak freely?"

"As long as yu don't swear."

"You get religion and expect everyone to change to your new standard. Before you 'got saved,' you weren't so perfect, and you're not so perfect now."

Surprised at the Sergeant's boldness, Garfield shook his head. "How dare you be so insolent? I've half a mind to take a stripe away for your insubord..."

At that moment Chaplain Charlie stood and put a hand on Garfield's shoulder. He moved his head ever so slightly. Garfield sighed, "Sergeant, that's all for now. Get out of my sight."

He turned to his enlisted aide. "Hart, I want a video conference in fifteen minutes. Get all the regular attendees on-line." He moved back to his desk, slammed his Bible shut and put it in a drawer.

After the sergeant and Hart left, Chaplain Charlie gathered his books. "General, the young man was right. You used to swear like a truck driver. You never swore around me. You thought you were showing me respect. In fact, someone who swears doesn't upset me. It's The Lord whom they offend. Many, including myself find it hard for you to be so strict. Especially since you have a history of violating the same commandment you get troubled over others breaking."

Garfield sulked. "You've been teaching me that I have to meet a new standard. I've been pretty good at not swearing the past two months. What's wrong with me insisting on my soldiers obeying the second commandment?" He sat back in his chair and crossed his arms. "Besides, other commanders have issued the same order I did."

"You aren't the other commanders. They don't have the testimony you do. You have to live the life you set up for yourself. In time you'll be able to make such a requirement. But for now you have to accept things you don't like."

Realizing he didn't have an answer, Garfield sighed, "You don't understand how much I want to serve The Lord. I can't lower my new standard, can I?"

Chaplain chuckled, "Sir, you need to grow in your faith. In time your testimony will hold, and people will see you for the Christian you've become. For now, you have to accept people for who they are. Trust me. You've got a lot to learn."

An hour later, Garfield looked into the camera. "Ladies and Gentlemen, we have our work cut out for us. You have your assignments. That's all. Dismissed."

He turned to his aide, "Get my car and driver. I need to brief the President."

"Yes, Sir." Hart grabbed both his and the General's briefcases and ran out the door.

Later as his staff car wove through the streets of Washington, Garfield rubbed his eyes. "Hart, I thought they might try something like this, I never imagined they'd be so successful. I wondered if Bobby Lee would have the leadership abilities his grandfather had. Maybe this was something he just took over and didn't think of himself."

#####

Appearing to feel self-conscious about his lack of stature, Rebel Secretary of State, Joseph C. Fendemere III stood in front of President Gressette and his Cabinet. He picked up a remote and with a nod to cabinet members, started his presentation.

"Mr. President, Vice-President, Cabinet Members, and guests; I've spent the past four-and-a-half months visiting all the countries in the European Union. We have many supporters, and detractors. Once the Federals feel the full effect of this blockade, I project our supporters will openly commit."

He paused and focused on The President. "Sir, if everything goes as planned, in seventy-two hours we'll have complete control of all Federal ports. Almost ninety-six percent of their shipping will be either cut off or re-directed to a ROA port. The cargo will be assimilated into our supply stream ..."

At that point the Secretary of Commerce leaned forward and interrupted. "Exactly how many ships do you think we should prepare for?"

Annoyed at the interruption, Fendemere coolly smiled, "Mr. Secretary, I don't have an answer. We don't know how many nations will recall their vessels. We don't know how the crews will react when our sailors board their ship."

The Rebel Ambassador to the European Community, sitting next to Gressette, pointed a finger at the Fendemere. "You sir, haven't considered the Union blockade in the 1860s was illegal. How do you plan to legitimize our blockade?"

Standing as straight as he could to appear taller, Fendemere smirked. *Why do I have to put up with these guys? Don't they realize how much I've done for The Cause? If I play my cards right I'll be the next President of our Confederacy.* "Sirs, I've done my homework. The original Northern Blockade was illegal because the Declaration of Paris, of 1856, stated that for a blockade to be legal, the blockaded country's coastline had to be rendered completely inaccessible. Also, a nation couldn't blockade its own borders." [i] "So if Mr. Lincoln said we weren't a nation, then their blockade was illegal. Since they didn't recognize us as a sovereign nation, they were violating the Treaty. We recognize the USA as a sovereign nation, and as of twelve noon today, we've restricted Federal ships from every inch of their coastline." He leaned toward the fat man across the table. "That, sir is how we'll legitimize our blockade."

He stood, smoothed his suit, "To answer your question, any vessel we capture will be taken to the nearest port that can handle the type of cargo in question. Whether its oil, or trinkets from China, we'll take care of it."

He opened a folder in front of him. "Mr. President, I suggest that we reimburse the ship owners for all cargo we acquire. That will prevent the shippers from having a complaint against us. It may cost us billions of Rebel Dollars. We'll be able to use or resell

[i] Seabrook, Lochlainn. *Everything You Were Taught About The Civil War Is Wrong, Ask a Southerner!* Nashville, TN: Sea Raven Press, 2012, pages: 133-136: Reprinted by permission of the publisher.

the captured product. The end result is the Federal economy will be in a shambles. The only means they have is to conduct an airlift over the North Pole. That will be costly and only bring in a trifle of what they need. They will have to ration essential material. Citizens who don't get what they expect as an entitlement will riot. This will cause General McClellan to take units off the battle line to deal with the civil unrest."

He closed his folder. "Sir, I request you allow the Federals to feel the full effect of our blockade."

Gressette nodded, stood, looked around the table, and back at his Diplomat. "Mr. Fendemere, you'll be given the time."

The Rebel President's Chief of Staff, also stood, and said, "Sir, we need to leave for Dallas."

Gressette checked his watch. "You're right." He picked up his cell from the table, and surveyed the men and women in attendance. "Dismissed."

DELTA – Getting Commo Up
(September)

Carlos' voice boomed through Dudley's phone. "Major, this is the third time this week Rebel patrols have come within a hundred yards of our compound. What are you and Van Ruiten doing about it?"

Dudley tried to get a word in edgewise as he held the receiver away from his ear and listened to the over-achieving Marine. Exasperated, he finally shouted, "With all due respect Lieutenant Colonel! Would you be quiet and listen?"

When the ear piece became silent he said in a slow controlled voice. "Sir, I've told you before, our soldiers are not trained experienced infantry, much less military police. I feel they've done quite well considering. We've freed up your staff so they could do their jobs." He slammed his fist on his desktop. "You need to understand that you'd be in worse shape without us, than you are with us."

The soldier heard Carlos' hand bang onto his desk. "I want to see you and your Battalion Commander now. We're going to have this out, once and for all."

An hour later Van Ruiten and Dudley sat in front of Carlos.

Dudley took notes of their discussion. *It'll take time, but I'll get even.* He glared back and forth between the short marine and his commander as they bantered.

She said, "Lieutenant Colonel when the first Rebel patrols arrived, we doubled our efforts. When that wasn't effective we tripled them and then went to sixteen hour shifts until Major

36

General McClellan sent an infantry and MP companies to assist us. They haven't had any more success than we did. If you don't back off, I've half a mind to take my soldiers where we'll be appreciated."

Carlos rose so he looked down at Marsha. "Lieutenant Colonel, I'll let you know when you can leave. Is that understood?"

She stood and looked the man in the eye. "I just realized," She winked at Dudley and then turned back to the Marine, I out-rank you. Last week you told me you were recently promoted, I was promoted fifteen months ago." She paused when he tried to interrupt. "And don't pull that 'President Barnes is a friend of mine routine. I've heard it too many times in the past few months. With the arrival of the infantry and MPs you now have three times the strength that you had when we first arrived. We're leaving tomorrow morning at 0600." She glared at him. "Put that in your pipe and smoke it."

Before Carlos could respond his phone rang. He pushed the speaker button and angrily said, "WHAT Gunny? You know I'm in a meeting."

"Yes, Sir, I understand, but General McClellan's Operations Officer just called. He confirmed that a tank company should arrive tomorrow afternoon. I thought that might affect your discussions with the Army."

He cancelled the speaker and looked at Marsha. "You will stay for an additional twenty-four hours, YOU WILL TRANSITION WITH THEM BEFORE YOU DEPART. I can't leave a hole in my security just because you think it's time for you to leave."

"Humph." Marsha plopped back into her chair. Dudley moved his head toward her. She leaned so he could whisper into her ear.

"Ma'am, it'll take us that much time to make a well-prepared departure. With your approval, I'll make the suggestion that the MP and infantry companies take over all fixed positions on the perimeter. I'll phase their external patrols in so they replace ours as we reduce the number of our patrols." He lowered his voice even more to ensure Carlos couldn't hear. "The last thing you want to do is to appear to have a disorganized departure. Really Ma'am, with the Pentagon and White House watching our every move, I strongly suggest we use extreme caution."

She took in a deep breath and let it out slowly, then turned to her adversary. "Lieutenant Colonel Tejada, the Major has a good idea. I'm going to leave and let you work the details out with him."

Carlos frowned and said, "Now wait a minute, Lie. . ."

Marsha put her hands on his desk and butted in. "One thing I thought you'd learn by now, is not to interrupt me when I'm talking." Before he could respond she continued.

"Major Dudley is my liaison, I trust him, and whatever you work out with him is fine with me. I have other tasks to." She stood, picked up her portfolio and stormed out.

#####

Rebel Captain Horning knelt next to a map. He circled a finger around a hill top. "We have an agent inside. He's given us the patrol schedule for the next twenty-four hours. A tank unit is arriving tomorrow. They will beef up the perimeter positions when the tanks are put in place." He paused to take a sip from a water bottle. "Tonight's roving patrols are manned by the support unit that's been on duty since the beginning. They've been on sixteen hour shifts for a month. This rotation is due to get off in two hours. They're exhausted; they'll be easier to overcome."

He stood and pointed to the Platoon Leaders and Sergeants, and then the map. You two will have your patrols enter here and here." Then he pointed to the remaining soldiers, "Your patrols will harass the Federals. I want you to make them think we haven't penetrated their perimeter. If you're captured you've all been given a role to play. In the end, if that happens we'll rescue you."

#####

Staff Sergeant Alexander called out, "Specialist Higgins, Thompson, Willoughby!"

The three men grabbed their gear and rushed to the front of their Squad Leader. Each man slid on the polished concrete floor as they came in front of the Non-Commissioned Officer. They checked each other out, after they finished they came to attention. Alexander walked around them and smiled. "As usual you all are well-prepared and ready. Get your ammo from Supply. Be sure to get a few cases of claymore mines. We leave in ten minutes. We'll be on the regular route. However, I'm going to reverse our course and go counter-clockwise tonight. The other patrols from our company will be on our right and left." He paused, pulled a pen out of his sleeve and drew circles on the map in front of him. The patrols on either side of us will be fifty meters away. We're leaving twenty minutes apart, that way one of our three patrols will have a better chance of surprising Johnny Reb."

The tall-lanky Higgins appeared puzzled.

Alexander put a hand on the young man's shoulder. "Don't worry son. Major Dudley came up with the idea. He's coordinated it with the infantry. They know the running password we've been assigned. If we're attacked just call out 'supermarket' as you approach one of our positions, they'll let you through."

He reached over and opened a case of claymores. "I need each of you to take three mines. We'll place these along weak spots in our perimeter. Dudley wants us to place them on our first trip around the perimeter."

As he talked he led them out of the compound. *I sure hope these youngsters learn well. They may not be alive for a second lesson.* Later he knelt in a clearing and opened a case. He looked up at Higgins. Remember son, I told you about these the other day. They're quite effective. He raised one up to reveal all sides of the mine. Then he demonstrated how to properly set it up. Higgins, you place yours up over there, and Willoughby on the other side of that rock. Thompson, save yours for later."

"See, it's that easy. You make sure the convex side is facing the enemy and the concave side is facing you. I've set up trip wires so if the enemy isn't paying attention they get sprayed with buckshot from the mine they trip. If I think they've made it past the wire then I can always pull these," he held up several lanyards for his soldiers to see, "then they get the full effect."

#####

Twenty minutes later, Higgins in the lead, the four-man patrol crept through the brush. Thompson deftly put his defensive devices in place as his partners scoured the area for the enemy.

Willoughby mouthed, "Sarge, what do you want us to do now?"

Alexander twisted the last wire in place. He whispered *Dudley gave me permission to follow my instincts. We're going to do another loop. We'll go clockwise this time, when we return we'll set up a defensive position on this side of the mines.* He raised his head, "Let's go guys."

They headed off and didn't notice a pair of camouflaged faces watching their every move.

#####

"Sarge," the Rebel private whispered, "what're you gonna do?"

The Rebel Sergeant smiled as he picked up his radio. "Listen and learn son." He turned his head and spoke into the mic, as he watched the Federal Patrol scurry off. "Alabama 4, this is 3. Bring four cans of that spray paint that's in the back end of our truck. Make it snappy."

He chuckled when he saw the puzzled look on his partner's face. "It's a trick the VC pulled on many Americans during the

Vietnam War. Be careful, we don't have a lot of time."

They heard the bushes behind them rustle just before a fellow Rebel pushed through a few trees and plopped a plastic sack onto the ground. "Sarge, I don't know what you're gonna do with this. Are you planning on re-decorating the forest?"

Everyone chuckled at the joke. The Sergeant low-crawled to the Federal position and fiddled with each of the mines.

#####

Two hours later Alexander's squad returned on-time. They quickly manned their positions. "Sarge," Higgins whispered, "I hear something on the trail."

Alexander and the others hunkered down and waited. When he knew the enemy was in range of the claymores they'd set up, he grabbed all the lanyards and pulled before the enemy could get a shot off.

BOOM, BOOM, BOOM, went all the devices.

The Rebel Sergeant checked Alexander's body for intel. "Hey you guys! Strip them of any information. We need to get out of here. Our job's finished."

His private shook his head. "I don't believe it! You painted the convex side of the mine the same color as the concave. So when those Yankees looked at their mines they didn't realize you'd turned them around." The young enlisted quickly obeyed and they all melted back into the brush before the Federal Quick Reaction Force could respond.

ECHO – Bobby's Escape
(September)

Bobby tugged at his parachute straps, checked all connections, and yelled over the roar of the engine. "See you in a few weeks."

His double nodded and shouted, "Yes sir!"

Gosh, it's been years since I've jumped. He leaned out the open side of the aircraft and leaped. *This better be good.* "Okay, that's eight, seven..." the wind rushed across his face as the ground sped toward him ..."three, two, one." He yanked hard on the ripcord. As the chute billowed above his head, his torso felt torn from his body. When his legs caught up with his chest, a gust of wind blew in from the west and distracted him. Before he could refocus, he straight-legged his landing. The wind dragged him and his parachute across a meadow. His right leg extended out. Excruciating pain screamed from his knee.

As he struggled with the cords to regain control, Bobby tried to get his good leg to slow his movement toward a highway.

He finally came to a stop just before a stand of sugar gum trees. *That must be state highway 64. I need to get moving south.* Favoring his good leg, he sat on a log, and pulled the chute over to him. After thirty minutes, he stuffed it in its case, and took a swig from his canteen.

He looked around, spying a thin log twenty yards away, Bobby leaned on his good leg and tried to hobble over to it. He fell, scraped his cheek on a rock, and all went dark. He woke, and tried to shake the pain raking his body.

He shouted in agony, reached out, and grabbed the branch. Bobby wiped the sweat off his forehead with his sleeve. Half-stood, and rested an elbow on a rock. He grabbed the stick and pulled himself up. When he regained his bearings, his throbbing knee almost knocked him down. He steadied himself between the stick and the rock, then started out.

Thirty minutes later he sat on a tree stump. As he caught his breath, he noticed a large hole in the old oak tree lying next to him. *What better place to hide my parachute?*

He reached into a chest pocket and pulled out a picture of a young woman. As he admired her face, he closed his eyes, smelled her perfume wafting through his head. He pictured her waist-length chestnut hair. "Bernadette," he sighed. "How can I work this out? I've loved you the entire time we've been in college. Now I have to give you up to carry out my life's work." He pulled out his cell phone, punched the speed dial and waited.

He mustered up the strength to sound normal. "Hi Sweetie, I need you to trust me. I can't talk much. I'm sending some people to bring you to me. Don't ask questions. I have a plan. If it works, we can get married. Are you still in Seattle?" He grimaced in pain.

A young woman's sweet voice came over the receiver. "I've thought of nothing else the past six months. It seems like it's been an eternity. Is there anything wrong? Your voice sounds strange."

"No, sweetie, nothing's wrong." He lied, "I've gotta go now. If you'll have me, I want to marry you." He leaned against a rock and caught his breath. To Bobby her voice was like sweet wine.

"If you don't you'll have a breach of promise suit on your hands. I wouldn't think of marrying anyone else. I love you and only you."

Bobby stared at his phone as he said, "Okay, Sweetie, I love you, too. See you soon."

Ten minutes, later he came out of a daze and struggled to stand. *Now, I gotta get outta here.* As he fought to rise, he mulled over his problems, tried to straighten up and move down the trail. His good foot tripped over a root, and he fell on his bad knee.

#####

Rebel Lieutenant Reiner pulled his binoculars from their case and spoke to his driver. "I see him. He's just about to land. OH NO. The wind's taken him at least three miles off target and into a grove of trees. It'll take me a while to get there. It looks like he could be injured. Get on the radio. Have them send an ambulance to the junction of state highways 64 and alternate 74. We'll guide them in with a flare."

As the Private spoke into the microphone, he stepped on the accelerator. After repeating his message he cut the other radioman short. Can't talk now, Gotta go!"

"I know this area Lieutenant. My uncle has a farm near here. Let's take that road, it's a short cut."

Reiner reached behind his seat with one hand to grab his first aid bag. "Go for it son. Focusing on the road ahead, Reiner ran a hand over his eyebrows while he shielded his eyes from the late afternoon sun. He said out loud, "He must've gone behind that clump of trees. This road doesn't go through."

His driver smiled, you're right sir, but I will." He sharply turned the wheel and veered off the road and through the brush. The truck bounced and swerved as the driver traversed the terrain. Moments later, he pulled to a stop.

Reiner grabbed his medical bag, "You stay here, stand on the truck bed, and send up a flare to guide the rest of our Platoon." He slammed the door and hurried through the brush.

Being a man of thirty-one, he easily traversed the remaining quarter-mile to where Bobby lay, gasping, and writhing in pain. *Okay, focus now. It's not as bad as it looks. I've got everything I need. Sure hope our patrol comes before the Yankees.*

Reiner kneeled. "Sir, you'll be all right. It looks like you hyper-extended your knee. It's painful, but not life-threatening. He pulled a cold pack and bandage from his kit with one hand, grabbed two sticks with the other, snapped the ampule in the cold pack, and then expertly wrapped the bandage around the makeshift splint. He peered through the sweat dripping in his eyes, and saw the ambulance crew lugging a stretcher along the trail.

"We'll have you out of here soon. Relax. I'm going to give you something for the pain. You'll wake up in the hospital."

The young officer stood, waved his right arm. "Hurry up, guys. We don't have all day."

#####

A USMC patrol sat while Lieutenant Benton scoured the horizon with his field glasses. "Sergeant, that small Rebel aircraft we saw overhead a minute ago, discharged a parachute. Mount up! We're going to get a prisoner." He pointed to a Corporal as he donned his gear. "Gunny, have him take point." He adjusted his backpack and stood in front of his Marines. "Most of you know that my older brother was a diver on the U.S.S. Lexington. He was wounded by a Rebel last April. I'll buy a steak dinner to the Marine who brings me a Rebel prisoner. If the captive has crucial information, I'll buy a steak dinner for everyone." He nodded, and the Corporal started to move out.

In unison, the Platoon shouted, "HOOAH."

#####

As the ambulance came into view, Reiner spoke rapidly into his microphone. "Yes General Grimes, he'll be fine. I'm not taking him to a local hospital. I've got a chopper standing by. . ."

ZING, POW, RATTATAT, TAT.

Reiner dropped the handset, and lay across Bobby's body. He drew his pistol, raised his head over a rise, and called out. "Driver, where're the rest of our guys?"

"On the run Sir. They're coming up behind you."

Reiner looked behind and shouted, "Give me a perimeter. Now!" *They got here just in time. We've got the future of our country in our hands. We have to make it.*

In minutes the Rebel Platoon had complied. The Driver arrived, positioned himself, between the main Yankee advance and Reiner. The withering fire from his carbine seemed to slow the enemy's progress.

As the young man low-crawled through some brush, Reiner saw a Yankee grenade fall from the sky and explode over his soldier.

Rebels reached the meadow. A Corporal slid next to Reiner, "Sir, I've got a stretcher. They out-number us three-to-one. Let's get outta here!"

The two Rebels slid Bobby's unconscious body onto the stretcher. The remaining members of their Platoon covered their retreat.

They carried Bobby for a half-mile, when they heard helicopters overhead. The first of the Comanche attack birds sprayed the Yankee positions with machine gun fire. The second sent a missile toward their vehicles in the rear.

After Reiner set his end of the stretcher in the middle of a clearing, a Sergeant crawled over to Bobby's Aide, "Sir, we've established a new perimeter. We're almost out of ammo, hopefully the choppers will give us time to get the two of you out." The NCO stuck his head up, put his hands to his mouth and shouted, "You, guide the first chopper in. As soon as it leaves, guide the second in, make sure you get every survivor aboard." Then he turned to another Rebel. "Have your Squad Leader gather up all Yankee prisoners, take care of all dead and wounded."

"Yes, Sergeant." Then the young woman ran off to complete her mission.

Fifty yards away a Rebel soldier moved into a clearing and started signaling.

Twenty minutes later, Reiner and Bobby were aboard a medical chopper. The young Aide unbuckled his seat belt and moved next to the crew chief and shouted into his ear. "Get on the radio. I want us to go straight to Camp Robinson."

As the helicopter crossed into South Carolina, the pilot motioned for Reiner to plug into the radio. Bobby, lay on the stretcher, his body shifting as the aircraft pitched to the right or left.

Reiner spoke into the mouthpiece, "Arrowhead 1, this is Titan 2. He's stable, gave him a shot of morphine. The medication's starting to wear off."

#####

The medical chopper touched down at 2055 hours. The stretcher crew reached the open door to the helicopter before the blades stopped. Reiner ran behind the medical staff as they pushed the gurney across the tarmac.

When they entered the emergency room, Dr. Wade McCall rushed up to the Lieutenant. "Thanks to you, we're going to be able to start the transition right away." At that moment, a doctor ran up to McCall. "Are you going to take care of him?"

"No, Doctor. I'm the President of his Council. Doctor Hampton and I need to work on his assuming complete control. I have faith in you and your ability." The Emergency Room Doctor turned, and caught up to the medical team.

Reiner and McCall entered a conference room. The first soldier to see them stood, before he could call the others to attention, McCall said, "Carry on." He surveyed the room and pointed to a man at the far end. "Corporal, who's in charge?"

At that moment a Sergeant entered. "Dr. McCall? I talked to you on the phone." He set a stack of papers on the table. "I made all the calls you ordered me to. They'll be here before midnight."

McCall put a hand on the man's shoulder. "Thanks, Son." He looked around and pointed to two lower-enlisted soldiers. "We don't need you anymore. You can leave. Thank you for helping us set up."

As the young man and young woman left, McCall leaned out the door. "Nurse, get me an administrator. We're going to use this room while Bobby's being treated."

He turned to Lieutenant Reiner. "I'm told you're his aide. Get the Watchers to provide extra security."

Reiner pulled a tablet from a cargo pocket and scribbled. "Yes, Sir. I'll have extra computers brought down too."

"Good initiative. Now, go check on how he's doing."

Bobby slowly woke as he lay on a gurney. "Uhh, did anyone get the license number of that truck?"

Immediately, McCall and a nurse jumped up and rushed to Bobby's side. McCall said, "If you're joking around, you can't be that bad off."

Bobby reached up and wiped his face with his free hand. For several seconds the sound of the IV pump was the only noise they heard. Then he glanced at the nurse. "Please leave, we have something to discuss."

The old woman shook her head, looked at Bobby, and stood her ground. "Sorry, Sir. I need to monitor your vitals."

McCall touched her on the arm and motioned for her to follow him. He turned to face her. "It won't take long. I'll watch everything, and call you if he needs attention."

Reluctantly, she left, walked across the hallway, and sat at a desk facing the door.

McCall returned to Bobby's bedside. "She's over-zealous. I'm sure she'll get over it." He reached behind and closed the cubical curtain. "Now, what's so important that can't wait to get out of here?"

Bobby's chin quivered. "W... w... we've been together for many years, we grew up in the same town. I have a decision to make and I don't know what to do. It'll affect everything." *He's not going to understand. Lord, you're the only one I have. I really need you to pull me out of this.*

Concerned about what his boyhood friend might be upset about, McCall pulled a chair next to the bed and sat, half on, half off the seat. "Go ahead, take your time."

Bobby tried to sit. He got up on one elbow and fell back onto the bed.

McCall sat and watched Bobby. "You'll learn. Don't move fast. If you want to sit up, I'll raise the head of your bed."

Grimacing in pain, Bobby nodded and pointed an index finger at the ceiling.

McCall picked up the remote from the over-bed table and raised the head of his friend's bed. "Okay, now, what's on your mind? Don't rush."

Bobby shook his head. "Don't have time. In the four years I went to college I fell in love with a northern girl. Her name is Bernadette Grayson. You'll find her contact info in my wallet. Get it for me, please. I told her I'd send someone to escort her here. Last I heard she's in Seattle."

McCall smirked as he went to the closet and retrieved the wallet. "Sure, I'll call her when we're done. So, what's the problem? We've had girls before. We like them, have our way with them. When we're done we move on." He paused, moved his glasses down the bridge of his nose, and said, "You didn't get religion on me did you?

"Sure did. We made a pact; that we won't even kiss or hug until our wedding day. That way we'd be able to savor our first physical relationship with each other." He struggled and rose up on one elbow. "We've kept that pact. I'm going to resign my position and marry her. My mind's made up." Then he slumped back onto his pillow.

At that moment, General Grimes and Doctor Wade Hampton came in. Grimes frowned. "Son, I heard you promise your grandfather that you would at least consider the woman he had chosen for you. I know he's not around anymore, but I have to hold you to that."

Hampton set his coat and hat on a chair and moved to the foot of the bed. "You don't have a choice. Catherine will be here in the morning. I expect you to honor your commitments. Understood?" He fingered the lid on the needle disposal container as he talked. "You won't like the only other option you have. You know too much."

Understanding the magnitude of the old doctor's comments,

Bobby frowned. "I'm not making any promises. I will guarantee that when I get out of here, if not before, I'm at least going to see my Bernadette." Then he folded his hands on his lap. "Ouch," he yelled, as the IV tubing reached the end of its limit.

McCall pointed a finger at Bobby. "Serves you right, you need to listen. We've got your best interest at heart." He stared at his watch. "She'll be here soon. I want you to get some rest. You have a big day ahead of you."

Bobby seemed to become more anxious as he stared back at each of them. "Well, Bernadette will be here soon too. It'll be awkward if the two of them are in the same room."

Hampton smirked, "We'll see, Son. We'll see. I usually get my way." He nodded to Grimes and McCall. "Let's get our meeting started. I'd like to have the transition ceremony soon." He glared at Bobby. "Maybe we'll do it at the wedding reception."

Bobby lay back and tried to ignore them. "I'm tired. I'm going to get some sleep." *If I ignore them maybe they'll go away.*

After the three leaders left, Bobby opened his eyes, and listened to the sounds of their footsteps fading away as they walked down the hall.

For the next hour Bobby napped fitfully. *What am I going to do? I'm only going to marry one woman. Bernadette!* He glanced at his watch, and thought, *its 0100,* I sure hope Bernadette makes it before this Catherine woman.

As he closed his eyes, he heard familiar high heels clacking down the hall. "That's not Bernadette. Oh no! She's the last person I need to see right now." He said softly under his breath.

Soon a woman opened the curtain and Deirdre Lee stepped next to Bobby, and stroked his head. "Oh Honey, I was so scared. I saw on the news when the Federals were shooting at you. I lost your father and brother to this war. I couldn't bear to lose you, too. Then Grimes sent for me. I landed five minutes ago." As she talked she hugged her son and peppered his head with kisses.

After a few minutes, the nurse came in. "Ma'am, I need him to get some sleep." Deirdre reluctantly stood and held Bobby's hand. "I prayed so hard for you. I was afraid your plane would turn into a ball of fire. Get some rest now. I'll be here. I'm so excited about seeing Catherine again. It's been years since I've seen her. She's such a nice girl."

Bobby clenched his teeth, and smiled as best he could. "I sure hope so, Mama."

Deirdre kissed him on the cheek and left to find Grimes.

As he started to doze off for the thousandth time, he woke with a start. Ignoring the pain, he sat up. *That's Bernadette's walk, I know it is.* "Praise the Lord, she came first. I hope I have time to explain everything to her before their choice for me shows up."

There was a light rap at the door. A woman's voice called out, "Bobby, is this your room?"

"Yes Sweetie it is. Come in, don't open the curtain, I don't want anyone to know you're here. I've got so much to say and not enough time to say it."

As he finished his command to his true love, a man's hand opened the cubicle. Standing there was Bernadette, Deirdre, Hampton, Grimes, and McCall. Everyone was smiling and laughing.

Apparently aggravated at being the victim of a practical joke he yelled out, "What's so funny?"

McCall stepped to the foot of Bobby's bed. "Buddy, let me introduce you to Catherine Jobe."

Bobby's jaw dropped into his lap. He closed it twice and couldn't speak.

Catherine moved next to him and lovingly stroked his head. "Sirs, I think we owe him an explanation. Shall I start?"

Hampton shook his head. "Not right now, we'll leave soon. You can explain everything when we're gone." He nodded at McCall, who stepped forward.

"Sorry for the deception, but you'll be taken upstairs soon. We're keeping you here so we can keep you out of the public eye. Tomorrow afternoon we'll schedule the transition ceremony and," he winked at Catherine, "if you want we can have the women start planning the wedding."

Still unable to speak, it was all Bobby could do to nod. The Rebel leaders and his mother left, the two lovers stared at each other.

Finally, Catherine sat back in a chair. "Since you seem to have lost your voice how about I tell you the short version?"

Bobby started to cough. *What's happening? Is this true? Bernadette and Cat the same woman? I don't believe it.*

She reached over and filled his water glass from a pitcher. She looked at him with adoring eyes. "I was raised in Mobile, Alabama. My lineage comes from Martha Washington, on my mother's side, and General Lee, on my father's. Last week, my Daddy told me that we're really third cousins, twice removed from your side of the family. I knew about General Lee's 'project' for years. I was sent north to go to school and, like you given a cover identity. Like you, I joined the ROTC program as a freshman."

Bobby sipped his water, then said, "Yes, but why didn't you tell me?" He took a deep breath, and absentmindedly took a handful of grapes from the bowl on his nightstand. Suddenly he snapped his fingers. "Wait a minute! My best friend in ROTC was Robert Anderson. After the fighting started, I found out that he was really Dewitt Jobe. Is he any relation?"

Savoring the nuances of her tale, Catherine squeezed Bobby's good hand. "He's a first cousin on my father's side. We're both direct descendants of the Dewitt Jobe who was hung by the Federals in 'Mister Lincoln's War.'"

They talked for hours. Then she reached over, and pulled a banana from the fruit bowl. "So you see, the other day when I saw that news footage showing you escaping from the Federals, I knew I had to make it to your side. I guessed that you are taking over from your Grandfather. I didn't know that our marriage had been arranged. I was hoping there was some way we could circumvent their plans." She winked at Bobby, "maybe even elope."

He scratched his head, "And to think everyone but us knew all along that we didn't know the other's identity was a cover, and that they had arranged for our wedding. I guess I wasted all that effort worrying about how we were going to resign, escape, and elope."

Catherine leaned forward in her chair, stroked the stubble of a beard on his face. They looked into each other's eyes. At the same time they winked, nodded, and shared their first kiss.

FOXTROT – Fendemere's Escape
(Late last Spring)

Major Fendemere hobbled down the hall toward Bobby's room. He flashed his badge and nodded to the Catawba Watcher at the door. He reached down and tapped the closed door with the tip of his cane. The sound of woman's shoes came near the door and Cat opened it.

"And who might you be?" she asked warily.

"I could ask you the same question young lady. I've come to see Bobby." He stepped between her and the door and hobbled over to Bobby's bed and sat on a chair.

Bobby woke, turned his head and smiled. "Mr. Fendemere!" He tried to sit up too fast and fell back onto his pillow. "I've gotta remember not to do that. He reached over, punched a button on a remote until the head of the bed was at the level he wanted. "It's good to see you." He reached out a hand and motioned for Cat to sit at his side. "Mr. Joseph Fendemere, this is my fiancée, Catherine Jobe. Cat, this is Mr. Joseph Fendemere. From what General Grimes tells me you almost single-handedly kept the Federal forces from leaving Europe and joining the fight against us."

Cat, apparently impressed, smiled and nodded her approval of the southern gentleman. "Mr. Fendemere, I hope you don't take offense at my being suspicious."

Fendemere stroked his newly grown goatee. "Not at all Miss Jobe. I've found that one can't be too careful these days."

Bobby stroked Cat's hair and said, "I heard you were stuck in Europe."

Fendemere grinned, and leaned back. "I was one of many Military Attaches who helped divert Federal assets." He stood, leaned over and grabbed an apple off Bobby's lunch tray. He munched on the crisp fruit, and started his story.

"Lieutenant Colonel Bostwick wouldn't accept any of the roadblocks I threw in his path. I finally had to resort to shooting down the aircraft I'd chartered for him."

Bobby interjected, "Ayers told me you guys had planned for every contingency."

"Yes we did son. I must say, that man made me use the back-up plan to my back-up plan to my back-up plan. I was pretty sure we'd get him in the end."

Cat leaned against Bobby's chest and focused on Fendemere.

The older man seemed to relish the opportunity to tell of his accomplishments. "I watched the 747 taxi down the runway. I punched a few buttons on my cell and waited. When the duty officer answered I said: 'This is Rebel Major Joseph C. Fendemere III. I have a message for General Lee. A crate for Washington D.C. just left L'viv airport. It weighs exactly four hundred three pounds. Thank you, no. I don't want to leave my number. He has it.'" He reached for his belt and retrieved his cell phone and demonstrated how he made the next call. "Then I called the National Guard Coordinator in Hoenfells, Germany."

He put the phone to his ear and continued. "Captain, have you heard the news?" He paused as if it was a real conversation. "That's right; I received word about it an hour ago. Listen carefully, it gets worse. I was just informed that a Delta Charter carrying a Battalion of California Army National Guard troops was shot down by a missile over the Atlantic." He paused, and nodded as if he was really talking to someone. "I agree with you, this is critical. I'm taking the Ambassador's jet and should be in your office in an hour or so. I need you to get me some information. Do you have a pen and paper? Okay, I'll wait."

He smirked as if he was following through with his plan all over again. "When I arrive I'll take charge of getting all units back to the states. I want you to have a complete, by-name list of every unit. Between the two of us we'll pull this off and make our President happy. Good bye for now." Fendemere reached over, snagged a banana from Bobby's fruit bowl and started to peel it. "I pretended to let him go, but I called out to him before he hung up." He licked bits of banana off his fingertips as he spoke. "Captain, if Washington's smart they'll call up the Civilian Reserve Air Fleet. You can reach me on my cell with all the information as soon as it comes in. I want to know when the aircraft leave and what units are on-board each one. Understood? Thanks, my plane's ready for me. I'll see you soon."

He returned his phone to its holster and winked at Cat. "Wow, just telling that story gets me excited."

Cat slid off the bed and straightened Bobby's blanket. "What I don't understand is how you guys tricked the Federal sub captains into shooting down their own CRAF flights?"

Fendemere stood, walked across the room and poured a cup of coffee. He stirred his brew and talked over his shoulder. "For years General Lee had been planting sleeper agents in the sub fleet. When the time came they were able to overpower the Federal crew on several subs. On others we were able to send phony radio traffic, and through that traffic, instructed the Captain to shoot down a missile that was disguised as a civilian airliner." He paused and scratched his head. "All told we were able to shoot down seven CRAF flights."

Bobby and Cat shook their heads. After finishing with Bobby's bedding, Cat moved back to her spot next to her man.

Fendemere pulled a chair close to him and propped up his bum leg on the seat. "I pushed my luck too far. After Hoenfells I went to England. By that time the Feds were on to me. As I was making my escape, a man with a familiar face rushed towards me as I rounded a corner. It turns out that he was Lieutenant Colonel Bostwick's cousin. He fired a lucky shot and hit me in the calf. I made it to my vehicle and made good my escape."

While he talked, the southerner absent-mindedly tapped his cane on the floor. "My Watcher was in the truck, he was able to evade the Federals and Brits who were chasing us. Then he administered first aid to my wound."

GOLF – Exchanging Vows
(Late September)

Catherine stood her ground. She tossed a knee brace at her fiancée. "You will wear this during the rehearsal, wedding, and the reception. It's important that we dance the money dance. My father's counting on us to pull this off. If your knee gives out in the middle of it, how is he going to get information for 'The Agency?' You may be in-charge of our military, but once we're married, you're accountable to me. Understood?"

Bobby sat on the edge of his bed. His good leg was in his trousers. "But. . ."

"No buts about it. I know the physical therapist told you that your knee is completely healed. But, she also said when you dance tomorrow night; the extra stress will weaken it. Mr. J. Hamilton Lee, if you don't support that knee you could do some permanent damage. NOW PUT IT ON."

Reluctantly, Bobby dropped his trousers and applied the brace. Ten minutes later he was dressed and ready. They walked hand in hand out of his room, down the corridor, and stopped in front of the elevator.

When Catherine leaned to push the call button, Bobby placed his cane, out of sight, and against a wall. Catherine purposely let Bobby in first. After he entered, she reached over, picked up the cane and held it in front of her man. "Lose something, Sweetie?"

Argh, he said under his breath, and then smiled. "Thank you, it must've dropped out of my hand."

"Yeah, right. You forget I've known you for years. Now behave or I'll make your life miserable. Got it?"

They stood in silence as the elevator descended. When the door opened, they both smiled for the crowd that awaited them.

Reiner nodded as he approached. "Miss Jobe, Mr. Lee, here's your copy of the schedule of events you approved earlier. If you'll follow me, the minister is ready." He turned and the couple followed.

At 1355 the next afternoon, the Ft. Bragg Chapel was filled with dignitaries from all over the world. Bobby stood, erect in his tuxedo. He shifted from one foot to the other, leaned over, and whispered to Dewitt Jobe, his Best Man. "Look at all the foreign diplomats. Fendemere told me the EU sent low-level representatives and want them to be as inconspicuous as possible. I guess they want to court favor on both sides."

Dewitt tilted his head toward the Chinese and Russian ambassadors sitting behind Grimes and Ayers. He barely moved his lips, "They and the South American diplomats are openly showing their support." Last night, on my way to the rehearsal dinner, I overheard Fendemere talking to the Mexicans and Cubans. He wasn't speaking only as our Secretary of State. He identified himself as the Chairman of 'The Knights of the Golden Circle.' He promised them a fast track if they want to enter the ROA. I really th. . . ."

At that moment, the first chords of Mendelsohn's 'Wedding March' were heard over the loudspeaker. All eyes turned to the rear of the Chapel.

Catherine started down the aisle, tall and slender. Her preference for simplicity was shown in her dress, made from the finest fabric, and designed by Vera Wang. As she started down the aisle, Bobby whispered to his friend, "Wow, she sure fills out that dress. The senior Catawba Watcher assigned to her told me they had the dickens of a time getting enough security for that shopping trip to Atlanta, I'm told she went to every store. No wonder it took a week."

By the time Catherine reached the altar, her father, a ROA General in full dress uniform, stopped and nodded toward Bobby. He stepped forward and accepted Catherine's hand. They smiled and walked in front of the Chaplain.

Fifteen minutes later, the Clergyman closed his Bible, peered around Bobby's shoulder, and turned the couple to face the congregation. "Ladies and Gentlemen, I present Mr. and Mrs. J. Hamilton Lee." They walked, arm-in-arm, to the back of the Chapel. In five minutes they stood in front of a receiving line. After hundreds of guests paid their respects to the bride and groom, everyone entered the reception hall.

The wedding party, and a few heads of state entered the Chapel, the photographer and her team, quickly and deftly performed their duties.

After the last photo was taken, Bobby whispered into Catherine's ear. She giggled, grabbed his hand and they ran off to change clothes.

An hour later they entered the reception hall. Bobby wore slacks and a sport shirt, Catherine, a royal blue suit, Bobby's wedding gift of a black Tahitian pearl necklace, with matching earrings exquisitely complemented her features. The first person to see them rose and started to clap. Soon everyone in the hall was applauding. The couple walked to the dais. Immediately, the waiters started to serve.

After the toasts were completed, the Master of Ceremonies tapped his crystal goblet. "Ladies and Gentlemen, in a few minutes we're going to have the money dance. General Jobe will start with his daughter. Mrs. Lee will begin with her son. Anyone wishing to join in, should line up at the table by the door. The attendants will accept your money, and then have you get in line. For those who wish to use credit or debit, we can swipe your card you will receive your receipt in an e-mail. I should note that one-hundred percent of the money raised will be given to the charities of your choice from the list on the table. Thank you in advance." He sat, and the orchestra started to play.

As the first notes came from the tenor sax, Bobby and Catherine strolled onto the dance floor. They twirled once around the parquet and each parent tapped their child's new spouse on the shoulder.

Catherine giggled as she and her father glided across the floor. *Daddy and I haven't had so much fun since Mama died.*

General Jobe whispered in her ear, "Cat, is your microphone in place?"

"Yes Daddy. Your technician put it in my broach. Bobby's is in one of his buttons." As her father twirled her around to the beat of the music, she looked at the line waiting for their turn. "Okay, let me get this, you want me to thank each of the diplomats by name, and then get them to talk about how they really feel about supporting us."

"Yes, I'm proud of you. I wish your mother had lived to see this. She would've been as pleased as I. The confidence you display will serve us well."

As the first song died down, Catherine hurried up her parting comment. "I hope your agency can use all the info we get."

The General kissed her on the cheek and squeezed her hand. "I'm sure it will."

After several dances, an English Earl took his turn with Catherine. "Sir, you have to be the smoothest partner I've had yet."

"Thank you Madam. My parents made sure I learned all the old and new steps as I grew up."

She leaned close to his ear, and whispered, "Thank you for your support."

The young English gentleman jerked his head. It appeared he understood that she meant more than supporting her favorite charities. "You realize that I'm not representing my government. Mr. Fendemere invited several of us from the EU on a fact-finding tour of your country. I must say, most of us have been impressed, but officially, we have to remain neutral."

The Earl spun her around and when he caught her again, she squeezed his waist. "I heard that once your father passes, you might become a member of the House of Lords. Is that true?"

It appeared the thirty-two year old man was pleased that such an elegant woman knew about his personal life. He squeezed her back.

As she spoke, her lips brushed against his cheek. "When that happens, can we count on your support?"

"Well, uh, I really can't speak to an issue until I examine all the factors involved."

"Sir, our time's almost up. I have a friend I'd like you to meet. I'll have her contact you. She'll give you all the data you require. If you give her what she wants, I'm sure she'll find a way to contribute to your support."

As she finished, the band stopped playing. Before she started clapping to show her appreciation for the band's performance, her hand lingered on the Earl's waist.

As her next partner approached, she quickly whispered, "I hope you guys caught that. Get someone in bed with him tonight. We'll get his support, one way or another." Then she smiled at her new partner. "Presidente, so good to meet you. Thank you for being here."

#####

Bobby and his mother twirled around the parquet floor. She leaned her head and whispered into his ear. "They told me your mic is working well. Be sure you don't knock it off as you dance."

"Yes Mama, I'm glad you're working with Cat on this project. I never expected you to approve of some of the activities she's coordinating."

"Sweetheart, I'm committed to doing what I can. I can't fight, but I can help. All I'm going to do is collate all the reports the ladies and gentlemen of the evening give us."

#####

It was one in the morning before the last strains of music died. At 8:00 am, General Jobe, Fendemere, Grimes, Ayers, Bobby, and Catherine met for breakfast to evaluate the information gleaned from the previous night.

Fendemere paused while cutting his sausage, "Catherine, I'm surprised that such a righteous woman as you would come up with putting those diplomats in such vulgar, compromising positions."

The General apparently surprised to hear that that part of their scheme had been his daughter's idea, jerked his head, and glared.

Catherine, sensing her father's distaste about her participation with such sordid details, reached over and patted her father's hand. "Don't worry Daddy. I'm not that kind of girl. Up until last night, I'd never been with a man." She took a sip of water. "But you didn't raise me in a convent. I know what motivates men. I know there are women who enjoy taking advantage of them. All I did was find those who wanted to further our cause. Is a woman who's promiscuous, any less a heroine for using her charms, than a soldier who charges up a hill and kills the enemy?"

She leaned over, and stroked Bobby's cheek. "Don't you agree?"

Bobby, startled by the revelation, he stammered for words. "Uh. uh. . . of course you're right, Dear. We need to give everyone a chance to show their patriotism."

HOTEL – Prisoner Exchange
(Late September)

Bobby cradled the phone on his shoulder as he waited for someone to answer. "This is Bobby Lee calling for General Garfield McClellan, would you be so kind as to see if he's available?" *I've got these Federals right where we want them. They don't have a chance. I know they'll fall for it.* He sat in his leather chair, tapped his fingers on the desktop when a woman's voice came back on the line.

"I'm putting your video call through now, sir."

"Lieutenant General McClellan, this is Bobby Lee. How are you today, Sir?"

The screen on his monitor pixelated, then Bobby's smiling face solidified. Hiding his emotions, Garfield pulled a tablet in front of him and motioned for Sergeant Major Hart to sit just off camera. "Fine, young man." He said tersely, "I received the notice that you wanted to talk. What can I do for you?"

"Sir, it should be obvious that our effort hasn't slackened. Your stealth gliders were a good idea, but we knocked most of them out right after you, supposedly won the battle. Our missiles took out your production facilities the next day. So it's going to be a while before you can mount another attack." Bobby smirked as he talked. "As you know, we have a lot of prisoners that are overwhelming our system. I'm sure your intelligence has told you we're getting ready for a big offensive. We need to make room for the prisoners we expect to capture. I'd like to discuss a prisoner exchange."

Panic came over Garfield. He hurriedly wrote on his tablet and shoved it over to Hart. The Sergeant Major nodded and rushed out. Garfield cleared his throat and tapped the desk in front of him as he spoke. "That can be arranged. How many representatives will you send?"

Bobby grinned when he saw the apparent strain on Garfield's face. He put his feet up on his desk. "Sir, along with myself, I'm sending Dr. Wade McCall, the President of my Council, and Generals Grimes and Ayers. Whom would you send?"

Garfield, thinking he was getting the best of the situation, smiled as Hart returned with several staff members. They sat across the table while he punched the speaker button. "Mr. Lee, it'll take a while to pull my team together, I suggest we plan for 1000 hours on Thursday, 29 September. That's in three days. I'll send representatives of suitable rank. Could you arrange for the meeting to be held in the Murfreesboro, Tennessee Courthouse? That town has special significance for some members of my staff."

"Murfreesboro is fine, General. I look forward to hearing from you."

Garfield hung up the receiver and pointed a finger at the two men sitting across from him. "General Duffield, you performed extremely well leading your Cavalry Gliders. And General Lester, I'm pleased with your performance in organizing the remnants of our Air Force into a viable fighting unit. I believe the two of you are the best we have to head up our delegation." He stood and paced the front of the room. "Gentlemen, I want you to scour the prisoner lists. This evening I expect a report with a prioritized roster of federal and rebel prisoners, especially the high-ranking prisoners they captured the first day."

As they walked out of the conference room, Duffield put an arm around his friend's shoulder. "Lester, I don't think the old man realizes the significance we play in this project."

Lester smiled, "And to think we'll be in Murfreesboro! If we pull this off we can eliminate the shame Brigadier General Forest caused our families back in 1862."

His grey-haired friend nodded. "When that rebel, Nathan Bedford Forrest, tricked your great-great-great-great-grandfather into making that erroneous report in 1862, it showed the type of unscrupulous liar he really was."

Lester opened a door and let his friend go through. "My ancestor was a good judge of people, a trait our entire family has demonstrated for generations. If it hadn't been for the fog of war, Colonel Lester would've realized that that Rebel was moving troops around his camp to make it appear as if he had many more soldiers than he really did."

They walked to their vehicle. Lester took out his key fob and unlocked the car doors. "This time we'll be the ones who'll come out on top!"

They both smiled and fastened their seat belts.

Bobby hung up the phone. He reached out to shake Dr. McCall's hand as he came into the room. Two majors carrying briefcases were right behind. "Doc, McClellan just confirmed they'll meet our delegation in Murfreesboro on the 29th. I'm assigning Grimes and Ayers to lead the team. The four of us will attend the meetings and set the stage for our trap, there's not much time, we need to prepare."

After releasing Bobby's hand, McCall pulled a tablet from a cargo pocket, and sat next to his young leader and boyhood friend. "Well, Sir, I think these two officers would make the best team." He glanced over to the two men sitting across from him. "I've nothing against Grimes and Ayers, but they're part of your grandfather's era. I want these men to be on my team. Their fresh ideas will let the world know you're in charge…"

Bobby slammed a fist on the table. "Grimes and Ayers have the insight that other officers don't. I can't think of anyone else who can pull it off. I don't care about making a statement for the history books. I want to win this battle. If rubber-stamping General Lee's policies will do it, then fine." He stood and pointed a finger at Mac, the whirr of the air conditioner hummed in the silence. "When the time comes, I'll develop my own policy."

He glanced at his watch. "I know we grew up with the men you want on your team. My grandfather started this project with Grimes and Ayers. They will finish it. I have something for the new guys to prove their worth. I agree we need to consider fresh ideas. You will include these two in planning the prisoner exchange. With the experience they get, there'll be a better chance of success. Understood?"

"Yes sir." Dejectedly, he sat and stared.

Bobby glared back. "I want them to observe how the old team does things. I don't want them discounting the old ways just because Grimes and Ayers are older than dirt." He pulled several pieces of paper from a folder, and slid them across the table. "Here's the background on their project. They're to come back to me with a plan for handling welfare and immigration issues for the ROA. Understood?"

The young doctor pursed his lips. "Sir, yes sir." Awkwardly the other men in the room looked intently at the table in front of them.

Grimes' image appeared on many video screens across the ROA. "Ladies and gentlemen, we come from different walks of life, different beliefs. Yet this conflict gives us similar goals. In the next hour you'll be given information about an opportunity. If you accept the challenge, you'll be given $1,500.00 in cash, and two credit cards with a $5,000 limit per month. You'll have two sets of clothes. Those of you with parachute training will be given extra credit if you jump. Those who don't have that training will be given a plane, bus, or train ticket for you to use after our helicopter drops you off. You'll be traveling in pairs. Let your coordinator know if you have a particular partner you'd like to travel with."

At the Bryan Federal Prison, Marshall Brown turned his attention from the big screen to the stack of papers in the folder in front of him. He scratched his head. "Hmmm, let's see. They want to drop me off outside Pierre, South Dakota. That's not bad. My uncle lives in Minot, that's not even 320 miles. I can steal a car and give the old boy a surprise."

Three days later, Duffield and Lester, wearing their immaculate army and air force uniforms, stood with their aides in the foyer of the Murfreesboro Courthouse. Duffield looked around. "So this is where it all happened over one-hundred-fifty-four years ago."

His friend stroked his mustache, looked around, and set his briefcase on a bench. "I can sense the history in this place. This is the town where General Nathan Bedford Forrest tricked our ancestors into surrendering." As he talked he looked around the foyer and up the stairs. "I wonder where the Rebels are."

At that moment they heard footsteps echoing on the landing to their right. They saw a rebel sergeant motioning for them to come upstairs. "This way Sirs." His southern drawl poured off his lips. "Your aides will wait there."

Duffield shook his head as the Federals started up the stairs. "Our team will stay together. You don't dictate anything to us."

The rebel sergeant shook his head. "I won't argue with you sir, but you really don't want to cross General Grimes."

Lester reached the top of the stairs first. "Sergeant, we don't report to him. Rebels embarrassed our ancestors in 1862. It's not going to happen again. We're in charge of this meeting. Now take us to him."

The young rebel sergeant grinned as he led the federals into a conference room, "Yes, sir. Anything you say."

Bobby, McCall, Grimes and Ayers stood as the Federals entered. Bobby reached out to shake his enemy's hand. "General Duffield, this is supposed to be an initial meeting between us. I don't want any detractors getting in the way." He paused, nodding to the Sergeant, "Escort the extra Federals to the Three Brothers Bar and Grill. Get them some lunch. Bring 'em back in two hours."

Duffield and Lester motioned to the rest of their delegation as they started to leave. Duffield held his hand up. His soldiers stopped and turned their heads.

Grimes stepped in front of the two federal officers. "Sirs, consider your next move. You have more to lose than we do. I suggest you go with the flow." Then he stepped back and spread his hand to allow the federals to pass.

Duffield and Lester stared at each other for a few moments and nodded to their team to leave.

Grimes, led the two Federals, their footsteps echoed through the large meeting hall until they entered a smaller room. *I bet these rubes think they're going to get one over on us. I don't think so.* When he reached the buffet table, he turned and glared. Dr. Mac and Ayers stood on either side of their enemies.

With a wan smile, Ayers pointed to the food and said tersely. "Gentlemen, I suggest we get to know each other over a southern barbeque."

"Humph" snorted Duffield. "Listen here. We don't have all day. We came to do a job. We have prisoners counting on us. We ate before we came, let's get down to business."

Ayers said, "Sir, even though you're our enemy, southern hospitality dictates that we be gracious hosts. If you choose to be rude, that's your problem. I pray to my Lord every day for you. You don't appear to have a gentle spirit."

Lester scowled and shook his head. "Religion has nothing to do with this. My Lord has given you what you deserved when we defeated you this fall. We have a conflict that you started the same as in 1861. We're going to finish it. We have to work with you, but we don't have to get to know you. We don't want to eat with you. We want to start the negotiations."

Duffield nodded, set his briefcase on the table, opened it, and sat.

Grimes loaded a plate with food. "Sorry you feel that way. But we're going to eat. Maybe we'll get something accomplished in spite of your attitude. If you choose not to participate, it's your loss. At my request, Chef outdid himself for you."

Lester breathed slowly and kept his temper. "Colonel, it's not that we're being rude. We came expecting to get to work right away. We don't want to waste time."

Mac leaned between the Federals and Grimes. "Sirs, there's no reason we can't have a working lunch." Glancing at the two men, he said, "We've gone out of our way to be good hosts," he paused, picked up two plates, and set them in front of the Yankees. "Now, let's not waste any more time."

Reluctantly Duffield and Lester each took a dish from the rebel. The silverware clanked against their plates as they each picked up a set of cutlery. Five minutes later, after the servants had filled their coffee cups and left, Grimes pulled a folder from his briefcase, and stared at Duffield.

"Sir, do you have a roster of prisoners you want to return to us?"

Duffield's plate screeched across the marble tabletop as he pushed it to the side and removed an envelope from a pocket.

"Yes sir. I have a list of the five thousand of your service members we've captured in the past, what fifteen months?" He slid the roster across the table to each of the Rebel officers. "Now, our records show that, including the officers captured on sneaky Saturday, you have fifteen thousand of our service members. Does that agree with your figures?"

Ayers ran a finger down the list of names and smiled. "Interesting, I understand and appreciate that you've done a good job of taking care of our prisoners." He said, "How many of your men and women do you think one of our prisoners is worth?"

Lester took a deep breath, "We'd like to trade one of our service members for three of yours." Then he looked at Grimes, back at Ayers, and then Mac.

Grimes smirked, "I think we can arrange the ratio you asked for, but we're talking about returning 40,000 prisoners."

Both Federals dropped their forks, and said, "WHAT?"

Ayers leaned forward, "You heard correctly. We aren't interested in negotiating for your service members we've captured. However, we have that many prisoners that we want to repatriate."

Duffield pulled a folder from his briefcase. He and Lester leaned so their shoulders touched, and skimmed through it. Lester looked up through his glasses that had slipped down his nose. "We haven't lost that many prisoners in the conflict. How did you arrive at that number?"

Grimes rubbed his chin and took a sip of his iced coffee. "We're not talking about exchanging your Prisoners Of War for our Prisoners Of War." Then he pulled a sheet from the stack of papers.

Dumbfounded, Duffield and Lester stared at the two rebels. Duffield stammered, "Th... Th... Then, where do you come up with that number?"

Ayers stood, retrieved a coffee pot from the buffet. "Anyone for more coffee?" No one answered. No, okay, then. You see we have twenty federal prisons in the Republic of America. These facilities were formally operated by the USA Bureau of Prisons. We did a survey and have a roster of over 40,000 criminals who were convicted of a federal crime against the north, these men and women are from the USA and we don't think we should bear the expense of incarcerating them any longer. That's why we initiated these talks."

Duffield stood and shook a fist at Grimes. "Sirs, this is criminal! We won't agree to any such exchange."

Lester nodded, and both Federals started to gather their paperwork.

Mac put a hand on Duffield's briefcase. "Why should the ROA pay for criminals who haven't committed a crime against her? We're willing to exchange the five thousand EPWs you have for fifteen thousand of our prisoners. The fact that our inmates weren't involved in the recent hostilities isn't an issue." He paused, "Of course then we have to negotiate what we're going to do with the remaining detainees." He smirked and continued, "Maybe we could exchange some of the remaining civilian prisoners for a price."

Red-faced, the two Northerners vigorously shook their heads and started to rush out the door. Duffield's briefcase slammed against his leg as it slid from the table to his side. "These negotiations are over. I knew we couldn't trust a Rebel."

Ayers moved to the door and held it open for the two men. "Sir, calm down, We didn't start Mr. Lincoln's War. All we've done is to remove your occupation forces from our country."

Duffield came up behind Mac and the two Rebel officers. "Mr. Lincoln's War? Where did you get your history lessons from?"

Grimes poked a finger at Duffield's chest. "The winners usually write the history. We've kept the truth alive for one-hundred-fifty years. It was the north who didn't want to negotiate in 1860 and '61. The same as you refusing to discuss this issue with us now."

Duffield stared at Lester for a few seconds. Then tilted his head toward the door. "Let's get outta here. We're finished." Then he turned toward Grimes. "Sir, you know how to get in touch with us if you decide to be realistic."

Ayers chuckled. "You've had your chance. We won't call you about this again. I guarantee you will rue this day." Then he ushered them out the door.

#####

Inmate Marshall Brown examined the contents of the boxes in front of him. *Let's see. They're giving me a laptop, 5G smart phone; two credit cards with a $5,000.00/month limit each, a M1911 .45 cal pistol, five hundred rounds of ammo, and $1,500.00 in tens, and twenties.* He looked around and saw the other prisoners were as dumbfounded as he.

Rebel Captain Henderson came to the podium and leaned into the microphone. "Ladies and gentlemen." He paused as the noise level diminished. "Thank you. If you'll set your boxes aside for a moment, we've assigned a counselor for every two prisoners. In a few moments, they'll review your itinerary and what we expect. I need you to remember that you're not being recruited into the ROA military in any way." He paused and took a sip of water from the glass in front of him.

As he put the glass down, he surveyed the audience. You are being released because you've never committed a crime against the

ROA. The USA doesn't want to negotiate for your release, so we're going to give you the means to start a new life in the north. Your counselor will give you two requirements: 1. obey all laws, and 2. never to return to the ROA." He stepped in front of the podium and spread his hands. We wish you well in your new endeavors. Before you agree, feel free to ask any questions of your counselor. After we've completed the paperwork, each of you will board a helicopter for your new home in the USA." Henderson came to attention, and nodded.

"Thank you for your time." Then he left the room.

Marshall looked around and noticed a stocky prison guard approach his table and motion for the prisoner next to him to move closer. As the prisoner obeyed, the guard sat, opened a file, and looked at the two men. "Gentlemen, I need to reemphasize the Captain's remarks. When you agree to this arrangement you aren't to return to the ROA under any circumstances. If you do, we reserve the right to re-instate your original sentence, or," He stared at each of them, "The right to execute anyone who doesn't comply with their commitment. Is that understood?"

Marshall nudged the old man sitting next to him. He shrugged. "I won't ever come back here. Where do I sign?" He reached into his box, grabbed a pen, and pulled the cap off.

The elderly prisoner shook his head. "Weeell. Ah don't rightly know…"

The counselor leaned over to Marshall's partner and said, "Doesn't matter to me. You're the one who goes back into solitary for the next month."

Startled, both prisoners said, "What for?"

"Simple fact that we don't want the Federals finding out about

76

our operation. We're going to ensure there's no chance for them to get an idea of the magnitude of our incursion into their economy."

Marshall looked at his friend and pointed to the box in front of him, "Which would you rather do, go into solitary or play with the toys in that box?"

"You've got a point." Then he took the pen from Marshall's hand, and hurriedly signed and dated where his counselor pointed.

Next evening as Marshall and his partner lined up with their carry-on luggage. He looked over and watched his partner slump to the floor. He knelt and yelled, "Is there a doctor nearby? This guy needs a doctor!" Then he started to loosen the man's clothing.

Medical personnel rushed to the scene and pushed Marshall aside. His counselor came out of nowhere and dragged him out of the way. Marshall reached behind him, grabbed his partner's backpack and slid it next to his own. In the fuss, he deftly opened the pack, pulled his partner's wallet, cash, and credit cards out, and slid them into his own. He let himself be led away from the commotion.

When they reached a table on the other side of the room, the counselor took a deep breath. "Marshall, are you willing to go it alone?"

"Yes sir I'd rather work alone anyway." *This keeps me from having to kill the old man when we arrive in the north.*

Henderson came into the room and raised a bull horn. "Ladies and Gentlemen, it's time to move out. Make sure you have your luggage. You won't be coming back here again." He pointed to the far door. "If you'll go that way, you'll board your aircraft in ten minutes. Most of you should be airborne in thirty. The rest will be gone within the hour."

He lowered the bull horn and the sound of shuffling feet echoed through the hall as the prisoners started to file out.

Twenty minutes later Marshall set his backpack on a seat in a Chinook helicopter. He nodded to the woman sitting across from him. The prisoner on her right leaned forward, "Hey man, don't you look at my woman that way."

The woman jerked her head at her partner, "I'm not your woman! You got lucky that I was chosen to be your partner. So back off."

Her partner stood and faced Marshall. "I still don't like your looks, so I suggest you behave."

As he returned to his seat, she balled her fist and rammed it into his pelvis. "I've had it with you Buster. I'm going with Marshall here." She cocked her head toward her new partner, leaned, and shouted over the noise. "That doesn't mean I'm your woman any more than I was his. Got it?"

Marshall shook his head. "Yes Ma'm, don't worry." He yelled back, "I'm into much younger girls. Maybe you can help me score."

He gathered his gear and checked his pockets. He winked at Cindy. He shouted over the roar of the helicopter's engines. "Ready? Got all your gear?"

Cindy patted her pockets and slipped her backpack over a shoulder. "Let's go."

The crew chief sauntered from the front of the craft and leaned between Marshall and Cindy. He shouted. "Make sure you hit the ground running. I don't want a problem like we had with the last team we dropped off."

Cindy put a hand on the crew chief's shoulder. "We understand."

Then the rear ramp lowered and revealed the rising sun. When the platform was a foot of the ground, they ran toward a line of trees a hundred yards away.

Two weeks later, Marshall glanced at his watch as he sat in a restaurant. "Cindy, I sure hope this girl you told me about shows up."

She waited while the waitress set their pizzas in front of them. She leaned over and whispered, "When have I failed you? The train doesn't leave 'til three am. It's not even eight now. That gives us time to feed this kid, "do your movie" and dispose of the body. We've done this six times, not including the boys you brought me. In the past two weeks, when have I failed you?"

Marshall picked a slice of pepperoni off his plate and stared at the entrance to the pizza parlor. "CeeCee, I have to admit you haven't botched a setup yet."

Cindy frowned. "I've told you I don't like to be called CeeCee. The name's Cindy or Cynthia."

At that moment, a young sixteen-year-old brunette stopped at their table. "Excuse me, Cindy. Sorry I'm late. I got lost. I've never been in a big city before." She hungrily stared at the third pizza at the table.

Marshall stood and admired the slender young woman. "Well, Cindy. You've definitely outdone yourself this time. She has just the shape we need for the lead in our movie."

The girl sat next to Cindy and giggled. "Oh this is so exciting. When do we start shooting? When do I have to start memorizing my lines? What's the plot of the movie?"

Licking his lips, Marshall remembered that he didn't have his prey in the trap yet. He reached out and patted the back of the teenager's hand. "All in due time, we need to get to know you a little better first. After dinner we'll take you to your hotel suite and talk a little more privately. If there's time we might even show you how you look on film. Would you like that?"

"Oh yes, sir. My mother and friends at home never thought I'd amount to anything, and now I'm going to be in a movie! E-gads!"

Cindy put a slice of pizza on the girl's plate. She opened a note pad and ran a finger down a list of names. "Uh, Loretta? That's your name isn't it?"

In between bites, she said, "Yes M'am, Loretta Johanson, from Pierre, South Dakota."

How can she possibly talk with that much food in her mouth? At least she has the body to do what we want. "Would you be opposed to taking your clothes off for this movie? It'd be done tastefully, and you wouldn't be harmed in any way. Every act will be simulated and hidden from the camera."

Loretta gasped at the picture in her mind. "B… But… But Miss Cindy, what you're asking me to do is…"

Marshall smiled a toothy grin. "Loretta, you can back out at any time." He reached in his pocket and pulled out a wad of money. "Here, we promised you $1,000.00 for the first week. You can have it in advance. If you don't feel comfortable with anything we ask you to do, you can leave and keep the money. Okay, Sweetheart?"

Reluctantly, Loretta looked between the two adults, and then down at her plate. "Well, if you promise I can leave any time, I want the…"

Cindy put her arm around Loretta's shoulder, and squeezed. "I'll be there the entire time. When he asks you to take your clothes off, I'll be there for you."

Relieved, Marsha took a sip of her root beer. "Oh Cindy, would you? You're the only one I can trust. I'll do it. Let's go, I'm ready. I can eat my pizza in the car."

#####

Two days later Grimes, Ayers, and Bobby walked onto the stage in the La Vern E. Weber Auditorium at Camp Robinson, Arkansas. Grimes moved toward the podium and nodded to the camerawoman that he was ready. The red light at the top of the Panasonic P2 camera flashed brightly and Grimes smiled.

"Ladies and gentlemen, thank you for coming today. I know it was difficult for some of you northern reporters to get here. I trust you've been treated well."

Several northern reporters laughed nervously.

Grimes surveyed the audience and called out, "Marc La Blanc, would you like the first question?"

Marc, surprised that he'd be given the privilege after last year's interview with General Lee, jumped up. "Yes, sir. For the record, I'm Marc LeBlanc with XYZ news." As his nervousness wore off, he became more confident. "Sir, I've known you for years. You told me before that you supported General Lee because your ancestors backed them back in 1861. Why would an intelligent black man like yourself and your ancestors support the racist southern culture?"

Grimes smiled at Marc. "I could talk for hours, but two points come to mind. First, when Sherman's soldiers came through the south they raped the black women first. Second, most of the plantation owners treated their slaves like family. When the southern men went to war, it was the slaves who kept the plantations running and sending supplies to the front. If antebellum society was so harsh and tyrannical, why did a vast majority of the slaves support the south? It was only logical that my ancestors do the same, and my family would continue in that vain."

Several northern reporters started to interrupt and correct Grimes' version of history. He raised his hand. "SIT. For over one-hundred-fifty years, you northerners have dictated history for us. Now, you're in our house. I told you the truth. I won't have you wasting my time with your lies." He turned back to Marc. "Did you have another question, Sir?"

Startled at being able to make another inquiry, Marc stood again. "Will you confirm that you've released murderers and rapists from southern prisons and set them free in the north?"

The reporters surrounding Marc were surprised at his boldness. Some moved away from him as if they were afraid they would be in trouble because they stood next to him.

So, he did get the message to ask that question, I bet he doesn't know that I wanted him to be first. "Mark, I appreciate your boldness. To give you a direct answer, we haven't released prisoners to the north. What we did is offer them to the Federals. They refused to discuss the issue. Two days ago, we took prisoners of the USA federal prison system, who've not committed a crime against the ROA, and given them the opportunity to start a new life. We have sent them back to the north. If these people, who've committed no crime against us, commit a crime in the north, then it's up to the northern authorities to apprehend them." Grimes surveyed the audience and continued. "We instructed each and every one we released that we expect them to obey all laws."

He held a hand up as several reporters tried to yell their questions at once. "We initiated negotiations with the north. We gave them an opportunity to receive the prisoners in exchange for our service members. Since they wouldn't negotiate, why should we bear the expense of incarcerating their criminals?"

A man up front jumped to his feet and shouted, "What about reports that many of the criminals you flew to the north have committed murders, rapes, burglaries? Aren't you guilty of aiding and abetting each one of those criminals?"

Grimes grinned as if he had wanted that question to be asked. "Sir, we didn't encourage any of these individuals to commit a crime. As I said before, we offered to turn these people over to the Federals. You called me a criminal when I haven't done anything wrong. Look at your history books and tell me that General Tecumseh Sherman wasn't more culpable than I could ever be held accountable for? I told you earlier, we've instructed the people we released to obey all laws. General Sherman either encouraged or ignored the fact that his soldiers were committing crimes."

With that comment, Grimes closed his folder, and left the stage.

INDIA – Section 8 & Section 9
(Beginning October)

Bobby stroked his newly grown beard and surveyed the audience in the large meeting hall for anyone he recognized. He nodded at a few, and then pointed to a man sitting in the front row.

"Ladies and gentlemen, I'd like to honor a man who's served our country well." He stood in front of the podium and motioned for First Sergeant Riley to come forward.

Riley reached for his cane and slowly stood. As he made his way toward the front, several in the audience started to clap. Bobby encouraged the crowd, soon everyone cheered.

When he reached Bobby's side, the young man put an arm around the old soldier. "Please, we have a lot of information to cover." Slowly the audience returned to their seats. "Thank you. Before we get started, I want to recognize Thomas Riley for his actions in last year's victorious battle for Vicksburg. If it hadn't been for his leadership after his commander was killed, the Federals would've cut through our lines. He's medically retired now, and resuming his career as a Social Worker by assisting me with our endeavors here in his home town of Amarillo." He turned, shook Riley's hand, and motioned for him to move to the rear of the stage and stand next to the other civilian leaders.

Bobby stood to his full six-foot height and adjusted his microphone. "I've called you to here to reveal our plan for helping the unfortunate." He waved at those standing behind him. "These men and women are tasked with instructing you in the way in which we are going to move forward. In the next few days, you and your staff will be interviewing everyone who was on welfare in the old system." He moved behind the podium and crossed his arms, "If you'll look at your program, you'll see that we have everyone scheduled for breakout sessions. I need you to adhere to the agenda. It's crucial that everyone is well-versed on every topic. In two days we start implementation." Then he turned and marched off the stage.

#####

(8 October)

Riley's driver pulled their car in front of the convention center. "First Sergeant, look at that crowd, and we're three hours early. There isn't a spot left!" He put the car in park, jumped out, and ran to open the passenger door for his boss.

He slid out of his seat, snatched his briefcase and stood, then moved toward the front door. He limped with the aid of his walking stick as he waded through the line of people who had queued up outside the hall.

Half-way up the sidewalk, a hand grabbed his shoulder. A middle-aged woman looked him in the eye, and shouted, "Hey, you're the guy who's gonna send us away from our homes and break our families up."

Riley shook his head, and raised his voice. "Listen up everyone. I promise, anyone who wants to work will get a job with benefits. Those who can't work will be provided for as you have been in the past. Those who need medical attention will receive it." He paused and looked at the woman in front of him. "We will not knowingly break up a family. The core of our belief is the family. Just give me a chance to get set up. In three hours we'll open, and start processing. If a family doesn't want to register under our new system, they will have the option of staying under the old one."

He turned, and out of respect for the popular war hero, the

crowd made a path for him. His heels clicked on the sidewalk as he rushed to the entrance.

When he reached the doorway, a big security guard left his desk and rushed for the door. Riley called through the glass. "Hello Sergeant. It's good to see you."

"Top Riley, I heard they medically retired you. I was hoping you were doing all right. I haven't seen you since you dragged me from that burning truck."

After the two men hugged, Riley spoke, "When they carted us away in different ambulances, I never thought I'd see you again."

The young man wiped a tear from his cheek. "Top, you ever need anything, you just come to me." He blew his nose. "They're ready for you. I was told not to let anyone in until you give the word."

Riley glanced over his shoulder and surveyed the line that now extended out of the parking lot and down the street. *We've got our work cut out for us today. We have to succeed, Bobby's counting on us.* He transferred his briefcase to his left hand and shook hands with his former Sergeant. "I'll leave word they're to let you in. Look me up when you get off work."

#####

Two hours later, Riley approached a microphone. "Ladies and gentlemen, it's time for me to fulfill the promise I made earlier today." He gauged the mood of the crowd in front of him, and took a deep breath. *Well, here goes.*

"When I finish explaining today's agenda, I need all clients who want a job to go to room 104. All clients who cannot work go to room 101, and all clients who need some sort of assistance for a disability go to room 110."

He paused, took a sip of water, and moved to the edge of the stage. "If your family unit fits into more than one category, go to the station you feel most fits your situation and we'll work out a solution to keep your family together. I don't have time for questions. Your Social Worker will deal with any issues. If something is too difficult for them, they'll bring your case to me."

#####

Twenty minutes later, as Riley heard chairs slamming and voices coming from room 104. He rushed down the hall, and shoved his way through the crowd to the main counter. "What's going on here?"

A large, white man in a sweaty t-shirt and jeans held Lilly up against a wall. He dropped the young social worker at the sound of Riley's voice.

Riley gagged as he passed the smelly welfare client and pulled the young woman up from the floor. Several clients started to pick papers up and straightened tables.

Riley turned to the unruly man. "What's the meaning of all this? We're here to help you..."

The rowdy man rushed Riley, pulled a knife from a pocket, and held it to the hero's throat. "Listen, PIG. The man promised me a car, and a large house. I aim to get it."

The security guard rushed in and broke through the scattering crowd. He knocked the knife out of the angry man's hand, and held him against the wall. "First Sergeant, I told you I'd be there when you needed me."

Someone in the crowd yelled, "Be fair to the man!" And started to rescue him from what they seemed to think was certain arrest.

Riley nodded thanks to the security guard. *Okay, we covered some of this in our training sessions. Let's see if I can pull this off.* He held his breath as he put his arm around the irate man and spoke to the crowd that had started to surround them.

"It's obvious this man's been through a lot. I won't be pressing charges. I'll personally work his case to make sure he gets everything he deserves." Then he led him away, to an alcove and had him sit. "Sir, stay here for a few minutes. Let me discuss your case with your Social Worker."

Then he and said to Lilly. "Let's move over there. I have a few questions." He stood where he could observe the unruly client and still talk to his employee. *Boy is she shook. I've gotta get her calmed down or she'll be worthless the rest of the day.* "Miss, uh," he looked down at her name tag, "Miss Jackson, how did you happen to be here? You're very young to be given this kind of responsibility."

Lilly, still visibly shaken from her experience, "Mr. Riley my father was a First Sergeant in an infantry company. He was killed early in the war. I was attending school to become a social worker. I applied for an internship when I heard about your program." She calmed down as she talked to the retired soldier.

After five minutes Riley put a hand on her shoulder. "Carry on with your other clients. I'll take care of this case. Do you have his file?" She reached into her briefcase and handed him the folder.

He walked over to the alcove where the unruly man sat with a scowl on his face.

Riley smiled and held out his hand. "Sir, I know we can work this out. Come with me, let's find your family." He helped the welfare client up and they walked down the hall, "Tell me, Sir, where are they?"

Seemingly surprised at being treated with respect, the unhappy client looked around. "My wife's over there along the wall with our two toddlers. Andres, who's our oldest, and our oldest daughter are in school."

Riley led the man over to his family. When he reached the young woman, the toddlers started wailing at the presence of a stranger.

He knelt, reached into a pocket and pulled out a bag of candy. The children quieted down. "Talk to me."

The husband, surprised that his children took to a stranger, stood with his mouth open.

Riley sat at a nearby table, and opened the folder. After reviewing it, he rubbed his chin, and said, "Sir, I see here in addition to a car, you really need a four-bedroom house to keep your four children. Is that correct?"

Surprised that he didn't have to argue to get what he felt his family deserved, the husband stroked his wife's arm. "Uh...Uh... Sir, that's exactly what I want."

Riley pulled out his electronic notepad, tapped a few keys, and then placed a call on his cell. He looked up at the couple while he waited for someone to answer. "Well, sir, would you mind if we paid to move your family to another town? I checked and we don't have a four-bedroom home available..." He held his hand up. "No, wait a second. Give me a chance to explain. If you agree to the move, we'll give you a gift card to pay for your relocation expenses. We'll pay for one month's lodging, food, and of course transportation expenses for your entire family."

Riley winked at the husband and whispered, "I'll put it in writing." He smiled at the wife. "You wouldn't mind a little three-hour bus ride, if that means your family gets a new home, and a car would you?"

Both husband and wife nodded.

Riley hung up his cell, "I hate answering machines, don't you?" Then he called out to a clerk who passed by. As he hurriedly scribbled notes on the stack of forms he said, "Son, take this family over to room 101. Make sure they go to the front of the line. Here's their folder. They get top priority. Make sure the rest of their family links up with them before they board the bus. Including any pets they have. I want them on the first bus north." He shook hands with both clients. Then he took the official aside, "Make sure they understand that when they leave here, they'll have a layover in Oklahoma, and then move to their new home."

The clerk nodded, and shepherded them away.

Almost immediately, Lilly came back and approached Riley and handed him another file. "Sir, I left a man in room 110. He's upset that we've denied continuing his Federal Social Security Disability Compensation. I didn't tell him that since the beginning of this war, we've been hacking into the Federal computers to provide entitlements to them. And that starting the end of this month we're changing the rules."

Riley looked up from the thick file, and took a deep breath. "Hmmm, I remember this case. I denied it three times. The fourth time he got an attorney. His appeal went to DC. They must've granted it." He set the file on a table, neatened it up, and put it under his arm. "I'll take care of this. Lilly, Go back and tell him I'll be there in twenty minutes.

She smiled, "Better you than me Boss."

After he finished lunch Riley, file in hand, walked into room 110. He sat the man's file in front of him. "Sir, I've reviewed your case." He glanced up and nodded at the door.

Unnoticed by the client, a burly man silently stepped into the room. "I see that as I, you walked in here with a cane. You seem to be an intelligent person. I agree that you have a disability that keeps you from your chosen. . ."

The Client interrupted, "So you're going to approve my claim?"

Riley smirked, "In a way, you will have a job. You will perform any duty within the limits your Doctor has prescribed. You will be. . ." He paused and ran a finger down a list. "Here it is, you're going to be assigned to the First Baptist Church of. . ."

"I ain't have'n nuttin to do with any church. I ain't gonna work. I want my money." Then the disabled client jabbed his fist into Riley's nose. Blood splattered over the papers between them. Immediately the guard pulled a Taser from his belt and zapped the client on the neck.

A passerby ran into the room, pulled a wad of tissue from a box on a table and pressed it against Riley's nose.

As the burly Sergeant dragged the unconscious client out of the room, he said, "That's twice in a day Top. Maybe I should pull a double-shift and stay by your side."

Two hours and fifteen hard cases later, Riley made a video call to Bobby Lee. As Bobby's image appeared, Riley self-consciously ran a finger over his bandaged nose. He winced a bit, and then smiled at his boss.

"What happened to you? I didn't know you were in a combat zone?"

Riley chuckled, "Had two problem cases this morning. The second guy made contact. I'm all right. Just a bloody nose."

He ran a finger down the list in front of him. "All one-hundred-fifty churches and the seventy-five non-profit organizations in our region have accepted our proposal. This afternoon they took three-hundred-fifty families off welfare in return for keeping their tax-exempt status. They've agreed to pay minimum wage and provide benefits to all those who are of working age."

He leaned back in his chair and scratched an itch on his nose. "As to the developmentally disabled and homeless clients who don't want to accept a job we've provided, they've been transported to institutions. When they're mentally competent, they'll be released. Next..."

Bobby interrupted, "We don't want any of them to be released unless they will go by our rules."

"Yes sir, I agree. Our doctors have enough medication to ensure that at least for the short term we won't have a problem in the institutions. As we wean them off the program, we'll evaluate whether they should be released back into our society or not."

Bobby smiled. "Good job. I'm impressed. Did you have any other problems?"

Riley lowered his head and frowned. Yes sir, sixteen arrests, two clients were injured, and three social workers were sent to the hospital. We'll be finished in two days."

Grimes had been in the background and leaned into the picture. "Riley, what about those who need to be relocated? Do they have a clue as to what will happen in two days?"

"No, sir, they don't. We gave them brochures for housing and automobiles for them to select from. Tomorrow, we'll finalize all their choices, give them their gift cards, and prepare them for the move to their new home."

Bobby looked at his watch. "Riley, it's time for my briefing from Austin, Texas. Good job. I look forward to hearing from you soon." He stood, leaned over, and terminated the call.

#####

Garfield shuffled the reports laid out on his desk. He peered through his glasses at Sergeant Major Hart, and General Prewkowski. "Look at these statistics. The criminals the Rebels sent north have caused a crime spree like we've never seen. I've had to deploy troops to almost every state except Arizona, Nevada, Idaho, Oklahoma, and Montana." He pushed the papers aside and they slid to the floor.

Hart rushed to pick them up. "Sir, what's so special about those states?"

Prewkowski glanced at the 52-inch TV, picked up the remote, and raised the volume. "Sir, look at this!"

Garfield and Hart focused on the large screen. Hart pushed a button on the remote and Marc LeBlanc's image took up the entire picture, "I've been informed the state legislatures of Arizona, Idaho, and Montana have, just moments ago, voted to secede from the USA and join the Republic of America. I..."

Garfield grabbed the remote and muted the screen. "Enough of this. We'll get the details later. We've got to focus on how to combat this crime spree the Rebels have sponsored."

Riley boarded a bus and faced the passengers. "I'm here to send you off with my blessings. I wish you well on your journey. Your trip will take about three hours. You all have lunches and this vehicle has two restrooms. When you arrive, show your paperwork to your new social worker. *Won't that Federal bureaucrat be surprised?* I guarantee they will honor every commitment I've made."

He walked up the bus' aisle as he talked. He reached the rear and headed back to the front. "Every adult among you has a debit card with $1,000.00 available on it. Spend your money wisely." He paused, and glanced around at the sweaty passengers. "Your money, car, and debit cards are all paid for with money from a northern financial institution, if you have any questions go to a branch for that bank. You will be able to pick up your car tomorrow morning. If the north wants a welfare state, then they can have all the citizens their economy can't handle."

As he came up behind the driver's seat, the bus door magically opened. He paused as he started to exit, he turned back to face the passengers. "This is a driverless bus. It is radio controlled and will be escorted through Federal lines by a company of our soldiers. Once you are fifty miles inside the USA. The bus will stop. At that time the soldier operating the remote controls will open the doors and you may go to your new homes."

#####

Two hours later President Barnes paced around the Oval Office. He shouted Garfield's name as he watched the video screen. "What do you mean? You let all those buses through our lines!"

Exasperated, Garfield put his hands on his hips. "Sir, with all due respect, you haven't given me enough troops. I had to take units off the battle line to handle the criminals the Rebels sent north. Then just as our troops arrived at their new assignment, the Rebels had army units escort two-thousand-five hundred buses laden with welfare clients carrying bogus paperwork. What was I supposed to do? Ignore the murders, bank robberies, rapes, and other violent crimes the local police force couldn't handle? And then when our line was the weakest, they dump all the welfare cases they can find on us. What more do you expect, Sir?"

JULIET – The State of Sequoyah
(Beginning October)

The whine of jet engines echoed through the motor pool as Captain Hampton squeezed between two tanks. He tapped the shoulder of a Lieutenant as the subordinate started to climb upon a vehicle.

"Lieutenant Jackson." He shouted. I need to see you, NOW."

Startled when he felt his commander's hand on his shoulder, Jackson jumped back and fell to the ground. A soldier carrying several ammo cases tripped over the officer, caught a loose box and continued on his way.

As he tried to get up, Jackson slipped back and called out, "You startled me, Sir!"

Hampton towered over the shave tail as he struggled. He stretched out his hand to help the young man. Once standing, Jackson stared at his Commander looming over him.

He motioned for Jackson to follow him to a corner of the yard. He set his clipboard on a table, folded his arms and glared at his Executive Officer. "What gives XO? First Platoon should've had their tanks ready an hour ago.

"Wh, Wh, well you see, Sir, some of the men had to go to sick call, so we got a late start Then …"

"Lieutenant, I'm tired of excuses. You get a handle on your men or I'll replace you. I remember you requested each of them to be transferred to your Platoon. Yet you seem to have issues with them that no other Officer or NCO has had before. I don't care if your Father's a Chief, get your act together. Understood?"

Not knowing what to say, Jackson stood at attention. After a few seconds he nodded. "Yes Sir. If you're finished, I'll get back to my men. Sir!"

Hampton scowled, "Carry on."

As Jackson saluted and turned to leave, the Motor Sergeant came and stood alongside the two officers. He looked at the Lieutenant and then the Captain. "Sir, repairs have been completed on the XO's tank. Seems they weren't conducting maintenance checks in the proper order. I've told his men over and over that before they put the engine in gear, they have to let the oil pressure get up to the proper level. I can't make it any simpler."

Hampton stared at Jackson the entire time the old Sergeant explained the issue. "We've addressed this before, need I say more? I need you on top of your game today and especially with the detail you head up tomorrow. Do I need to spell it out?"

"Yes, Sir, I'll be ready." Then he ran off.

The crusty Sergeant moved in front of the Commander. "Sir, aren't we being too hard on him? After all he just graduated from ROTC. I don't know if he's up to tomorrow's mission."

"Hampton shook his head. "No my friend, he's a good kid, comes from strong Cherokee stock. He needs a kick in the seat of his pants. Hope he learns his lesson before this war kills him and his men."

He snatched his clipboard from the table, and moved to where he could watch Jackson from a distance.

Apparently motivated by his Commander's threats, Jackson ran from tank to tank, yelling at, and directing his soldiers. He grabbed one Corporal by the collar and dragged him to the side of an M-1 tank, pulled a technical manual out of another soldier's hand, and opened it to a chart. "I've told you before, perform your maintenance checks by the book, and don't skip any steps. Got it?"

The NCO took the book from the officer, "I promise I'll never forget again."

Jackson glanced around and saw other members of his Platoon standing and gawking. "The same goes for the rest of you. I'm tired of babysitting. Start doing things as you've been trained or I'll get someone else to do your job." He stared at several sergeants and other NCOs. "Understood?"

Some men said, "Yes, Sir." Others nodded. All turned back to the task at hand, getting ready for battle.

No sooner had Lieutenant Jackson departed when a Lieutenant Forrest ran up and saluted. "Sir, you wanted to see me?"

Hampton led the younger man aside and steered him through the mass of soldiers. "Here's the plan. There's a chopper waiting at the airfield to take you to Ft. Riley. When you get there, tell Lieutenant Colonel Duffield that we want to prevent another embarrassing situation for his family. We've received intel that at 0500 tomorrow, the Rebels are going to launch a massive attack toward Wichita. We plan to fall back from Oklahoma City to just inside the Kansas border. We'll turn around once we're behind him and launch a coordinated counter-attack. We need the running passcodes and the transponder frequencies for his unit. You give him this letter. We served together at Ft. Irwin back in 2012. He'll recognize my signature. Tell him as soon as we pass the Oklahoma/Kansas border, I suggest he attack any Rebels that come in sight. I believe they'll be about a quarter-mile behind us."

The skinny man chuckled, "This is brilliant. I'll leave right away. We'll suck those guys into a trap."

The Blackhawk helicopter touched down just past midnight.

Forrest and his Sergeant rushed to a waiting Hummer. As their Federal driver darted across the tarmac, the red beam from the Officer's flashlight bobbed up and down in his mouth as he talked. "Here we go. Take us to your Commander's quarters."

Moments later their boots shuffled up the stairs to the second floor of the Senior Officer Quarters. The two knocked on room 212, and waited to hear, 'Enter.'

He reported, and presented Hampton's letter to Duffield. "Sir, I'm to return immediately with your response." They stood at ease and waited for Duffield to look over the memo.

Duffield, wrapped in a plush terrycloth robe, looked at Forrest, and said, "Son, do you know the connection between our families?"

"Uh, no sir, There isn't one."

"Oh there's no doubt about it, why with your facial features and the fact that last week, my uncle was embarrassed by a relative of yours, I can't be too sure."

"Sir, if you have any doubts, you can double-check my credentials. I won't be offended. Captain Hampton will vouch for me. If you still have his cell number from when you were stationed at Ft. Irwin, he can answer any questions you may have as to my veracity."

"I just might do that." The Federal officer opened a drawer, pulled out, and powered up an old cell phone. Tones chirped as he punched the numbers into his newer phone and waited for the line to connect. Before he put the phone on the desktop he pushed the speaker button.

Captain Hampton's southern drawl came through the instrument. "Lieutenant Colonel Duffield, very good to hear from you. It's been a while hasn't it?"

Still not convinced, Duffield drummed his fingers on his desk top. "What rank were you when I saw you last?"

A quick reply echoed through the room, "Second lieutenant."

"Okay, what did we talk about?"

"That's an embarrassing thing to mention in front of my men. It's worth it if it'll convince you. I had just reported that I'd lost three soldiers in the desert for three days. You were quite upset. Then for some reason, after chewing me out, you took me aside and gave me some excellent guidance."

Apparently startled by their by-the-book Commander's past indiscretion, Forrest and his Sergeant glanced back and forth between Duffield and the cell phone.

Duffield turned the speaker off his cell. "I take it you didn't notice your Lieutenant has the same name as my ancestor's nemesis?"

Even though the speaker was off, Hampton's laugh was heard throughout the room.

"I knew you'd catch my joke. I promise you he's on the up and up. If you trust my loyalty to the USA, you can trust his."

Relieved, Duffield reached over and punched several buttons on a landline. "S-2, bring a copy of the running passwords and transponder codes."

Within minutes there was a knock at the door, a Sergeant walked in, handed an envelope to his Commander, and stood at attention. Duffield kept his eyes on Forrest.

The Federal Officer opened the envelope flap and a thumb drive fell onto his desktop. He scooped it up, and flipped through the list. Then he looked up at the man through his glasses, which had slipped down the bridge of his nose. "They can take this copy right?"

"Yes, Sir."

"Where do they sign?"

The Sergeant produced a clipboard and placed it in front of Forrest. "Sign here, for the hard copy. And here for the thumb drive." Forrest scribbled where directed. The Sergeant placed the papers and the thumb-drive back in the envelope and handed it over."

#####

Larry scowled as he searched around the room for someone. A young Captain spoke up. "Sir, the Intel Officer came down with kidney stones. She'll be out several days."

That's outrageous. Lord, how am I going to pull this off? First I have to live down my Civil War ancestor's reputation, then my Uncle goes and falls for the Rebel's prisoner scheme, I need her insight. With her family connections she knows the Rebel mind better than anyone. He shook his head. "ALL RIGHT THEN, you give her report."

He turned and faced his staff, "Ladies and Gentlemen, we've been given reliable information about a Rebel raid. Our source expects the first attack around 0500. Every unit will be in place in two hours. I've instructed the Commanders of the Oklahoma National Guard to flow through our line, then turn, and become our Quick Reaction Force. I gave them the current running passwords." He paused, took a swig from a bottle of water, and wiped dribble from his mustache. "I've ordered extra canister rounds for the battle. I want them used on every Rebel Infantry formation that comes across our path. The buckshot in those rounds will definitely clear the way for our troops. Intel will signal me as soon as they see the Rebel Comanche helicopters. At that time I want a volley of M-PAT rounds at each one. The radar on each shell will detonate the projectile when it gets close to the chopper. My favorite is the Sabot rounds that will make mincemeat of their tanks." He chuckled, stroked his mustache, and smiled, "Let's go around the table. Any questions? Any problems?"

Later Larry snapped his binder closed and stood. Everyone at the table rose, and smartly saluted. He returned their salute and left.

#####

At 0200 hours the next morning, Hampton stood in front the Company Formation.

Unnoticed by most, several armed men were positioned around the back wall.

"Hampton pulled a paper from a cargo pocket. "I have here a message from Governor Harrison." He unfolded the paper with one hand as he put his reading glasses on. "Fellow Citizens of the Great State of Oklahoma, as of midnight I've disbanded the state legislature, and declared a curfew for the entire state. The Five Civilized Tribes have assumed control of all state functions, we've petitioned for admission into The Republic of America. The reasons are many, but we Native Americans have had grievances against the Federal Government for centuries. Need I remind you of the Trail of Tears? We tried to play by their rules when in 1905 we requested a state of our own, The State of Sequoyah. The National..."

A soldier yelled at the top of his lungs, "No, never! Several other men ran for the nearest exit. Immediately Jackson and the armed men on his detail dropped to a knee and fired. Several fell, writhing in pain. A few came to a sliding stop and held their hands up. Jackson fired at one soldier who slumped forward, blood spurting from his neck.

As soon as the first shot echoed through the hall, the remaining soldiers in formation hit the floor.

A medic ran toward the closest downed man. He unzipped his combat lifesaver bag, and slid on his knees next to the fallen soldier. He deftly placed a bandage on the wound and applied pressure. Then relaxed and slumped onto his haunches.

He sighed, looked up at Jackson, and said, "Why?"

Jackson rubbed his pistol and moved the safety in place. "He's Tongkawa. His ancestors killed my great-great-great-great-grandfather back in the early 1860s, just because he supported the

Union. I don't care about this war. When I realized he was a direct descendent of those barbarians, that sealed his fate. I'd planned to kill him when we went into battle, their race doesn't deserve to live."

When he heard the first shot, First Sergeant directed several soldiers to help the medic.

Fifteen minutes later, after the wounded and dead had been removed. Hampton and First Sergeant regained control of their men. "Listen up! Those who ran weren't cowards, we're in a war. They've chosen the other side. Some paid a high price for their convictions."

He paused and moved closer to formation. "Regardless of what just happened, we have a battle to get ready for..." He continued to inform his unit of the Governor's message. "Now as for tomorrows plan ..."

Forty-five minutes later, he said, "Any questions?"

He marched off the drill floor and into the conference room where First Sergeant had placed Jackson under guard. He sat in front of his XO and slid a tablet of paper in front of the young Officer.

"After I finish with you I want a complete statement. I want to know why you think the Tongkawa deserve such treatment."

The full-blooded Comanche scowled. "You expect me to show remorse? Huh, it wasn't your ancestors who were massacred. The Tongkawa have never paid for their crimes. It's up to this generation to own up to their past. I've sworn to my father that I would kill as many of them as possible. My family has always supported the Federals. I didn't know or care what the governor was going to do. I only want to get revenge for my ancestors."

Hampton stared wide-eyed as he listened to the Warrior. He glanced up from the notes he was taking. "Wait a minute. I remember you talking about how you were this Christian who believed in the saving redemption of the sacrifice Jesus made on the cross."

Jackson peered through his glasses, which had slipped down his nose. "That's true Sir. There are times when The Lord expects us to carry out his plan. Look at King Saul who didn't kill all the Amalekites. The Tongkawa are just as bad."

"You can't claim you were fulfilling The Lord's plan. There's nothing in the Bible that allows you to pass judgment on innocent people."

The young officer sat up. "Captain, it's well documented that when the Tongkawa raided our village in the 1860s they butchered everyone they could. Afterwards they celebrated with a barbeque. My ancestors were the main course." He sat back and folded his arms in front of him. "Believe me the entire tribe doesn't deserve to live."

The Captain raised his head, "You've got to be kidding me. That's so outrageous. They were Rebels. That's why they were fighting your people. There's no evidence, and never has been, of such an atrocity being committed."

He rose, and called out. "First Sergeant, send the MPs in." He lowered his eyes, "Rebel Lieutenant Jackson, it's my duty to inform you that I'm required to investigate your actions. You're under arrest and will be confined until that inquiry is complete. Do you understand?"

Defiantly Jackson stood, crossed his arms, and said, "Of all people, I expected you to support me."

#####

As Hampton inspected Headquarters Platoon, Rebel Lieutenant Red Cloud followed. The new Executive Officer took notes about deficiencies. Twenty minutes later the two men walked to the front of the formation.

Hampton handed a thick folder to Red Cloud. "Lieutenant, even though you haven't had time to prepare, I need you to follow this operations order. If you don't think you can handle it, I'll get someone else."

After thumbing through the file, Red Cloud placed it under his arm. "Sir, from what I've heard, all units were given the same basic plan. Yours seems similar to Bravo Company's. When I was tasked to replace Jackson, I requested to be allowed to bring my entire Platoon." He stood at attention. "I'll integrate my old unit into this one. We'll be ready. I should mention that I was raised in some of the towns we'll be maneuvering in. I don't anticipate any problems."

First Sergeant yelled out from across the drill floor, "Sir, we're ready for our brief."

Hampton moved in front of his tank, ran a finger down a page on his clipboard. He scanned the Motor Pool. "Okay, everyone's here. Nothing's changed from our last briefing. Remember, unless they try to interfere with our operations, no civilians are to be fired upon. After we deliver our packages to Wichita, we'll commence our true mission. You are to take out any asset which the Federals could use against us. Use your discretion. Consider our mission as the same type of maneuver as Sherman's March through Georgia. The only difference is we won't commit any war crimes. Once that is completed all units are to follow their designated route back here. Any questions? No? Good, First Sergeant, move 'em out. Let's get going."

Red Cloud, tapped his fingers on the side of the tank as they rumbled north on I-35. He reached down and pulled a pair of binoculars from inside the tank and focused on upcoming bridges, he nodded to the Sergeant standing in the open hatch of the Bradley Fighting Vehicle alongside. He turned his head and winked at several children staring at him from one of the three busses in the next lane.

One six-year-old boy opened the emergency window held up a puppy, pointed at him, and waved.

Red Cloud pulled a candy bar from a pocket and tossed it through the window.

The boy snagged the treat ripped off the wrapper, and waved.

He smiled at the boy, then picked up the microphone and flipped the intercom switch. "Listen up everyone, our exit's coming up…" *Blast it all.* He yelled into his microphone. "Driver, you missed the exit, and the Bradley on our left followed us. Thanks to you we're off course. The fuelers, and the rest of our Platoon made it. With all this traffic, we've gotta go five miles out of our way to get back on course. STEP ON IT."

He flipped the switch from *intercom* to *radio*, "Arrowhead 6, this is Arrowhead 2."

The Commander's southern drawl came through over the engine noise. "Go ahead 2, this is 6."

"Sir, we missed the off ramp, I've directed my driver and the Bradley next to us, to speed toward the next exit."

Hampton's voice came through the microphone. "2, what part of your anatomy are you thinking with? You're in an Abrams tank. Make a U-Turn, go against the flow of traffic. Part of our mission is to disrupt the Federals, make the best of the situation."

"Sir, you're not here, you don't see what I see. I can't comply without endangering my crew and an awful lot of civilians."

Hampton gritted his teeth as he spoke, "Lieutenant, I don't care how you do it, but you get both vehicles back in line."

Red Cloud gulped, switched on the intercom and said, "Driver, turn here. Go through that sound wall, the rest of our Platoon should be about a block away." He switched back to the radio. "Sir, I'm making my own short cut. We'll be back in line soon."

As he put the mic back on its hook, the driver yanked the controls and the tracked vehicle lurched to the right, surged up the side of the highway, and smashed through the block wall. The Bradley rocked back and forth as it followed its bigger brother.

His vehicle bounced from the hilly terrain. His driver's voice came through his headphones. "Lieutenant, we have a problem. Our front fuel tank is empty. The rear tank is down to a quarter. We need to find 300 gallons of jet fuel now."

Red Cloud slid from standing in the hatch and sat on the seat. He rummaged through a flight bag and tore a Wichita city map as he pulled it out. He spread the biggest piece over his legs. *I went to college in this town. There's gotta be fuel around here. Aha! There it is.* "Driver, make a right at the next street." He stuck his head out of the hatch, leaned to the left as the vehicle traversed around a corner, and pushed the intercom button. "That's good, now go into that gas station."

"Sir, we can't get fuel here. We need jet fuel."

"I know what I'm doing." He stood high in the turret and called out to the Sergeant in the Bradley. "Have one of your soldiers tell the attendant I want her to open the pumps we pull up too. She's to authorize us to pump as much as we need."

The red-haired sergeant appeared startled. "Sir, why would she do that? What're you going to pay with? A credit card?"

Red Cloud called out over the intercom, "Gunner, traverse the turret and point it at the front door." Then he yelled at the Sergeant through the mike as he pointed to the clerk. "Tell her that's my authorization."

He chuckled at the cashier's reaction. Her eyes bulged out even before the Sergeant entered the building. He continued to shout through his mic at the Bradley, "I want the remaining soldiers to set up a perimeter around this property. Move all civilians across the street. If they argue, shoot 'em."

Red Cloud and his driver watched the soldier through the

window. The young man's arms were flying around as he apparently argued with the clerk. When she noticed the tip of the tank's gun barrel pointed at her head she timidly nodded, and her hands flew over the cash register. The red-headed sergeant ran out and over to pump number nine. Two other soldiers exited the rear of the Bradley, walked over to two civilian vehicles and took the hoses out of the customer's hands. Other soldiers brought empty five gallon fuel cans and filled them up on the customer's credit cards.

Twenty minutes later they'd topped off all tanks. While the soldiers strapped the fuel cans in place on their vehicles, Red Cloud called out to a soldier who ran by. "Corporal, get whatever food's cooked, pack up lunches for everyone. Bring plenty of water. I won't complain if you bring a few cases of beer."

Smiling, the young NCO yelled out as he ran off, "Yes, Sir."

Frustrated at his mistake, Red Cloud slammed his fist on the side of his tank. He rubbed his hand and happened to see a police car on an overpass. "Gunner, sabot round, two o'clock."

"Sabot, round, yes sir."

As the shell moved into place he listened to the sound of his tankers below. *That's music to my ears.*

His vehicle barreled down the road at fifty-five miles an hour, the turret traversed to the right. "Gunner, fire when ready."

When the tank fired, smoke belched from the muzzle, he watched the round soar toward the bridge. A lone police officer stood looking at the tank barreling down the road. He didn't have time to react before the round struck his cruiser and obliterated everything within thirty-five meters.

Red Cloud slid inside his tank and closed the hatch. Debris from the explosion rained on top of the turret. "Good job guys, that's one Federal cop who won't bother us. Now that we've caught up to the rest of the convoy, let's drop off our packages."

He reached down and spoke his southern drawl into the microphone. "Remote operators, get ready to drop off your load."

Three voices chimed over the loudspeaker above him. "Yes, Sir, ready here."

Like clockwork the Abram Tanks and Bradley Fighting Vehicles from the task force formed a perimeter around the supermarket parking lot the buses had pulled into. The rear door of the armored vehicles lowered and a squad of infantry took positions behind several pickup trucks and dumpsters.

Two NCOs from each Bradley ran to the bus doors as they opened. They escorted the passengers into the store. Each Sergeant called out, "Hurry along now, move along, let's go, you're almost there."

Once all the passengers were inside the market, the Sergeants yelled out, "Everyone, out of the door way. They waited for several mothers to pick up their children, and move well inside the store. Then they disabled the entrance.

#####

"Arrowhead 2, this is Arrowhead 6, over."

There was silence over the air.

"2, this is 6, come in 2 over."

The Commander paused, "2, what's your ETA?"

"Sir, we just arrived and are in position."

"Very well, 2, 6 out."

KILO – The Enforcer
(Mid-October)

"General Grimes, Lieutenant Ronald Sherwood is here."

Grimes scribbled a note on a file, set it aside and pushed the intercom. "Send him in."

Sherwood entered, set his briefcase on the floor. "Sir, you sent for me?"

The old black Rebel nodded for the policeman to sit in a chair. "Son, I have another assignment."

The officer adjusted his pants as he sat where directed. "Yes, Sir, I came as soon as I received your call."

Grimes moved from behind his desk and sat in a chair next to Sherwood. He handed him a thick envelope. "Here's your assignment. Nothing new, just the largest we've given you to date. You shouldn't have any problems. Our contacts have assured me your escape routes will be secure."

The Police Lieutenant opened the flap on the envelope and speed-read the pages in front of him. "Sir, I reserve the right to change this plan. Last time the original almost failed. I know how you feel, but it's my life on the line. If you don't agree, then you can get someone else." He paused, stared at the senior officer, and then said, "With all due respect, Sir."

Grimes frowned. *This guy could be a problem. The General gave him too much leeway. Oh well, he's the only one who can handle the mission.* "General Lee told me you had a tendency to be direct. This is the most complex task we've given you. You have ten targets, in three states. We have it all laid out."

Sherwood didn't blink and responded. "General I always bring several disguises and necessary documents to support each. I was a rookie when I first started with General Lee. I've worked with you guys for over a decade. Surely I've demonstrated that I can think on my feet and adjust in the field."

The black man drummed his fingers on the table. "I have to agree with you, that last mission we gave you was poorly planned." He rose, reached across his desk and checked his calendar. He sat back down and smiled. "All right, we'll do it your way."

They rose, shook hands and the lanky man departed.

#####

Sherwood tapped his fingers on the console of his rental car as he waited for someone to answer.

"Yes, Ron. What do you need?

"Chief, my Army Reserve Unit just gave me another assignment."

"Another! That's the second this month. When I agreed to have you transferred here, I never thought they'd pull you out on so many missions."

He rested his head on his headrest while he listened to his boss on the rental car's bluetooth. "Listen, you may be in-charge of this town's police department. But when we joined their cause, we gave up our independence. We've both taken their money for years. We don't have a choice. There have been a lot of people who haven't followed through. We both know they have to be taken care of. If we don't, others may follow their course."

The Police Chief's exasperated voice filled Sherwood's car. "I understand that, I'm loyal to the organization. We have a small department here. Cases are piling up on your desk. I'm beginning to have a hard time justifying why I'm allowing you to take so much time off."

"I can see where that's a problem for you. Tell everyone my mother's dying of cancer. I'll have someone fax you the doctor's verification. Will that help?"

The aggravation in his bosses' voice was evident. "Argggh! I hope this will end soon. This is getting to be too much."

"Thanks Chief. I'll see you in about two weeks." Sherwood pushed 'END CALL' on his cell and got out of his car.

He entered his hotel room, set his briefcase on a chair, pulled out his scanner, and checked for bugs. *Hmmm, two areas seem suspicious.* He picked up the room phone and pushed '**O.**'

"Front desk."

"This room is unacceptable. I'm checking out. Please have my bill ready when I reach you."

The clerk's voice responded through the earpiece. "Sir, is there something I can do to make this right?"

"No young lady. I don't like the view from this window."

"I can transfer you to another room."

Yeah right, if they put bugs in this room, how long will it be before they bug the other? "No, I've changed my mind."

Two hours later Sherwood had checked into a non-descript hotel across town. After not finding any devices in the new room, he retrieved Grimes' envelope from his attaché and ran a finger down the list of names. He pulled his cell from his shirt pocket, and punched a few numbers. After he put it on speaker he started to change into a disguise as a woman's voice came forth.

"Mayor's Office."

"Yes, Ma'am, my name is Anthony Jones. I'd like to know if the Mayor could see me at noon instead of one o'clock."

"Let me put you on hold."

Music played in the background Sherwood laced his boots. As he tucked the extra laces into the top of his boots her dulcet voice came back. "Yes, the Mayor will be able to see you at noon."

After hanging up his phone Sherwood checked his false mustache in the bathroom mirror before he applied a wig to his bald head. Pleased with his image, he grabbed a uniform jacket and left.

He walked into the Mayor's office and paused at the secretary's desk. "Mr. Anthony Jones to see the Mayor."

The woman's eyes widened as she looked up from her computer screen and saw him for the first time. "Aren't you handsome?" Then she composed herself, and acted more professional. "Yes, Mr. Jones, go right in, he's expecting you."

Sherwood walked through the open door and silently shut it behind him.

The Mayor rose and extended his hand. After pleasantries had been exchanged the politician gestured toward a seat by the window. "Shall we? What can I do for you? My 'Cell Leader' told me to expect you. Care for coffee, tea?" He turned and didn't wait for an answer.

Sherwood nodded and sat.

The official carried a tray over to his guest and set it on a ledge in front of a bay window. He snapped his fingers. "Oh, I forgot the creamer," and rushed back to the buffet.

In the few moments he was gone; Sherwood pulled a vial from his coat pocket and quickly slipped three clear droplets of poison into the Mayor's cup. He waited for the old man to be seated and pour the coffee.

The old bureaucrat smiled, "Now, Mr. Jones, what is it that you want to see me about?"

Sherwood leaned back in his chair. "Mr. Mayor, I've been sent to see you about your commitment to the cause. It seems you're no longer as enthusiastic about the tasks you've been assigned."

The smiled faded from behind the grey goatee. "Uh, just what tasks are you talking about?"

Sherwood reached into his vest pocket and pulled out a single piece of paper. "It seems you were responsible for several tasks prior to last April. You haven't fulfilled any of them. It seems that you contacted a Federal Agent and attempted to inform them of General Lee's plans." He sneered as the elderly gentlemen drank from his cup. "You see that Agent was in fact one of ours. It was a sting operation. You were one of ten individuals who failed the test. I've been tasked to repay you for your treason."

A look of panic came over the southerner's face.

"Don't worry sir. You won't suffer long. In a few moments I'll have your secretary call 911." He leaned forward and lowered his voice to a whisper, "It won't do any good though. You'll be dead before I sound the alarm."

The old man's eyes widened and slowly closed. His head fell forward onto the floor.

Sherwood stood, straightened his jacket and walked to the outer office. "Miss? The Mayor seems to have a problem. You might want to call an ambulance."

As the young woman whirred into action, Sherwood calmly walked out the door.

#####

He adjusted his uniform, applied an auburn wig and rubbed his chin. *That new blade did the trick.* Before he fastened his utility belt, he applied a dab of armoni perfume to each wrist. He walked out the side entrance of his hotel. When he reached the corner of the building he glanced around for witnesses. Finding none he calmly walked to his rental car and pulled out of the parking lot.

His watch alarm sounded as he turned a corner. *Okay, right on time. Now let's see if the target will. . . Aha, there he is.* He reached onto the seat beside him and pulled a blue light out of a bag and placed it on the roof. Seconds later he switched the light and siren on and pulled behind a brown Mercedes. As the driver pulled over he put his hat on his head and stuffed the long hairs of his wig inside his hat.

Sherwood walked up to the driver's side, in a perfect falsetto voice he said, "License, registration, and proof of insurance please."

The thirty-year old woman stopped texting on her phone and looked up at the female officer's face. "Just what have I done Ma'am? And who are you? My husband's a City Councilman, we know all the cops on the force. Especially the females and I don't recognize you."

Sherwood did a double-take when he looked down at her. *What? A woman?* His pistol was drawn, she'd seen his face. *No choice now.* "Nothing Ma'am. Your husband was supposed to be driving this car."

Confused, her hands shook as she handed the documents over.

Sherwood put his pistol against her chest and fired twice. He reached across the dead body, retrieved the woman's cell. His fingers flew over the buttons on the phone as he added to the message she'd started to her husband. *Hmmm, she started with:* HONEY I'VE BEEN PULLED OVER AT THE CORNER OF FIFTH AND MAIN. He deftly added, A FEMALE OFFICER I DON'T RECOGNIZE IS ACCUSING ME OF SPEEDING.

He pushed SEND and pocketed the phone. Sherwood opened the trunk and pulled out an emergency kit. After putting several reflectors behind the dead woman's car, he moved his around the corner. Just before the Councilman's vehicle screeched to a halt, he pulled the blue light off the roof, removed his wig, bra, and uniform top.

The man opened his driver's door before the car halted. He ran over several safety cones as he hurried to the passenger side and slid onto the seat. "Honey, are you all right?"

Sherwood was right behind him. "Councilman? Don't move."

The middle-aged man froze mouth open as he stared at his wife's bloody body. "Wh, why? What did she ever do to anyone?"

Sherwood put his pistol at the councilman' head. "That'll be enough. Don't say anything else."

His body shaking with fear, the politician nodded.

"Good. Your wife's death is your fault. You were supposed to be driving. She sealed her fate when she saw me. Your destiny was determined when you failed to keep your commitments last April." Without waiting for the man's response he pulled the trigger and shot the man behind the ear.

He calmly pocketed his revolver as he unbuckled his utility

belt. In moments he was on the highway out of town. *Well, three more to go and then I get to. . .* His bluetooth rang. He checked the display on his cell and answered. "Hello Pastor. I've been waiting for your call."

"Good morning Deacon Sherwood. I trust your Reserve Duty is going well."

He pulled the rental car alongside a dumpster and tossed half of his disguise inside. "Good morning to you. I'm glad you were able to get everyone to agree to my participating in our meeting via my cell phone."

"It wasn't a problem Brother. We're honored to have such a dedicated patriot as a member of our church. We realize that sometimes we need to accommodate your secular responsibilities."

Two weeks later he called General Grimes. "General. Mission accomplished. All ten traitors have been eliminated, each one by a different means. Nothing will be traced back to us and our cause."

LIMA – Grimes' March Through The North
(Late October)

Hampton pressed his mouthpiece closer to his lips. "Lieutenant, I don't care how you do it, but get both vehicles back in line with your Platoon." He switched his receiver off and tapped his boot on the gunner's head. When the Corporal responded, he pointed at the local map that had fallen on the floor.

He took it from the man sitting below, fastened the map to his clipboard, and surveyed his convoy. *Good, Red Cloud's two vehicles are the only ones missing. We may pull this off.*

He switched the control to 'radio.' "Let's not have any more hiccups. Pay attention now." He listened as the clank of his platoon's tanks clattered down the road.

Several crisp, "Yes, Sirs," came back over his headphones, and he watched each team leave his convoy on cue and peel toward their individual assignments. He pictured in his mind what the scene must look like from the air. *One-hundred-twenty-four teams, spread out across the entire ROA/USA border. Each one a part of one simultaneous attack.*

He raised his night vision binoculars to scan the horizon and found Duffield's formation. He switched the NVGs off when he realized the sun was starting to creep through the storm clouds coming over the horizon. "Okay, Federals are right where they said they'd be." *Knew I could count on old Duffy.*

He switched to the Federal frequency. "Pinnacle 6, this is Arrowhead 6, over"

Duffield's voice blared through the airwaves. "Hamp, you're right on time. Knew I could count on you. The Rebels are a mile away."

As a light rain started to fall, Marc Le Blanc's driver brought his XYZ News van to a screeching halt in front of a large supermarket. Before the wheels stopped turning, Marc was out the door, recorder in one hand, rain slicker in the other. He rushed to a large bus that had just pulled up. Soldiers had formed a perimeter around the parking lot.

Marc shouted into his producer's ear. "Don't know why the Rebels are leaving us alone. Let's take advantage of it."

His assistant left and started to direct disembarking passengers in the reporter's direction. Marc selected the most desperate looking characters to interview. Most weren't interested in anything except getting out of the rain. After three families brushed past him, Marc reached down to help a young woman struggling with three children and several large suitcases.

She shook her head. "I can manage, go away."

Marc, keeping a grip on her families' luggage, tilted his head. "There's enough room for your family over by that door. At least let me help you get that far."

Reluctantly, the woman followed. She kept a tight grip on two of her children. "Andres, hold onto Sissie's hand. You're the man of the house while Daddy finds us something to eat. Make sure she behaves."

Beaming with pride at being given responsibility, the six-year-old obediently gripped his sibling's hand. "Yes, Mama." His eyes bulged, and he shouted, "Mama! That's the man who gave me the candy bar."

Marc paused his interview as the two adults stopped and watched Red Cloud's tank clank across the parking lot and halt fifty feet away. Before her son could move, his Mother put her hand on his head. "Stay, don't go near that thing. That man's busy and doesn't have time for you."

Andres sat with his back to the storefront window, put Sissie's hand under his arm, and pouted. The adults resumed their conversation.

Red Cloud jumped from his vehicle and motioned for a Sergeant to come to his side. The soldier put the remote control he'd been using to drive the bus under his arm and ran to the front of the newly arrived tank. Even though they were out of earshot, many by-standers understood from the officer's hand motions that he wanted the bus moved out of the area. The bus driver saluted, and then jumped into the shotgun seat of a hummer.

The panel in the Sergeant's lap lit up. His hands flew across the instrument. The bus came to life and started to move.

As soon as the vehicles' front wheels started to turn, Andres jumped up and looked around. "Piper, Mama? Where's Piper?"

Aggravated at the interruption, his Mother shook her head. "Your puppy's around, don't worry."

When they resumed the interview, Andres put his little sister's hand in his older siblings, left them sitting against the wall, and ran. Unseen by the remote driver, Andres boarded the bus just as the front door closed.

#####

The Remote Driver fastened his seat belt and secured the panel into the rack in front of him. "Corporal, take me up to the light. I saw a police motor pool around the corner. That'll be the best target." Then his hands continued to make adjustments.

#####

Andres' Mother, startled when she heard the turning wheels crunch on the pavement, screamed, "Where's my boy?" She checked in the immediate vicinity and became more panicked every second.

Red Cloud happened to catch a glimpse of the youngster's head bobbing up and down as he ran through the inside aisle of the bus. *If the bus is moving, the driver knows where he wants it to go. Can't stop the bus. Gotta save the boy!* He ran forward, and caught up with the front door as the wheels slowed for a turn. His hands forced it open. He slid inside and fell flat on the floor.

"Come here boy. We have to get you off this bus."

Andres screamed. "My puppy!" I can't leave my puppy!" Then he resumed crawling under the seats to snag the small terrier.

Red Cloud got to his knees and scooted towards the boy and his dog. As he neared the rear wheels, the dog snarled and snapped at the Rebel's hand. The Rebel Officer reached around a seat leg and grabbed the dog by the nape of his neck. He struggled with the movement of the bus, and finally stood. He started to the front, paused to let Andres jump into his arms. When they reached the front door, he put his weight on his rear foot, and kicked the door open with the other.

#####

A Wichita Police Officer stretched his lanky legs as he ran toward his patrol car when he saw a bus moving toward the motor pool. He ran where the bus was going to be. As he reached the front door it popped open and a boy holding a dog flew toward a fence post. He snagged the boy in mid-air. They rolled on the asphalt. Piper broke free, and ran under a bush.

Ten seconds later the bus exploded in a row of police cruisers.

#####

As he listened to his old friend, Hampton kept his main radio on the company frequency. "Gunners get your rounds ready. First two rounds are to be sabots, right at their rear filters. Those penetrating rounds should take them out. After that, fire at will.

Use your own discretion as to the type of round."

Again, each tank commander responded.

"Bradleys, keep your squads inside until I give the word. Have your gunners watch for enemy aircraft."

Fresh voices could be heard over Hampton's speaker.

"Yep, Yeah, and then a loud Rebel yell screeched over the air waves." After a pause, a deep baritone voice spoke, "Sorry, Sir. Couldn't resist."

Laughing to himself, Hampton checked his watch. "Alright, here we go, everyone should be at their turn. NOW!" He flipped the switch to the Federal frequency. "Pinnacle 6, don't know if you realize it, but when we were at Ft. Irwin together, I found out that you had an affair with my wife. She died last year. I've waited all this time to get even." He flipped back to the company frequency.

"FIRE!"

The turret on each tank in his task force traversed and aimed at the rear of a different Federal tank. At his command, two rounds in quick succession from each Rebel vehicle met their mark. In seconds the battlefield was ablaze with bursting vehicles and bodies jumping out of tanks only to be mowed down by Bradley machine gun fire.

In minutes the battle was over. Hampton climbed from his vehicle and waited for a Texas National Guard tank to pull up next to him. He mounted his friend's vehicle and vigorously shook his hand. "That was awesome. Just like we've been training these past few months."

#####

Garfield entered the briefing room, Command Sergeant Major Hart tossed the General's briefcase on the table so hard it slid to the far side, fell on the floor, and flopped open.

A Sergeant knelt and picked up the papers that were strewn on the floor. The General plopped into a chair, the seat snapped as he leaned back.

Several Soldiers rushed to his aid. He brushed himself off while someone brought another seat. *Lord! You're supposed to be helping me. It's like everything's been going wrong since I started following you.*

Once settled, Garfield stared at the officer in front of him. "Abe, tell me the bad news first. As if it could be any worse than the blockade news you gave me yesterday."

Garfield's new Chief of Staff, Brigadier General Prewkowski, picked up a remote and scrolled through several slides before he spoke. "Sir, here's the big picture as of 0800 this morning." He aimed his laser pointer at the map of the USA. "The entire west coast is blockaded. Only two tankers made it into San Pedro last night, two more were sunk." The red dot slid across the map and flickered up and down the east coast. "Here we've had more success. Six tankers made it through. However, more and more shipping companies are refusing to carry our cargo."

Abe opened a newspaper in front of him. Turned it around and slid it over to Garfield. "At this time the average gas price in the North is $10.95. President Barnes is talking about extending gas rationing from odd/even to odd/even with two days of no sales to non-government vehicles."

Garfield frowned as he ran a finger down the newspaper column. "Ski, I don't see how it can get worse."

Somberly, Abe clicked over to another screen. A map of the former USA morphed into the current battle positions. "Notice the red flashes along the forward edge of the battle area. At each of those one-hundred-twenty-some odd sites, the Rebels have launched an attack with a company of tanks, and Bradley Fighting Vehicles. For some reason each unit has three or four civilian buses in the center. At this time we're not sure…"

An Aide rushed in and whispered into Garfield's ear.

Garfield pointed at the wall. "Ski, get the news on the screen."

Quickly, Abe snatched the remote and complied. Immediately XYZ news popped up on the one-hundred-five inch TV.

President Gressette's image pixelated for a few seconds and then came into full view.

"…yesterday's release of Federal prisoners was accomplished with a minimum loss of life. Those prisoners haven't committed a crime against the ROA. We tried to exchange them for POWs held by the Federals, but they didn't want to work with us. Since they had become a burden on our budget, we had no choice but to release them."

Gressette glanced at his watch. "In conjunction with that, we've revamped the Federal welfare program. Our program is only interested in providing for those clients who are willing to work. The Federals want to coddle welfare recipients and play Santa Claus. So as of today, we've started releasing those ROA residents who don't want to be hard-working members of our society. We've escorted them to Federal territory, where they can be cared for in the manner which the Federals have let them become accustomed to."

Gressette shuffled a few papers in front of him, then resumed. "On another note…"

MIKE – Diplomacy
(Late October)

Ambassador Joseph C. Fendemere III sat, in a large chair and nodded to the man sitting across from him. "Yes, Mr. Prime Minister. Today's news has been very favorable. The blockade has been in effect for two weeks, we've seen a drastic drop in traffic."

The Prime Minister checked his watch. "His Majesty will see us soon. You realize this is an off-the-record meeting. I can't have the fact that we're considering recognition leaked out."

Mr. Prime Minister, thanks to Cat's Cats you won't have any control over that. "Yes, Sir. We understand. Especially with having just ascended the throne. President Gressette is pleased that I have this opportunity to discuss the King's and your feelings with the rest of the European Union members."

"Well, yes, I see, but you have to realize you don't have the wholehearted support of the Crown."

Fendemere raised an eyebrow, "Oh really, well Sir, you have to realize the level of economic aid the ROA gives to the EU all depends on the strength of the support we receive. If you get my meaning."

The Prime Minister glared at the Ambassador. With a very measured tone he said, "Sir, I fully understand the significance of your comments. However, you need to realize that Great Britain has had a long-standing relationship with the Americans. We don't like being forced to take sides, when we should be neutral."

Controlled anger flared in Fendemere's eyes, "Sir, your claims of neutrality are a little hollow. It was the repositioning of your satellites that hampered our operations during the initial days of this conflict. President Gressette is fully aware the only reason you're even considering recognition is the Rebel Dollar is the strongest currency in the world. That we are debt free and have a balanced budget. But as long as we understand each other, we would like to privately convey your wholehearted support of the ROA when I speak with the rest of the EU this coming week."

A butler entered, stood in a doorway, and nodded. The Prime Minister stood and led the Rebel Secretary of State into his audience with the King.

Twenty minutes later, Fendemere looked straight in the young monarch's eyes. "Your Highness, as I told your Prime Minister, my President is willing to help the EU in stabilizing the European economy. We're sure you understand that support comes at a price. But it is well worth the commitment."

The monarch frowned at the Rebel diplomat, and rose to his feet. Taking the hint that the meeting was over, the Prime Minister and Fendemere stood also. They immediately left.

Once the butler closed the door, they walked to the far side of the room and stood by a bay window. "Mr. Ambassador, you have a lot of gumption to speak to my King they way you did."

"Sir, my fellow soldiers are fighting for their lives. I don't have time for niceties. I was respectful, I reminded him that we're winning and the USA is losing. We know where your sympathies lay. All I did was point out that the EU needs to be on the winning side. I know you don't like it, but you need all the economic assistance we can give."

With a scowl, the English leader summoned an aide to escort the Rebel out.

#####

One week later, Fendemere stood in front of several low-level bureaucrats. "My Aide is passing out a folder with information about the trip we have planned." The room went dark and the screen filled up with scenes of the South.

After an hour of questions and answers, the Secretary of State came from behind the podium. "So you see, ladies and gentlemen. We have a full two weeks of activity lined up. You'll tour the ROA, in addition to our agenda; you may visit any city, site, or point of interest. In the end you'll have the true picture of who we are and an idea of what type of support you can give us."

Several bureaucrats surrounded the Rebel. A tall man leaned forward. "Sir, how safe will we be?"

Fendemere had started putting files in his briefcase. He peered up through his glasses. "Every location we take you to will be secure. We control the press on the North American continent, but that's harder to accomplish over here. Just because the European media believes the ROA is losing, doesn't mean that we can't and won't prevail." He glanced into the faces of the other attendees.

"Any other questions?" He snapped his attaché shut and spun the combination lock. "That settles it. I'll see you at Heathrow in two days. Remember if you need anything on the trip," he winked at several of the men, "we'll provide it for you."

Later that day, the Ambassador paced back and forth as his aide checked his hotel room for bugs. The woman set the scanner down. "The room's clean sir. Will you need anything else today?"

He pulled his cell from a jacket pocket and shook his head. "No, that will be all. See you tomorrow for breakfast." After she left, he hit the speed dial and put the phone on speaker as he started to change for dinner. A woman's southern dulcet voice flowed through the air.

"Director's Office, this is a secure line."

"This is Fendemere. I have a party of twelve. They'll be arriving in two days. It'll have eight men and four women. Have Cat's Cats arrange the itinerary for all of them."

"Yes, Sir. Do you want the same level of service we gave the tour that came for the wedding?"

"That would be fine."

NOVEMBER – Battle for Wichita
(Early November)

Larry Duffield searched the horizon with his night vision goggles. *No Rebels yet. Still early.* He sat back in the turret of his tank. His fingers danced on his computer's touch screen. He pushed the talk button on his radio, "Okay everyone, the Oakies are in sight. Radar shows the Texans a clic behind. First Platoon, loosen your formation and let them through."

Immediately tanks and Bradleys maneuvered to pre-arranged positions. "Excellent, First Platoon, all Oakies are accounted for. Any vehicles in front of you are Rebels, FIRE AT…"

Before he could finish, the Oklahoma Rebels fired.

#####

Hampton peeked through the periscope as his tank scooted past the forward edge of the battle area. He swiveled around and tallied the Federal tanks surrounding him. He clicked his microphone, "Listen up everyone. I count fifteen enemy tanks in front of us. Fire at will."

In seconds every Rebel tank opened fire. The casings from Sabot rounds littered the battlefield. The projectiles streamed toward their prey. Several struck the Federal vehicles in the rear, while others slammed into tank treads. Road wheels flew off and bounced across the Kansas Plains. As Hampton had ordered the battle to commence, a few USA tanks adjusted their position. Consequently, the shells aimed at them missed their mark.

Hampton screamed into his microphone. "I count seven killed, four disabled and not moving. Second Platoon, go after the three that are regrouping on the south side." He paused and focused his night vision goggles, "Third Platoon, go after that tank on the north side. That's the Commander's tank. I don't want it destroyed. I'll be there soon to take the crew prisoner."

He slid hard onto his seat, slammed, and dogged the hatch. He spun the turret around and yelled. "Gunner, canister on that Bradley, NOW!"

Gunner nodded, as the loader complied. Sensing the breech was closed; Hampton spoke, "FIRE!"

In seconds, twelve Federal Infantrymen lay dead or maimed from the buckshot. Then silence filled the Plains.

Hampton looked at his watch. The entire battle had lasted less than five minutes. *Lord I guess that's what planning and praying accomplishes.* "Driver, pull up next to that Command tank. I want to take Duffield prisoner myself."

Hampton's vehicle pulled alongside Duffy's. Both turret hatches opened. Duffield pulled his pistol and aimed it at his former friend.

"Captain, what do you think you're doing?"

The Oklahoma Rebel smiled, "True to your family's reputation, you fell for another Rebel ruse. Look around, you'll see more than a pistol aimed at you, I suggest you drop that peashooter. You're my prisoner…" At that moment two Battalions of Rebel Tanks and Infantry sped past. After the noise died down, the Rebel continued. "Sir, those troops, and others, are headed for Ft. Riley and the Wichita rail yards. Thanks to your help, we Rebels will occupy Kansas for the duration of this war."

#####

Garfield watched the blips on the screen in front of him and slammed his fist on the table. "I need more troops! What happened to all the troops I ordered moved to the front?" He glared at Sergeant Major Hart, then back to the screen. "Get Ski on the line.

I want answers."

"Yes, Sir, right away Sir." He rushed to the far side of the room and punched numbers into the land line.

Garfield stood and paced in front of the large TV. "Look at that line, one-hundred-twenty-four breaks. Count them, Sergeant Major! How am I supposed to fight when I don't have enough troops to cover the line?"

A Sergeant entered and stood next to the General. "Sir, I have several reports from northern cities. You might want to read them."

Irritated at being interrupted, Garfield grabbed the file from the young man's hand and tossed it on his desk. "I'll deal with these later."

At that moment XYZ news flickered on the large screen hanging on the wall. Everyone's eyes turned to catch a glimpse of Red Cloud tossing Andres and his dog into the hands of a Federal officer. As the segment ended, Marc LeBlanc appeared on the screen. "This has been an interesting day here outside of Wichita. My cameraman happened to catch the clip you just saw." The camera panned out and Red Cloud and Andres appeared at his side. "We have here the soldier who saved the life of this boy and his dog." He turned and placed the microphone in front of Andres. "Andres, tell me, what were you doing inside that bus?"

Enjoying the attention, Andres waved to the camera, "Hi Mama."

Marc moved the mic lower for the boy. Andres held the squirming puppy, tail wagging, and licking his master's face. "I saw Piper's head in a window. I didn't want him ta go away. I was trying to catch him. He just kept running. He thought I was playing."

The Reporter moved toward Red Cloud. "Well Captain, why did you risk your life for a little boy you didn't even know?"

The Cherokee patted Andres' head. "Marc, I have twin boys his age. I knew the bus was loaded with explosives. I couldn't bear to be a part of that scenario. I was just in the right place at the right time."

Andres' mother's profile came on the screen and took him away. The camera tightened to Marc and Red Cloud. "Captain, why would you put explosives on a bus loaded with civilians? Wasn't that risky?"

Apparently aggravated at being put on the spot, Red Cloud glared at Marc and then stared into the camera. "Marc, we don't have unlimited resources. We had safety procedures in place that kept the explosives harmless, until my driver decided on a target. I haven't heard what's happened in other battles, but our purpose was to bring those who don't want to live in our society to where they'll be happier, and to cause as much damage as possible to the Federal infra-structure. Our purpose is to do more damage in the north than General Sherman did when he marched through Georgia back in 1865."

Surprised at the Rebel's frank answer, Marc tilted his head. "Wait a minute, how can you equate what you've done to General Sherman's March through Georgia?"

"Marc, you've been taught the history of 'Mr. Lincoln's War' from the Federal point of view. Sherman wanted to prevent Southerners from continuing the fight. That's our goal, we're doing everything we can to deny the Feds from having the assets they need."

At that time the camera panned out to show the burning bus in the background.

Garfield picked up a remote and turned the TV off.

His Aide reached over and picked up the papers that had been brought in and skimmed them. "Uh, Sir, you might want to rethink that. These requests are from thirty cities, some hundreds of miles from the battle line. It seems the prisoners the Rebels released are creating havoc throughout the North. They're robbing banks, and murdering innocent civilians. Governors of ten states have declared martial law, and are also requesting you support them."

Garfield shook his head. "We can't. I can barely cover the battlefront. How can I send the divisions of troops it would take to restore order?"

At that moment, Hart spoke up from a corner. "Sir, I have General Prewkowski on a video call. Shall I put him on the big screen?"

"Yes, definitely." The monitor flickered, and then Abe came into focus. "Ski, what's happened? You've failed on every section! What have you done with all the troops I sent?"

Waving a stack of papers in his hand, Abe frowned. "General, we're holding as best we can. We're spread too thin to be effective. I sent the divisions you sent me to Colorado, Missouri, and Kentucky. We did better there, but we're still in a desperate battle. I don't know how, but in some cases the Rebels have gotten behind our lines and won the day. I'm only getting sketchy reports, it doesn't look good…"

Abe pushed a few buttons and his image moved to the top left of the screen. Several charts and maps appeared and he continued. "Gaps in our line are massive, twenty miles in some cases. We've lost the states of Kansas and West Virginia. I also heard on the news that Oklahoma, Nevada, Montana, Idaho, and Arizona have seceded. General, I need at least six more divisions if you want me to recover."

Garfield shook his head, "I…"

Sergeant Major Hart rushed in and interrupted. "Sir, I have a message from General Grimes. He's offering terms if we surrender."

Garfield's head jerked toward his enlisted aide. "What! Surrender, no way. Americans don't give up so easily. You send a message back that the only surrender I'll consider is his."

Hart came to attention. "Yes, Sir, I'll send that off."

Garfield's head turned back to the large screen. "I'll give you three divisions, no more."

"With all due respect, General, that won't be enough. We're…"

"Boom!" After the explosion there was a bright flash and the screen went blank.

OSCAR– Attack On The Bunkers
(Early November)

"What happened? Get Ski back on the line!" Garfield hurried to the phone and as a sergeant punched several numbers. Pandemonium set in.

Hart rushed to a radio and called for Ski's headquarters. "Potomac 6, this is Jefferson 6P, over." There was static on the line.

The room shuddered at the same time the TV went blank. A light fixture fell and struck the General on the head. As he fell an aide rushed to his side, pulled a pressure bandage from a cargo pocket and wrapped it around the old man's forehead. "MEDIC!" He called out.

In the corner of the room the radio crackled to life. "Jefferson 6P, this is Potomac 5. 6 is unavailable."

Gunshots echoed from the hall, boots stomped past the unhinged door to the conference room. "Over there, cover me!" Then the thump of a grenade reverberated into the room. BOOM! And the door fell from the resulting blast.

Hart carried the microphone as far as the cord could reach and stretched his neck to see how the General was. "Potomac 5, our 6 is down and unconscious. The Deputy Commander's out of touch. Find General P and inform him he's in command. Over."

A hurried voice came over the speaker, "Jefferson 6P, copy that. We've been hit, but are operational. Our base is under attack. We're bugging out. Will contact you every…" Then BOOM! BOOM! The sound of small arms fire broke through the air.

#####

As soon as he felt the heat from the bomb blast, Prewkowski grabbed his radio and slid under his desk. His aide rushed into the conference room.

"You okay Sir?" When he heard his commander on the radio he stuck his head into the hall and shouted. "Sergeant, find a detail to guard the General!" Then he called out to a female officer as she ran down the hall. "Colonel, Commander wants a damage report." He picked up a rifle from a dead soldier and ran back into Ski's office.

"Thanks, Sergeant. I heard you send a detail here, make sure Security estab..."

Machine gun fire reverberated through the walls. Pistol drawn, Ski crawled toward a broken window from under his desk. "Driver, jump out this window, get reinforcements, then bring my vehicle and security detail."

The young soldier snapped his helmet strap, nodded, and jumped out the window. A single shot zinged through the man's shoulder, came through the window, and ricocheted off the concrete walls. "I'm hit Sir! I'll be okay. I can make it to safety." His arm dragging, the lad firmly gripped the handgrip on his weapon with his good arm and pointed it in the direction he thought the Rebels had fired from.

Ski poked his head and pistol through the window and provided cover fire by shooting at several Rebels on the other side of the motor pool.

Immediately a Federal Sniper fired covering shots. The Driver scurried around a corner and out of sight.

While Ski's back was turned several Rebels stormed in. "Drop it Soldier!"

Ski turned pointed his weapon, when he saw a rifle muzzle peek around a corner he dropped out the window and ran after his

Driver. He ran a zig-zag path down the alley to safety.

#####

Two days later, Ski and his Driver arrived at Ft. Indiantown Gap. The new Federal Commander jumped out of the car before it came to a stop. "Sergeant, find out where we're staying. Unload our luggage. Be back in an hour."

Favoring his wounded shoulder, the young man put the car in park. Exiting the vehicle, he retrieved Ski's briefcase, and handed it to him before he reached the sidewalk. He saluted, "Yes, Sir. It's almost dinner time. Shall I pick us up something?"

As Ski turned he called out over his shoulder. "Thanks, I forgot neither of us has eaten since breakfast. Thanks to your driving, we escaped and missed all the Federal patrols."

Before he entered the front entrance, a somber Hart rushed through the lobby, opened the door, and greeted Ski. Garfield's aide took his new commander's briefcase. They walked up to the security desk, and Hart signed the log. "Sir, we didn't know when you were going to arrive. We'll have your badge ready in less than an hour. His arm swept around the room. "We should have this all cleaned up in a few days. This building wasn't as damaged as the original headquarters bunker."

He paused as Ski stopped to get a sip from a drinking fountain. "You're a sight for sore eyes. Did you have any problem getting here?"

"Yes, quite a bit. The other day, my driver and I just barely escaped the Rebels, then, both yesterday and today, we dodged their patrols."

The sound of their clomping boots echoed through the corridor. Hart paused to open a door for Ski. "Sir, we have a regularly scheduled briefing at 1900. It will be quite full. Twenty minutes ago, we received word that President Barnes, his Chief of Staff, and the Secretary of State will be here. They're coming for the memorial service. Their chopper lands in two hours."

Ski stopped and stared out a window. *I don't even have time to get familiar with the situation. I hope he doesn't expect answers right away. Yeah, right.* "Sergeant Major, I need every staff officer here." He checked the clock on a far wall, "let's say in ten minutes. Tell them I don't expect a pretty presentation. Bring their notes. I need to know what my options are before he gets here. He doesn't care what my problems are. He wants answers." *Talk about jumping into the frying pan. I may even get fired before my first battle.*

At exactly 1900 hours a scowling President entered the small auditorium. He nodded to several officers. Ski crossed the room, and saluted. "Mr. President, you sure made good time. It's been years since I've seen you. I wish things were better."

After returning the salute, Barnes sat in the center seat in front of the room, rubbed his bald head, crossed his arms and frowned. He turned to Ski, and said, "I don't see how things could possibly be worse. I appreciate the fact that you've just assumed command. But our back's to the wall. I have to make some hard decisions. I've just been informed that the Chairman of the Joint Chiefs escaped from a Rebel prison. We'll see what input he has about your performance," he lowered his voice, "or lack of. Are you ready?"

Ski, visibly shaken, struggled to regain control. *I may not have all the answers, but with the briefing I just had, I can wing it.* "Sir, I'm as ready as can be expected. I sense you need immediate results. I don't know if that's going to be possible."

Apparently, not happy with the tone of Ski's voice, Barnes pounded the arm rest next to him. "No! That's not acceptable. Congress wanted this taken care of in six months. That time's up in a few weeks. I need answers." He paused, and pointed a finger at Ski. "You weren't my first choice for this command. Since the Rebels still have so many generals in their EPW camps, I don't have a choice. Let's get on with this. Prove me wrong."

Ski nodded. The first officer stood and introduced himself. Two hours later, Ski rose and faced his Commander-In-Chief.

"Sir, as my staff has indicated, all categories of supply are critical. We have rioting in all major cities. Two days ago, an hour before his death, General McClellan ordered five divisions of troops to assist the governors in maintaining martial law. The units along the forward edge of the battle area are spread so thin, as to be ineffective." He stood to his full height. "Mr. President, I understand that we can't surrender. I wouldn't even consider it, but at a minimum we should agree to a truce."

Barnes jumped up and stood nose-to-nose with the taller man. "If I'd known you were such a coward, I'd have found a second lieutenant to take command."

Ski swallowed, *this guy's been in combat. He knows what I'm going through. Something's wrong. Why can't he accept the obvious?* "Sir, I have tanks running out of gas in the middle of battle. I have soldiers, just out of boot camp, fixing bayonets against a fully armed Rebel unit. And you call me a coward? I call you unrealistic. If . . ."

Lyle, not having said a word the entire presentation, rose and put a hand on the general's shoulder, and then he moved between them. He looked back and forth.

"Sir, and General, let's calm down. Mr. President, I know you don't believe he's a coward. You've told me many stories about his bravery when he served under you. This isn't getting us anywhere."

Secretary of State Carter stood, and motioned for the General's staff to leave. Then he motioned for both to sit, and he laced into both. "Mr. President, I've known you for years. I know the pressure you're under. But that's no excuse for berating the General in front of his staff." He half-turned toward Ski. "And you Sir, know better than to talk back to your Commander-In-Chief. So both of you behave. We have too much at stake, too much to lose."

He walked back to his seat and picked up his water bottle. After taking a swallow, he pointed the plastic container at Barnes. "You, Sir, are not being realistic." He stared at his boss and pointed a finger at Ski. "And you, Sir, need to realize that even agreeing to a truce could be political suicide. We have to find common ground."

Carter pulled a folding chair over, straddled it, and leaned his elbow on the seat back in front of him. "We need to buy time. What's wrong with a truce? We have to sell that concept to Congress. They don't understand how desperate we really are. Hopefully in three months or so we'll have our supply problems solved, our G-15s will be in full production, and we can get the upper hand." He glanced at the clock on the wall. "We've had a long day. You've toured two battlefields, and changed time zones twice. You need rest, let's reconvene tomorrow after the viewing, and then see what we can come up with."

Still scowling over how Barnes had embarrassed him, Ski stood. *Alright, focus now. I need to wrap this up and get out of here.*

An exhausted President took a deep breath and after Ski extended his arm, shook the General's hand.

Twenty minutes later Ski stared at the papers on the mahogany desk in front of him. *I don't understand it. I've been faithful. Why doesn't Rabbi Cohen call me back?* A knock at the door brought him back to the present.

"Sir, the Chaplain would like a word with you. Do you have time?"

That's all I need right now. A Bible-thumping preacher, he's the one who ruined a perfectly good drinking partner. Haven't been able to really tie one on since he got Garfield to stop drinking. "Sure Sergeant, bring him in."

Chaplain Charlie quietly entered, and in his mild voice said, "Sir, I know it's late, but I wanted to introduce myself. Do you have time?"

"Sure, just don't start preaching to me. I'm not in the mood."

"Yes, Sir. I understand. You've got a lot on your plate. After all, you've just assumed command."

Ski motioned for the clergyman to have a seat. "Well, what do you need from me?"

"I wanted to review a few of the details for General McClellan's Memorial Service. Tomorrow's the viewing, and the service will be at 1100 hours the day after."

Ski and Chaplain Charlie sat facing each other across the conference table. "Chaplain, I know that he wanted a Christian service. That's okay with me. But some of the other soldiers who died in the attack were Jewish. I want to be sure they have a proper service."

"Yes, Sir. I asked a local Rabbi to come and assist in that matter." He set his organizer down. "General, I've known you're Jewish, can I ask a personal question?"

Suspiciously, Ski peered over the rim of his glasses. "What type of question?"

"Are you a practicing Jew?"

Ski leaned back in his chair with his arms firmly planted on the table top. "And what business is that of yours?"

Nervously, the cleric cleared his throat. "Sir, my main task is to be a spiritual advisor to the commanders in the unit I'm assigned. If you want I can preach to you. But I need to understand where you are spiritually."

"Well, I guess it's okay, if that's all you want the information for." Still a little suspicious, he relaxed, scooted his chair closer to the table, and nodded. "Ask away."

"Why are you a practicing Jew?"

"That's direct and to the point. I guess it's because my father was one. Both of my paternal great-grandfathers were Rabbis in Poland before they immigrated through Ellis Island in the early

1900s."

Taking care not to ask direct questions about the General's unwillingness to consider Christianity, the Chaplain leaned forward. "Sir, do you keep the Sabbath?"

"As much as possible. With this war, I've had to make a few exceptions. I think The Lord understands."

Charlie nodded. "I agree, we're fighting The Lord's battle. We can't always keep the Sabbath." As he talked, the Chaplain started to nervously tap a pencil on the table top. "Well, when you are able to honor the Sabbath do you ever start a fire? Do you travel more than a quarter mile from your quarters?"

Aggravated, Ski shook his head. "No I don't start a fire, and I don't see any requirement to restrict how far I travel on the Sabbath."

The clergyman smiled. "Sir, every time you, or your driver, start a vehicle you start small fires in the cylinders of the engine. Any time you travel more than a quarter mile, you're breaking the Rabbinical Law. How can you, as a practicing Jew, reconcile that with your beliefs?"

Ski scowled at the minister. "Boy, are you legalistic."

"Well, Sir, do you think a practicing Jew should follow the old Rabbinical Law, as required in the Pentateuch?"

"Definitely. That was drilled into me from childhood."

"Then why don't you offer blood sacrifices to atone for your sins?"

Apparently taken aback by a question that seemed to come from left field, Ski frowned. "What a stupid question! Civilized people don't conduct themselves that way. Besides, it would take a qualified Levitical Priest. I don't think any exist. And, I'm not a sinner. I'm a good person."

Gaining confidence as he observed the Jew's reaction to his comments, the Chaplain tilted his head. "Okay, tell me this, when did The Lord Jehovah change?"

Shaking his head, Ski fidgeted with a pencil that had been sitting on the table top in front of him. "No, of course He's never changed. He's The Lord. He's perfect. If he changed, then he wouldn't have been perfect in the beginning."

"So is there a logical reason for what he requires of us to change?"

Ski frowned, stood, and gathered his papers. "I see where you're going. I don't have time for this."

Chaplain Charlie rose at the same time. "Let me leave you with this, if The Lord Jehovah didn't change his requirements, how can a practicing Jew be right with him if he doesn't address the issue of blood sacrifice? After all, throughout the Torah didn't He demand payment for every human's sin?"

"Like I said, this meeting's over!"

PAPA – Truce Negotiations
(Mid-November)

Lieutenant General Prewkowski entered the West Wing, walked through a door, and stopped at a desk. "Excuse me, Miss, I'm looking for the Oval Office."

The middle-aged woman smiled at him as she peered through her glasses. "Aren't you sweet." She rose and moved toward a far door. "This way, General. You're not too lost." They walked down the hall, she knocked twice, and went through the open door. "In here, Sir." She stood inside the Oval Office. "Sir, General Prewkowski is here to see you." She stepped aside, let Ski pass, and left.

He marched to the front of Barnes' desk and saluted.

Barnes stood, returned the salute, walked around his desk and moved to a couch. "General, let's sit over here. I have some things I want to discuss before the others arrive. Secretary of State Carter may make it back from his round-the-world tour before we finish. I want him to lead the negotiations. Your task is to support him and stand in if something goes wrong."

Ski pulled out a thick folder from his briefcase. "We have many weak spots on our line. I'll have to assign every soldier we have in reserve to strengthen our border. I need at least two-hundred-fifty-thousand more troops to pull this off."

Barnes nodded to show he understood. "Carter will be in charge of the negotiations. I want you to ensure the integrity of the battle line. Before we get into those issues, we need to review the parameters I want the two of you to follow in your discussions with the Rebels." He pulled a sheet of paper off the table top.

"Here's a copy of Robert E. Lee's Will." He placed it in front of Ski. "Nowhere is there any mention of Lee wanting a conspiracy to resume the Civil War. Be sure you emphasize that their entire movement has been a sham for almost one-hundred fifty years, especially since last spring."

Ski skimmed Lee's Will. "It's amazing that so many had to die for a lie." *Those Christians, always fighting for their 'God.' At least when my ancestor's fought for Jehovah they were fighting for the true God.*

Barnes handed a file folder to the General. "I don't expect them to surrender just because they've believed a lie. I want you to start with that. Then I want you to bring up these speeches by Jefferson Davis and Alexander Stephens. In these discourses their ancestors talk about slavery being a cause of the Civil War, even though today's Rebels insist that it wasn't, and are offering five acres of excess federal land as an apology. What a sham!"

The President paused to take a sip of water. "We can't offer immunity for the leaders, but we must have a dialogue. You need to buy us time. We need two months before the new plant has enough stealth gliders available to make a difference. Also, we have a secret weapon, and when it's fully operational, it will swing the tide of battle in our favor."

The General added the papers to the pile in front of him. He looked up. "Mr. President, these will come in handy. I've done my own research. I'll be ready when we meet General Grimes and Bobby Lee tomorrow afternoon."

Barnes shoved several papers aside and pulled a tablet from an end table. "In fifteen minutes, Vice President Underwood, Senate Majority Leader Isaacson, and the Speaker of the House Diamond, will be here. Congress has been working overtime. They may have the solution to our troop strength problem."

The outer door opened and a secretary ushered in the Vice President and Congressional leaders. Ski rose, and Barnes made the introductions. "Mary, can I assume from the smile on your face, you have good news?"

Everyone sat. The Vice President handed an envelope to Barnes. "Sir, as promised, it passed easily. The Diamond-Isaacson Draft Bill is ready for your signature."

Barnes opened the packet and skimmed the document. "Abe, would you explain this bill to the General?"

The side door to the Oval Office opened and the Secretary of State rushed in. Appearing exhausted from his travels, Carter slumped into a Queen Anne chair next to General Prewkowski.

"Bill," Barnes said, as he put a hand on his friend's shoulder, "I haven't seen you this tired since my first Presidential campaign."

The envoy nodded. "Mr. President, I haven't slept more than two hours at a time in the past three days. I average a total of four hours a day, and when you throw in the jetlag," he paused, "enough of that, I was able to meet every Chief of State on your list." His head slumped, "I wish I had good news."

Everyone in the room jerked their head in his direction. The ticking clock on the wall chimed and brought them back to reality.

"Bill, we don't need any more bad news. You've got to have something positive."

The Statesman shook his head. "Even the favorable tidbits I have are not much to brag about. Each of our friends, some of our neighbors, and even our enemies gave us verbal support. But there the good news ends. Many of them have succumbed to public opinion in their country. It seems Fendemere's spent quite a few Rebel Dollars offering economic aid. In effect, the Rebels have bought recognition on the world stage."

Bill paused, rubbed his eyes, and continued, "The Chinese are getting ready to call in the loans we owe them. The Russians are talking to the World Bank. They want to replace the US Dollar as the world standard with the Rebel Dollar." With tears flowing down his face, the exhausted diplomat pulled a tissue from a box and wiped his eyes. "Sir, my trip was a complete failure. If you wish, I'll submit my resignation in the morning."

Barnes stood and moved next to his long-time friend. "I'll never accept your resignation. You get a good night's sleep. We'll talk in the morning. I need you fresh and ready to deal with the Rebels tomorrow afternoon."

The President looked over at the Senator. "Let's get back to the D.I. draft bill you ran through Congress."

The politician turned toward Ski. "General, this bill reinstates the draft. We need males and females between the age of sixteen and sixty, regardless of military experience. Women will be deferred if they have children under ten years of age. We're giving you two categories of recruits, those with the military background and those with no military experience. It will take three months to setup and organize, but…"

Barnes interrupted, "General, if they don't surrender, which I admit is unlikely, the outcome of your negotiations with Grimes needs to be a truce. When your draftees are trained we'll break it. Now, tell me how you'll make use of the three-hundred-fifty thousand service members I hope to give you?"

Surprised, Ski stopped taking notes and dropped his pen. "Uh, Mr. President, may I speak freely?"

"Sure Ski, by all means."

"Sir, you must feel desperate to ask Congress for this bill. Sixteen-year olds? Sixty-year olds? Women? For a society to take these measures is a sign of pure desperation. This is the type of thing Hitler resorted to at the end of World War II. I admit things look bad, but I've only recently assumed command, I'm still sorting my options."

The Vice President interjected, "General, women have been kept out of power too long. Females have an enormous amount of intellect. It's about time our society started to tap that resource. If they do it by drafting women, then it's a start."

Barnes scowled in Prewkowski's direction. "Our society's in great shape. We need resources. We need soldiers, marines, airmen, and sailors. When we finally win, we'll release everyone from active duty. I'm going to give you tools to fight this battle. It's not for you to question where the tools I give you come from. It's for you to use them."

It appeared that Ski was unmoved by Barnes' and Mary's comments. He started to speak, swallowed hard, looked down, and scooped the papers in front of him into his briefcase. "Sir, I have a lot of work to do. If you'll excuse me I'll get started."

As Barnes stood, the Congressional leaders also rose. "Ski, I expect a preliminary plan from you in the morning. You have your instructions. Dismissed."

#####

At exactly 1400 hours the next afternoon, a Federal convoy pulled to a stop just outside the parking lot of the Appomattox Courthouse National Park. The gun trucks and fighting vehicles made a hasty perimeter around a limousine. The limo driver jumped out, his weapon at the ready. Ski exited and motioned for a Lieutenant to come over.

The young woman ran to his side. "Yes, Sir."

The Yankee Lieutenant put a hand to her forehead, shielded her eyes, and scanned the terrain.

Ski said, "When we pull up in front of the courthouse, I want a perimeter around the limo. They're to provide security and commo for us."

Ten minutes later, tires crunched on the gravel driveway. The Federal vehicles stopped, and a soldier ran over to the passenger side and opened the door for Bill. Ski stepped out right behind. A flock of reporters tried to surround them.

Several tried to get their attention. "Mr. Secretary!" Another voice chimed in, "General!" Several other correspondents tried to force their way close to them. Federal troops formed a cordon around the men and broke through. They walked toward the building. Ski opened the gate for the Secretary of State.

At that moment Marc LeBlanc squeezed through a loose spot in the line of Federals and yelled in Bill's ear. "Sir, is it true that you're going to surrender to the ROA?"

Bill and Ski turned and glared at the young Rebel reporter. The Secretary shook his head, "We're as strong and as viable as ever. We're here to see what the Rebels have to say. I don't expect anything major to come out of our talks." Bill and Ski turned and briskly started up the walk.

Still suffering from jetlag, and a lack of sleep, Bill rubbed his eyes. "I think it's odd they want to have these talks here." *I don't feel so good. Why did I let Barnes give me this assignment?*

"I don't trust them. They always have something up their sleeve," whispered Ski.

Bill paused when they were halfway up the walk. "I know what the President said, but I want you to take the lead. If necessary, we'll take a break for a private conference."

Sensing the exhaustion in the career politician's demeanor, Ski put his hand on his partner's shoulder. "I'm ready." They walked on in silence; the only sound was a bird chirping in the distance and the scrunch of Ski's boots on the path.

They reached the stairs, and looked up to see Grimes and Bobby coming out the north door. Grimes smiled. "Mr. Secretary, it's good to see you again. It's been what, three years?"

Bill and Ski exchanged handshakes with the Rebels. "Yes, it's been at least that. I think we bumped into each other in a Pentagon hallway during the summer of '12."

They walked into the same room that Grant and Lee had met

on that day long ago. Bobby pointed to the southern side of the room. "Gentlemen, if you'd sit on that side."

Ski turned his head and checked out the area. Bill waited for his eyes to adjust to the dim lighting. *I've taken the Park Service tour here many times. They've cleared everything out to make room.* Then he turned and glanced across the hall into the other room. All exhibits had been removed. He noticed a lavish buffet.

A waiter entered, and stood next to Grimes. "Sir, would you like me to serve lunch?"

Grimes tilted his head toward Carter and Prewkowski. "I know you've been on the road for a while, we've prepared a light lunch."

Ski smiled. "General, one thing I've learned is, never turn down southern hospitality. We'd enjoy whatever you have prepared. I hope you didn't go out of your way on our account."

Bobby motioned everyone to move to the buffet. "This way please. As a matter of fact, I did. We know northern rations are a little sparse. We thought you might enjoy something special." A broad sweep of an arm ushered them toward the food.

Garfield told me this kid was rude. That was an understatement. "General Grimes, let's make this a working lunch."

The four men moved around the table. Bill was the only one who put small portions on his plate. Grimes glanced over Bill's shoulder, "Mr. Secretary, are you feeling alright?"

Bill set his plate down and took a deep breath. "General Grimes, I just have a touch of jetlag. I've done quite a bit of traveling this past week."

"So I've heard, Sir. You seem to get around don't you?"

As they moved to their seats, Ski spoke up. "General, Mr. Lee, we appreciate the hospitality and you providing the location for this meeting. But enough of this chitchat, shall we get started?"

Startled at such directness, Grimes put his plate down. "Ok, if you want, bottom line up front, that's what you'll get. We expect you to surrender this afternoon. If you do, the ROA will offer an economic aid package to rebuild the damage from our conflict."

Ski dropped his dish onto the tablecloth. Fried chicken and spareribs fell off his plate and onto the floor. "Sir, we're still strong, we have plenty of resources, and assets available. We're here to consider a truce that may develop into a cease fire. But surrender, no way."

Bobby pointed a drumstick at the Feds. "Sirs, I hope you're not depending on your stealth gliders, or your new secret weapon. We destroyed Boeing's plant in Everett, Washington a while back. We know where the new plant is. We also know that you think you've fully developed a Star Wars Defense Shield. Well, it may work now, but we have the frequencies, codes, and passwords to render it ineffective."

Startled, Bill took a sip of water. His hand shook as he brought his glass to his lips.

Grimes noticed out of the corner of an eye. "Mr. Carter, you just returned from visiting your supposed allies around the world. How much support did you find? How long do you think you can hold out?"

Ignoring his adversary, Bill nodded to Ski.

Ski pulled out two sheets of paper from his pocket and passed them over to the Rebels. "Sirs, you've been fighting for a lie. This is a copy of General Lee's will. It doesn't mention any conspiracy to resume the Civil War." He leaned back in his chair, crossed his arms and said, "So you've caused all this carnage for a lie. What do you have to say for yourselves?"

Bobby was speechless at the allegation. Grimes smirked. "General, it's true what you say about the General's will. However, our ancestors had the foresight to realize that as in the antebellum era the north would try to control the south. They recognized that after we lost the first conflict, the north would try to impose its way of life on us. Our ancestors used deception as a tool to keep our way of life alive." He tossed the paper back across the table. "This paper doesn't mean anything."

Ski, leaned forward, "What about the war crimes committed by you and other leaders of the ROA?"

"War crimes? What war crimes?"

Dumbfounded, Ski slammed a fist on the table. Several glasses toppled over, water seeped into the tablecloth. "What about the carnage caused by the prisoners you sent north? What about the upheaval you caused when you sent welfare clients across our border? The two of you are responsible for every murder, rape, robbery, and crime committed by these criminals from the first minute you sent them into our society."

Bobby turned pale at the possibility of being charged with a war crime. Grimes smiled. "Nothing that's happened since last April comes close to the crimes committed by Federal troops during the original conflict, especially during General Sherman's March to the Sea. Your historians wrote the history and claim Sherman as a hero. Now you're trying to make him a hero in our schools."

The Rebel General looked at both of his adversaries. "Sirs, you've brought up minor issues. The fact is that our blockade has been more effective than we thought possible. Your citizens are starving and rioting in your streets. We have the coordinates of Boeing's plants. As we mentioned before, we have all access information for your Star Wars Defense Shield." The black man paused, opened a file folder, and slid a one page document across the table. "This outlines our surrender terms. You have forty-eight hours to accept, or we'll send another forty thousand prisoners and welfare clients north. Think of how your economy will handle the infusion of the real and counterfeit money they bring with them."

Bill and Ski took the paper and read the document. As if on cue, both stood. Ski spoke first. "Sirs, we'll get back to you." They both turned and walked out.

That evening, Bill and Ski sat in a tent a mile south of the Appomattox Courthouse. Ski pointed a Cuban cigar at Bill. "Mr. Carter, the Rebels may have zeroed in on Boeing's plant, may have the details on our Star Wars program, but we haven't lost yet. I haven't come this far to give up because the ROA seems to have the upper hand. We've got to come up with a solid plan."

Bill's iPhone rang. He immediately put it on speaker. A woman's voice came over the air. "President Barnes, calling for Mr. Carter."

"Carter here. Thanks for putting my call through."

As his image appeared on the screen, Barnes' voice snapped through the air waves. "Well how did negotiations go? Was Grimes reasonable?"

"No, Sir, he wasn't. They demanded our surrender. The Rebels claim to have the location of Boeing's new plant, and the data on the new Star Wars program. They threatened to release more prisoners and send additional welfare clients north."

"SURRENDER. Over my dead body."

Bill jumped up and spoke directly into the speaker. "Sir, they have some valid points. Their blockade has been effective, our supply line is non-existent. Even if you gave Ski three-hundred-fifty thousand combat veterans, we're going to be lucky to hold our line. You're living in an ivory tower. We need to face facts."

The two mediators watched the small screen as Barnes slammed a fist on his desktop. "No! Not on my watch. You will follow my orders to the letter. Understood?"

Both men nodded. "Yes, Sir." Then the phone went dead.

Bill walked over to the table and tapped a finger on the map in front of Ski. "When he gets this way, there's no reasoning with him. He'll calm down. I'll work with him. How are you going to overcome this?" Then he drew a line across the North American Continent.

Ski touched a stack of papers. *I don't have to like the draft he implemented, but I'd be foolish not to use whatever troops he gives me.* "Here's my plan. We agree to a cease fire, not a truce. I need it to last at least three months."

Bill thumbed through a few pages. "I see you plan to split combat-ready units into three elements, then promote every soldier by at least one rank. At that point you'll fill all three with one-third of their strength coming from draftees with military experience. The remaining will have no military experience. Given three months, you hope seasoned combat vets will mold the rookies into some semblance of a soldier. Will we have the time? And will the units be viable on the battlefield?"

Rubbing the stubble of his five-o'clock shadow, Ski mused. "In World War II they did something similar, only they split the units in two, and then filled the lower ranks with draftees. They didn't have the deadline we do. Today, I'm at least getting some draftees with combat experience." He paused to re-light his cigar. "I think I read Grimes correctly. Even though they think they're winning, they're as tired of this as we are. They'll agree to a cease fire, hoping it will become permanent. My experience has been that small factions on either side will not be able to hold to the terms of any agreement for long. We'll use any incident we find handy as an excuse to resume hostilities."

Bill jerked his head toward the General. "Now you're sounding like Barnes. There's no way I'm going to let him dishonor the USA by intentionally breaking a truce. You're suggesting the same thing. Why?"

Ski spread his hands, and said, "Mr. Carter, I'm not planning to break a truce or cease fire. However, incidents do occur." He lowered his voice, "When something happens, I'll take advantage of it."

Bill scowled and motioned for Ski to come to the table. Two hours later they shook hands. Bill walked the soldier to the door. "I'm glad we came to an agreement. Let's get a good night's sleep. Tomorrow's a big day."

#####

When the Federals left, Bobby reached for his phone. "General, you've taught me a lot the past few months. I'll be forever in your debt. Is your Doctor sure about his diagnosis?"

The old man, seemed to be caught off-guard by the concern in his protégé's voice. He sat and put his head in his hands. "No, my prostrate is the size of a walnut. Five months ago she told me I had six months. Last week, she gave me two months. I've taken you as far as I can. You've done well. Sir, there's nothing else I can teach you. Lieutenant General Ayers will be available any time you need him. "

The young Rebel leader reached over and put a hand on the black man's shoulder. "General, I still need you. I'm not ready." *Lord, I can't do it. I need his guidance as much as yours. He's the tool you've given Grandfather and me.*

Grimes put his hands on top of Bobby's. "Son, the eaglet needs to leave the nest. You have many who will support you. Remember, The Knights of the Golden Compass are behind you."

Bobby wiped his eyes "Sir, we've met with them several times. I only hope they can pull it off."

Grimes picked up a cup of coffee. He pointed it at Bobby before he took a sip. "Remember, between them, and President Gressette, you have all the support you need. I'm seventy-five years old. It's time for me to let someone else step forward." Grimes tilted his head toward Bobby's I-pad.

Bobby punched a few numbers. "This is Bobby Lee for the President." While he waited for an answer, he nodded at Grimes. "General, anything special you want me to mention?"

The old black man looked up after staring at his withered hands. "You might mention they reacted as expected. Tomorrow we begin the serious talks."

Bobby held a finger up, pushed the speaker button on his video phone, and spoke. "Mr. President, did you hear what General Grimes said?"

Gressette's voice boomed through the phone. "That's good news, Bobby. Grimes, I want the surrender agreed to tomorrow. Understood?"

Both negotiators jerked their heads toward each other. Grimes responded first and leaned into the screen. "Sir, we need more time. Bobby's been handling the Federals quite well. But we can't guarantee they'll ever agree to our demands, much less by tomorrow."

The Rebel President smiled. "Then you boys have some overtime to put in. Don't you?" The phone went silent.

Both envoys stared at each other. Bobby reacted first. "General, was he this hard to deal with before we started all this?"

"General Lee was running the show then. He was hard, but in a different way. Believe me, we don't have a choice." He sat next to Bobby. "Son, I've seen your test scores. You have more potential at this time in your life than your grandfather when he took command." He squeezed the young man's shoulder. "Remember, the Doctor says I don't have long. Let's get started."

At 0800 the next day, all four adversaries sat at a round table and glared at each other. After a few moments of awkward silence, Ski said. "Gentlemen, we have considered your proposal."

The two Rebels looked at each other.

Ski shifted in his chair. *Here goes. Give it your best shot, soldier.* "General Grimes, Mr. Lee. At this time, after considering your initial proposal, we need to study our options in more detail. We're countering with a complete three month cease-fire on all fronts. That will give us time to work out the details."

Bill leaned across the tabletop and tapped a finger, and said firmly, "That would mean no aggressive activity against any Federal unit. Is that understood?"

Surprised that they hadn't received a complete rejection, Grimes nodded. "Mr. Secretary, it wasn't us who started this war. Your Mr. Lincoln caused the problem back in 1861. Our ancestors responded and..."

"Who was it that fired the first shot at Ft. Sumter? If that wasn't starting hostilities I don't know what was." Bill interrupted.

Bobby laughed. "Sir, I can tell you were educated in the North. Our ancestors had every right to secede. We asked the Federal troops to leave Ft. Sumter. They refused. As a sovereign state, we had every right to force a foreign power to leave our boundaries."

As Bobby spoke, the Secretary of State walked to the coffee pot. "Anyone else care for a cup?" He poured and mixed his cup before he continued. "The Confederate States of America have never been sovereign states. The Rebels in the first conflict were just that, Rebels."

"Humph!" Grimes retorted. "Mr. Lincoln recognized the CSA as a sovereign state when he ordered the illegal blockade of our shores. According to 1860 international law, a blockade was only legal if it was used against an independent nation."

Ski had been watching the southerners and Bill. He pulled out some papers. "I've heard that line before. I haven't found anything in my research on the Internet that supports such a premise. The fact remains that logically a government has every right to suppress any civil unrest in whichever way it deems necessary."

Bobby interjected, "Sir, I studied at Stanford. I received a Masters in U.S. History. I did research at the Hoover Institute of War and Peace. My study supports our position. Now, if..."

"Enough. We can debate all this some other time. We have a conflict to settle." Bill said.

Grimes nodded. "Mr. Carter, you suggested a cease-fire. Can we assume you mean in place?"

Ski pulled out a map. "I suggest the original borders of last April."

Bobby shook his head. "Several states have joined the ROA since then. We won't give them up. And, I might add, we're not going to give up any of the recent gains we made in Kansas, West Virginia, and Pennsylvania," he paused and let the magnitude of his comments take full effect, "until after a peace treaty is signed."

Bill scowled. "That would give credibility to your illegal actions. We can't agree to that."

Grimes reached across the table and took Bill's coffee cup from him. "How about a refill? You take cream and two sugars, right?"

"Thanks."

While Grimes poured the coffee, Bobby commented, "Sirs, we're talking about a cease-fire, not a peace treaty. That means we stop wherever we are, and cease fighting. That doesn't mean we retreat, or give up any gains." *Besides, if you could force us to retreat you wouldn't have agreed to these discussions.*

Four hours later, everyone gathered their reference materials and stood. "Bobby motioned to Grimes. "General, if you would be so good to have someone bring the hard copy of what we've agreed to.

Ten minutes later, Lieutenant Reiner, returned and handed three notebooks to Ski. Bobby pointed "General, there's an extra copy. Included is a CD. Shall we meet in three days to finalize everything?"

Not trusting their enemy, but realizing they needed to keep a civilized tone, Bill and Ski accepted the material. Ski looked out a window. "It looks like it's going to rain." He turned and put on his field jacket. "Yes, that should be fine. We'll meet at 1000 hours, we'll host the next meeting at Ft. Indiantown Gap. Will you be ready?"

#####

The Rebel helicopter hovered over a field at Ft. Indiantown Gap, Pennsylvania. Grimes pointed out the window. "Bobby, it looks like they're ready for us. Get a look at all the security."

"Bobby tilted his head so he could see past the General's hand. "Yes, they have over five times as much as we did when they visited us."

The chopper jolted when it touched down. Both men unbuckled their seat belts. Grimes called out, "It's show time, Boss."

Twenty minutes later they were ushered into a conference room. A large buffet spread along the far wall. Bobby looked around. "Sergeant Major Hart, where is Mr. Carter and General Prewkowski?"

Hart approached and saluted Grimes. "Sir, they're on a tele-conference with President Barnes. I expect them shortly." He waved a hand at the food. "Please, help yourself."

This has to be intentional, how rude can they be? That's a purposeful insult. There's no excuse for being late. Grimes returned the senior NCO's salute. "No problem, I understand." He turned to Bobby. "Mr. Lee, hungry? Let's grab a plate."

As the Rebels filled their plates, Bill and Ski came into the room. Bill walked up to Grimes. "Sorry we're late. The President had some issues he wanted to review."

Grimes put his plate down and shook Bill's hand. "Don't worry. I understand how Presidents can be. Shall we get started?"

The five men sat around the oval table. Several waiters entered and poured beverages.

Hart pulled pages from a folder and passed them out.

Bill set his copy aside. "Our President agreed to the terms we discussed earlier this week."

Grimes cut into his Monte Cristo sandwich, then pointed a knife at the diplomat. "My President wasn't happy with our product. But he realized this will take time, and that he needs to be patient."

QUEBEC – Jennifer's Command
(End of November)

A light rain fell. First Lieutenant Jennifer Eagleton put her clipboard under her arm to keep her papers dry. She yelled over the roar of the engines. "Listen up! First Sergeant Kelly and Staff Sergeant Michaelson will lead this mission. First Sergeant, you mentioned you had replacements for the two soldiers? The one who broke his arm and the other who had a Red Cross Emergency?"

Kelly looked up from the roster he was scribbling on. "Ma'am, I'll assign two drivers as soon as you finish" Then went back to his roster.

Jennifer resumed her Safety Brief. *These soldiers have really come a long way in the past few months. I can't let up on them or they'll slip back into their old ways.* "Each driver has strip maps showing the route to the Logistical Release Point. You'll pick-up four pallets of Meals Ready to Eat, ten thousand gallons of JP-8, ammo for Brigade, and return. Even though there's a truce, I want you to be sharp. I don't trust these Rebels. Keep your air guards up. Sergeant First Class Jimenez, where are you?"

Hector, standing in the rear, raised a hand, "Here Ma'am."

"Good, have you made sure all guns are checked out?"

"Yes, Ma'am, I had the Armorer examine the head space and timing on each machine gun. I took the liberty of putting an extra can of ammo on every truck."

"Good idea. While they're gone you're the Acting First Sergeant, report to my office in thirty minutes."

Hector noted the time on his watch. "Yes Ma'am. I'll be there."

Shielding her eyes from the sun that had poked through the rain clouds, Jennifer glanced at her soldiers. "New recruits, be sure you listen to your Sergeants and the combat vets who're with us." She paused, and pulled a sheet of paper from her clipboard. "This is a priority mission, so you'll miss this afternoon's ceremony. Because of our combat record, General Van Ruiten put us in for a Presidential Unit Citation. She'll present us with a streamer for our company flag this afternoon."

Everyone cheered. "Hooah!"

The red-headed commander came to attention. "First Sergeant, I need to see you before you leave." Then she yelled over the din. "Dismissed. Let's get this show on the road."

Kelly ran against the tide of soldiers rushing to their vehicles. He reached Eagleton's side. "Yes, Ma'am."

Jennifer tapped her pen on the clipboard. "We need all the fuel you can get. I sent a detail to Supply. I want you to fill every five gallon fuel can that will fit on your trucks. The General expects the Rebels to break the truce. The troops we support will need every drop you can get. Understood?" She nodded. They exchanged salutes. Kelly ran to his hummer.

Jennifer moved onto toward the drill floor. She turned her head and watched every soldier on the detail as they ran through the rain soaked Motor Pool to their vehicle. Several made a last minute check of their engine, a few looked underneath for leaks, and others kicked the tires. A Sergeant ran to roll the gate open. After fighting with the lock he yanked it, and it fell to the ground. *Atta boy Soldier, that's the spirit!*

#####

Twenty minutes later, as their vehicle bounced over a back mountain road, Kelly tapped his driver's arm. "I see your combat patch. Where were you in Iraq?"

The young sergeant focused on the road and maneuvered the Hummer through traffic before she glanced at Kelly. "I was in Baghdad for six months. I was an interpreter for an Engineer Company."

"Interpreter? That's a good MOS. How'd you get to be a driver? Why did you only serve six months? During that time, combat tours were twelve."

She checked the rear-view mirrors, and then said, "First Sergeant, it's a long story. I don't want to bore you."

Kelly reached for the microphone, and called out, "Headquarters, this is Romeo 4. Passed checkpoint 1. All clear, out." He turned to his driver. We've got three hours to get there and three hours back. I'll keep whatever you tell me in confidence."

The thirty-year old soldier shifted in her seat. "Well Top, back in '06 my Company Commander informed me I was going to interpret that evening. It wasn't unusual; he often had meetings with Iraqi Officials."

She paused to turn a corner, "By the way, Top, all vehicles are still behind us."

Kelly unfastened his seat belt, turned, and looked out the passenger window. "Yes they are. Spacing's good too."

The vehicle straightened out. As she pulled onto the highway, she resumed her tale. "Supposedly he had been invited to a feast with the Mayor of a small town thirty miles from our base. During the forty-five minute drive, he told me this was a high-priority meeting. If everything went well, the Mayor was going to help bring a band of insurgents to support us."

Kelly sliced open his MRE with his knife, and sorted through the bag. "Wow, if he'd pulled that off, it would've been a feather in his cap."

She adjusted the visor to block the rising sun. "Yes it would've. We arrived a little early and he introduced me to the Mayor. We sat at a typical Iraqi feast. The town's police chief, and two other minor officials were there also. I realized later they were interested in me, not any discussions Captain Morgan Lee had in mind."

"I've heard about those feasts. You were lucky to enjoy one."

Her chin quivered, "F, F, First Sergeant it was horrible. I've never told anyone the entire story. You see, after the meal, the Mayor complimented the Captain on bringing what he wanted. All of a sudden his mood shifted. He rose from his seat, walked behind me and pulled out the bobby pins that held my hair up."

She turned toward Kelly. "He caressed my hair and then my shoulders. He told the Captain, 'When I attended Harvard I was always partial to American blondes, never had a red-head. We'll just go in the other room. After we're done, I'll sign the papers that will bring the insurgents into our sphere of influence. My man will have your $10,000.00 in an envelope before you leave.'"

Kelly's eyes widened as the young woman continued. *Wow, which side was her commander on?*

"I grabbed the Mayor's hand and twisted his arm behind him." She paused and took a deep breath. "That creep only smiled and twisted it back. I wasn't strong enough. He called out to the Captain. 'She's a feisty one. If she's a virgin. I'll double my price, and each of my friends will pay $5,000.00 for their time with her."

She reached into a cargo pocket and pulled out a handkerchief. After blowing her nose she glared at Kelly. "My own Commander was pimping me out and tried to call it a mission!"

Apparently embarrassed by the young soldier's tale, Kelly moved in his seat. "What did you do? How did you get out of the situation?"

As they drove on, she moved her head to check traffic, and controlled her emotions. "Top, we were required to set our weapons aside as we entered the Mayor's home. I always kept a pistol hidden at my side. I pulled it out, put the gun to his head and told Captain Lee, 'Sir, it's time we leave.'"

After twenty minutes of silence, Kelly reached for the mic, "Headquarters, this is Romeo 4. Reached checkpoint 2, all clear, out." He shoved the litter from his lunch into a trash bag. "I'm amazed you handled yourself so well. But how did you wind up getting sent home six months early?"

She laughed, "It seems Lee was well-connected. It was my word against his, until I pulled out my tape-recorder. He'd forgotten that I always brought it to make sure I could review my work later on. With the tape, they decided to transfer both of us to different bases. He was posted to Germany. I was given an early out, and $50,000.00. I wasn't going to take it, at first. But I realized that I didn't want to remain in an organization that covered up that type of behavior. Then I was drafted. The induction center sent me to your unit."

Kelly reached over and touched her arm. "We don't put up with anything like that. If you have any problems you come to the Commander or me."

"Thanks, Top. I think I can trust you."

As the hummer turned the last corner and moved into their destination, Kelly spoke into

the mic. Headquarters, this is Romeo 4. We've arrived. No incidents. Out." He unbuckled his seat belt and climbed out of the vehicle, ran across the field, and called out. "Lieutenant! Ma'am?"

A young woman, standing twenty feet away, looked up. "Kelly, you're early. Have your cargo trucks back up over there. The tankers know where to go. Have the ammo trucks stay put. I'll have the forklift bring the pallets to them."

Kelly saluted, turned and watched his crew following the

Lieutenant's instructions. Forty-five minutes later the convoy was loaded, lined up, and ready to depart.

"Lieutenant, I don't like the idea of just trading tankers with you. But Eagleton told me that was the new procedure. How come we're only getting 7,500 gallons?"

Appearing frustrated, the woman shook her head. "First Sergeant, it's like we're fighting this war on a budget. Last week we were short of MREs. This week it's fuel. Next week, who knows? The only way I was able to fill your ammo request is that, due to the truce, you're not firing as much, so you requested less. You're lucky I'm giving you that much. As soon as General Van Ruiten's order came through I stopped filling the second tanker we had set aside for you. Those extra fuel cans won't be filled. "

Kelly, displeased, said, "And how do you expect us to support the Brigade?"

The young woman took Kelly by the arm and moved around the corner. "First Sergeant, I know you're frustrated, I can see it in your face. I've known you for years. I remember when you were a Specialist. But I can't have you use that tone in front of my soldiers. We all have to adjust. Got it?"

Not liking what he heard, but realizing he didn't have a choice, said, "Yes, Ma'am." The young First Sergeant saluted, turned, raised and circled his arm over his head, then called out to his convoy. "Mount up, let's go."

As he buckled his seat belt, a Private ran up. "Top, my brakes aren't building up pressure. The air brake alarm won't go off."

"Private, that truck's always been like that, the pressure will build up eventually. Get in your vehicle and get moving. Take it easy until the alarm goes off. I can't afford another delay."

The fifty-year-old Private appeared frustrated. "B, but…"

Kelly, aggravated at the older man's persistence, interrupted. "Private, I'm in charge. I've driven that truck before. I know how it handles. We don't have time to dilly-dally. Get your vehicle on the road!"

The Private trotted to the end of the convoy and climbed into the cab. As he fastened his seat belt he commented to his co-driver. "Sarge, you were right. He wouldn't listen to reason. I've half a mind to stay back."

The man next to him put a hand on his wrist. "Calm down. It'll be okay. We've had this problem for years. It'll make it. I promise."

"Listen, Sarge," he shouted over the buzzing alarm, "before I was drafted last month I was driving the civilian model of this truck cross-country. I don't have a good feeling about this. I've been doing it for decades. Ten years ago I had the same difficulty. I was hauling 2,500 gallons of fuel, turned a corner too fast, and the load started to slosh. The vehicle in front of me came to a quick stop. My brakes failed. I turned the wheel too hard, and the trailer tipped over. In aftermath the fuel exploded. Four people died. Look, if our brakes go out we may have to bail. If I have to I can disconnect the trailer in less than a minute."

Ten miles away, three Rebels put the finishing touches on two roadside bombs. "Sarge, I'll just pull some of that brush on the mud and get rid of our footprints. With all the rain we had it'll take a while. I'll meet you over by that rock."

His Sergeant lifted two crates onto a truck. "Good." He turned his head toward the other side of the road. "Corporal, do you have the remotes ready?"

The young NCO called out, "Yeah, Sarge. I left them in the case by the birch tree. Tell me, I thought we were in a truce. Why are we setting up IEDs that are against the terms of the ceasefire?"

The older soldier put an arm around his subordinate. "Son, the terms are that we won't take any aggressive action. These devices

166

are defensive. We won this area in battle. If the Federals come this way, we need to be able to defend our sector with a minimal loss of Southern lives. Now, get in position. I need you on that hill to spot any enemy activity. Got it?"

A Rebel Private came running up, out of breath. "Hey, I hear a convoy coming. It might be Feds!"

All three reached their hiding places as Kelly's hummer turned the corner.

The old tank commander struggled to hold his poncho down so it covered the hatch opening. Rain came down in buckets and flowed into the hatch of his Abrams tank. Traveling at sixty miles-per-hour, rain pellets stabbed at his cheeks. The hem of the poncho flapped in the wind. He keyed the mike as he looked through his binoculars. "C-1 this is B-12."

"Go 12."

"Top Kelly, be advised, I just spotted a motorcycle moving up on our right side."

"Sergeant, is the cyclist making any threatening or suspicious moves?"

"No, he's kept pace with us. Wait a minute. He's pulled out his cell. He's taking pictures."

"Not suspicious enough. Keep an eye on him."

"Will do. Hey, he's just sped up. Now he's alongside the tanker ahead of us. He's taking a picture of it, too." The Sergeant dropped the mic and focused his binos. He picked the handset up and clicked it. "Top, I can't read the license plate, and part of the frame's broken. The top says, 'Valley,' bottom says, 'High School Cross Country.' The plate's muddy, the last character's an '8, B, or 3.' Whoops, there he goes again. He's sped up around the corner. He's weaving around on the trail. Probably, going to take more pictures."

Kelly's voice came over the speaker in every vehicle in the convoy. "Listen up. We have a lone cyclist coming up on the right. Be cautious. If he makes any threatening moves, shoot to disable his bike. I want him as a prisoner." *This is a big coup. I gotta make sure we handle this Rebel right. We can't afford any mistakes.*

Several voices came over the speaker. "Yes, Top."

"You got it."

"Yup."

Kelly tapped a finger on his mic. Then keyed it, "Reaction Team, if something happens, be on the alert. Make sure you get him. You got that Corporal?"

A confident voice blared through the speaker, "Yes, First Sergeant!"

The Tank Commander un-holstered his pistol and made sure it was loaded and the safety was off. When he raised his head to scan the road in front of them, he noticed a man's head in a tree a few yards ahead.

Kaboom! The vehicle in front of them tried to maneuver around the first tanker that had instantly become a ball of fire.

The Abrams driver rotated his controls and veered around the fuel truck.

As the old driver turned the wheel to straighten out, the rear trailer wheels of the second tanker fishtailed into the flames created by the first tanker, and exploded.

Kelly's voice boomed over the radio. "Reaction Team, MOVE, all drivers go to rally point 4."

The tank commander took charge of the Reaction Team. "Corporal, send a detail to search for that cyclist. You take the remainder of your team and search the woods to the north. I saw a man's head in a tree. It could've been a spotter for that roadside bomb. I want him alive."

The Bradley Fighting Vehicle behind the tank veered to the left and slid to a stop in a muddy meadow. Immediately, the rear hatch opened and five soldiers exited, their boots splattering mud in the air as they instantly fanned out and secured the area.

#####

The second Bradley sped off in the direction of the cyclist. After following the muddy cycle tracks for a mile, the sergeant-in-charge ran to a hillock and called out to his team. "Over here guys, I found him." Then he ran over to a trail bike that had run into a tree. He knelt next to the injured cyclist. "Medic!" he called, then checked the man for injuries and rolled him over.

The Medic unzipped his aide bag as he ran. "I got him Sergeant. My guys'll bring a stretcher." Then he started to evaluate his patient.

The Sergeant grabbed a Private and moved him over to the smashed cycle. "Get some help. Load his bike onto that cargo truck. Be sure to collect all the pieces. Lieutenant Colonel Williams will want to have it analyzed. As he turned to leave, his eye caught the cyclist's fanny pack. "Wait, let me have that pack." He reached down and grabbed it from the Medic's out-stretched hand.

"Thanks Buddy." He ran over to a tree stump and dumped the contents out. He called out to a passing soldier. "Get me a radio. I gotta call this in." Minutes later, a soldier brought him the instrument. "Thanks. Go tell Doc I want to leave in ten minutes."

"You got it, Sarge." The young man ran off.

The Sergeant called out the names of the spy's possessions to himself as he listed the items he found on his tablet. "Cell phone." He moved some scrap pieces of trash and revealed a student ID from Valley High school. He flipped the card over. "Seems his name is Jay Bourne. Yeah, right. Likely story." He put the card back in the pack and resumed making his list. Two candy bars, tablet, colored pens, mini-binoculars, small first aid kit, mag…"

The Medic came up, picked up the cell phone and tossed it in his hand. "Sarge, we've loaded him into the ambulance. I've told the driver to head straight back to base. I'll see you there."

The Sargent grabbed the Medic's arm. "Oh, no you don't. The ambulance will go to the rally point with us."

"Sarge, my patient woke up. He's in pain. I need to get him to the Battalion Aid Station."

"I won't take the chance. It's too risky. You'll stay with the rest of the reaction team. Besides, if we get hit again, we'll need your services. Our potential wounded are more important than this spy."

The Medic started to speak, but his Sergeant held a hand up. "It's not open for discussion." He shoved everything back into the fanny pack. "I see they're ready for us. We're leaving now. Let's go."

Apparently upset at being forced to delay his patient's medical care, the medic frowned as he hurried to get into the ambulance.

Five miles away and fifteen minutes later, the tank, and the remaining reaction team vehicles rumbled up to the rally point. Kelly waited for the NCOs to join the impromptu meeting he'd called together in the afternoon mist.

Kelly looked around and pointed to the Sergeant-in-charge of the quick reaction team. "Where's the Bradley?"

The Sergeant moved to where he could be seen. "I sent him after a Rebel I think I saw in a tree. They checked in ten minutes ago. They searched the area and found a cache of C-4, grenades, and rifle ammo. They'll be here soon." The rumble of the Bradley was heard before it came around the corner. It parked next to where the men and women were meeting.

The Corporal and a lanky man were sitting, facing each other. They turned and looked at the soldiers standing on the ground. Both men stood and walked across the top of the vehicle. The Corporal pointed to the rear, and motioned for everyone to move with them. They shifted to the back hatch.

The Corporal sat with his feet dangling over the opening. "First Sergeant, we met this guy." He pointed to a lanky man sitting next to him. "This here's Jimmy-John. He has moonshine still about a mile back. I heard on the radio about the hummer fuel tanks getting hit by shrapnel. If you can get the holes patched, maybe you can trade for some shine. You know army engines will run on anything flammable. I told him he could ride on top as part of his payment."

Kelly motioned for the two men to join them. As they climbed down, Kelly spoke to the NCOs in his convoy. " Here's what we have. We had fourteen killed. That includes all four tanker drivers, and the ten replacement soldiers we picked up when the cargo truck they were in flipped over in the explosion. We also lost all 7,500 gallons of JP-8, and..."

At that moment a Private ran up. He paused to catch his breath. "First Sergeant, the mechanic took some twigs and whittled them into pegs. He tapped them into the holes, it's not a permanent fix, but it'll work till we get back to base. But we don't have any fuel."

The Corporal and Moonshiner stood next to Kelly. Tell me Jimmie-John, just how many gallons do you have?"

"Waall, Ah got ten barrels out back, an anotha fourteen at my otha still back at my farm."

"Humm." Kelly stroked his chin. "Are they thirty or fifty-five gallon drums?"

"Both. Ah have six thirties and four fifty-fives here. On my farm I have seven each."

"I'll take five of the thirties. What do you want in trade?"

Jimmy-John put his hands in his pants pockets and looked into Kelly's eyes. "Waall, Ah'd like five pallets of that deeehydraated army food you soljurs eat."

Kelly looked at his watch and then back at the Moonshiner. He put out his hand. "I don't have time to dicker. I'll give you two-and-a-half. That's my final offer."

Jimmy-John smiled a toothless grin at Kelly. "Done."

Jennifer nervously tapped her fingers on the desktop. *She's gotta approve a quick Court Martial. We can't spend weeks dealing with this. He's a spy and should've been shot on the spot. Oh well, now that we have him here I can't execute him without giving him a fair trial.* When the phone stopped ringing, she took it off speaker and slapped the receiver against her ear. "First Lieutenant Eagleton for General Van Ruiten."

"Yes, Ma'am, I'll put your call through now."

"General Van Ruiten."

"Good evening, Ma'am. Did you receive the request I sent regarding the Court Martial?"

"Yes, I did. Lieutenant, I must say it disturbs me. You're accusing a sixteen-year-old high school student of spying. That's serious."

"Yes, Ma'm. For me it's even more so. My oldest son is almost seventeen. You see there's just something about him that doesn't ring true. First Sergeant Kelly and I have both interrogated him. On the surface his story seems true. We confirmed with his history teacher that he did have an assignment to document military activity. His birth certificate and his history seem to pan out. But in addition to his name, he has a certain air about him that makes us suspicious."

Van Ruiten sighed. "Lieutenant, there could be any number of reasons for a child to have the name, Jay Bourne. Don't let that prejudice you. I'm going to approve your request. I know that during a trial the truth will come out."

Jennifer heard ruffling of papers over the connection.

"Here we are. I'll appoint Lieutenant Colonel Williams as the presiding officer. I'm short of JAG officers. I'm taking Lieutenant Colonel Dudley off the Wounded Warrior Program. He'll be the Defense Counsel. Do you think there'll be a problem between Williams and Dudley? After all, Dudley was Commanding Officer for both of you just a few months ago."

"Yes, he was. But whatever I thought of Dudley as a Commander is different from his performance as an attorney. From what I've been told, both he and Williams are good lawyers. I know neither of them are experienced JAG men, but I think they'll present a fair trial."

Jennifer heard the sound of a briefcase being snapped shut. "Lieutenant, call your Battalion Commander. By the time you reach him, he'll have his orders from me. I'd like this wrapped up as soon as possible."

"Yes, Ma'am." Jennifer replaced the cap on her pen and slid a few papers in a file. Then the line went dead. She raised her head when she heard a knock at her office door. "Enter."

Michaelson stuck his head in the door. "Ma'am, First Sergeant is ready to resume the interview with the prisoner. Do you want to be present?"

She gathered her patrol cap, briefcase, and jacket. "No, I'm going to Battalion. I'll be back for the 2000 meeting. Have my driver meet me in the motor pool."

"You got it Ma'am."

#####

Lieutenant Colonel Dudley set his attaché case on the table between his client and himself. "Well, young man. Seems as if we have our work cut out for us. By the way, I've noticed the work you did for a friend of mine."

The young man jerked his head up and stared at his attorney. "Sir, did you say what I think you said?"

Dudley removed a file folder from his case and opened it. The air conditioning whirred in the background. He smiled. "Yes, I've known we had an operative in the area for quite some time. Didn't know who it was." He paused and glanced around the room. "Don't worry. My aide swept the room for bugs. I don't trust these Federals to obey the rules."

Jay looked inquisitively at Dudley. "Y...,y..., you mean you're not a Federal attorney?"

Dudley laughed. "No son, I've been a sleeper agent for decades. I was wounded last July. Rather than have me sit around and do nothing, they decided I can be a defense attorney. Sort of convenient, isn't it? Now, let's get down to business..."

Two hours later Jay stood. His chair legs screeched across the tile floor. He stretched his lanky frame. "Sir, that's it. Do you think my cover will hold? I've had this ID for so long its part of me. I'd like to get back to a regular unit and get some real fighting in."

"All in due time, son. Right now we have to get past tomorrow. I don't think the trial will last more than three days. We need to decide if you're going to have a panel of officers, a panel of officers and senior NCOs, or have the presiding judge decide your fate. I recommend you go with a panel of officers and NCOs."

Jay shook his head as he doodled on a tablet in front of him. "No, Sir. I'm going to have a panel of officers. I just get a good feeling about the situation. Do you know who they'll assign as the judge?"

As he stood to leave, Dudley commented, "Yes, it'll be Lieutenant Colonel Williams. He was a First Lieutenant a year ago. He's a fine young officer, thirty years old, a competent attorney…"

Jay turned pale and fell into his chair. The old piece of furniture collapsed under his weight and he lay sprawled on the floor.

Dudley dropped his attaché and ran to his client's side. "Jay, what's wrong? Why would the judge's name be a problem?"

As Dudley, put his arm around the boy's shoulder and helped him up. Jay said, "I'm all right." Then stood, brushed himself off, and scooted the broken chair into a corner.

The young man pulled another chair to the table and sat. "You see, in 2006, before I joined ROTC, I was engaged to a girl. Her name was Vanessa Williams. I think the judge is her uncle. He was upset when I ran off and left her six months pregnant."

"Let's be realistic, Son," he said. "Michael Williams is a common name. This man came from Maryland. Most likely, we don't have a thing to worry about."

After three days of trial, Jay and Dudley sat at the defense table, waiting for the judge to return from lunch. They chatted back and forth in low tones. Every once-in-a-while one of them would glance at the door on the far side of the room. They knew destiny would walk through it at any moment. The ceiling fan squeaked, and the room reeked of sweat from so many bodies.

In one quick movement the door opened, and Lieutenant Colonel Williams entered.

The bailiff rose and called out: "ALL RISE."

Before he sat, Williams tugged at the hem of his uniform jacket and straightened it out. He put his glasses on and read a few pages. When he finished he rubbed his chin. "Madam Prosecutor. Have you finished with your closing argument?"

Jennifer rose and nodded. "Yes, Your Honor."

"Lieutenant Colonel Dudley, are you ready to present your closing argument?"

Dudley, in contrast to his appearance at the beginning of the conflict, was dressed in an immaculate uniform. "Your Honor and members of the Jury. The Prosecutor has accused this young high school student of being a spy. She's suspicious of his choice of a name. We've explained that after being bounced around in foster homes for years that he chose the name Jay Bourne. That name stems not from his being a Rebel Spy, but from a young man's fantasy. We've provided his birth certificate and his educational records from Kindergarten through his Senior year. His history teacher told you that he was working on a planned project. He was trying to document the conflict for future generations. Not one shred of evidence has been shown to demonstrate that he was working for the Rebels. Now…"

Twenty-five minutes later, Dudley spread his hands in front of the court. "Your Honor, Ladies and Gentlemen of the Panel. Please, do what is right and fair. Acquit my client."

Williams cleared his throat. "Ahem." His eyes moved from the prisoner to the jury, Jennifer, and then Dudley. "It's a little out of order, but I have a few questions for the accused." He turned to squarely face Jay. "Son, have you ever been fly fishing?"

Jay stood, and for the first time during the proceedings, he looked the judge straight in the eye. In a strong firm voice he said, "Yes, Sir."

"Are you right or left-handed?"

"Left-handed, Sir."

"Roll-up your left sleeve."

Dudley jumped up. "Your Honor, I object. What's the relevance of this line of questioning?"

Williams frowned and turned to the defense attorney. "Overruled. You'll see the relevance soon." Then he turned his head back to Jay. "Let me see if I understand everything. You are Jay Bourne, a high school student from Valley High School. Do you have any scars on your left arm?

"Y…, y…, yes, Sir."

The Judge turned to the jury. "If I'm right he has a long scar on the top of his left forearm." He turned back to Jay. "Roll-up your sleeve."

"Yes, Sir." Jay said quietly, his hands shaking as he unbuttoned his sleeve.

"Now, hold your forearm up for everyone to see." Jay held his left arm up to reveal a six-inch scar."

The Judge spoke to the jury but kept his eyes focused on Jay. "I can tell you how he got that scar. In July, 2005 our family was fly fishing in a river. My nephew Matthew and he were horsing around. Matt cast his line without checking where Jay was. His fly caught Jay's left forearm. It left that scar.

The only sound in the courtroom was a window blind slapping against a window frame.

Williams leaned forward in his chair, "Just a few more questions and I'll give the panel their instructions. Now, aren't you the Dewitt "Dee" Jobe who was my niece, Vanessa's fiancé?"

Jay/Dewitt stared at the judge, then said, "Yes, Sir."

"Didn't you leave to attend Texas Christian University on a ROTC scholarship in September 2005?"

"Sir, Yes, Sir."

"One last question and I'll give the panel their instructions. At the time you left, you knew you were the father of her unborn child, didn't you?"

Jay/Dewitt stood very erect, and in a firm voice said, "Yes, Sir."

Williams put his hands face-down on the table in front of him. Everyone sensed the trouble quivering through his shaking body. When he closed and then opened his eyes, it appeared he was in complete control. Over the next two hours he gave the panel their instructions.

The next afternoon every eye in the courtroom was on two doors. The left door was where Williams would enter the courtroom. The right door was where the panel would come through with Jay/Dewitt's destiny in their hands.

As they waited, few people held muffled conversations.

At 1445, Williams came through the door.

Immediately the Bailiff jumped up. "ALL RISE."

Everyone rose. Williams stood erect, panned the courtroom and then sat. Almost immediately the right door opened and the jury walked in.

After they were seated, Williams asked, "Mr. Foreman, have you reached a decision?"

A Major rose, paper in hand. "Yes, your Honor. We have a unanimous ruling."

"Very well. Mr. Bailiff, would you please read the verdict?"

The Bailiff moved from his position and accepted the decision. He moved back and stood just to the left of Williams. "We the panel have determined that Dewitt "Dee" Jobe is guilty of espionage." Then he folded the paper and handed it to the Judge.

Williams accepted the judgment and placed it in a folder.

"Sentencing will be tomorrow at 0900." He picked up his gavel and rapped it on the table top.

#####

At exactly 0900 everyone was in place. Williams appeared as if he hadn't slept. The bags under his eyes were more pronounced than normal.

With a tired voice he addressed the panel. "Have you reached a decision as to a sentence?"

The Foreman rose. "Yes, your Honor."

Williams nodded and the Bailiff walked over and accepted the ruling from the Major. Then he returned to his normal position. When the judge nodded again, he unfolded the paper and read: "We the panel, having found the defendant Dewitt "Dee" Jobe, guilty, sentence him to twenty-five years at Leavenworth."

Jay's foster parents, who had never believed he was a Rebel spy, sobbed, and consoled each other.

Williams accepted the paper. He placed his hands face down on the table in front of him and addressed the court. "It is at my discretion as to whether the panel's recommendation is carried out. Now, after reviewing..." Over the next hour he explained his options to the court. Finally he stood, and for the first time Dewitt and everyone in the courtroom, noticed that Williams had a pistol strapped to his right hip."

"The defendant will stand."

The defendant and Dudley stood.

"Rebel First Lieutenant Dewitt Jobe, you have been found guilty of treason, and of being a spy. Since you are definitely an officer on active duty in the ROA Army, and since you were captured out of uniform, you leave me no choice. The research I've done leads me to believe that I should order your death by firing squad. However, under the circumstances..." He pulled his pistol, pointed it at Dewitt and fired one round.

Dudley caught his client as he fell and laid him on the floor. As his attorney struggled to stop the bleeding, with his dying breath Dewitt said, "I regret that I have only one life to give for my country."

ROMEO – Percy Dunlop Escapes
(Early November)

Captain Percy Dunlop paced back and forth in his cell. *I can't believe was so stupid that I could be tricked into shooting down that aircraft. I know I was conned, but it's still my fault. I've gotta find a way out of here.*

The sound of footsteps and a cart coming toward his cell brought him back to reality.

Sparks stopped in front of his commander. "Captain Sir, I've been given Trustee Status." He lowered his voice to a whisper as he handed a snack to Percy. "Several of us are organizing a breakout. We're going to take you and XO with us. We don't have room for anyone else. "

Both glanced around. Not seeing any guards, he nodded. Sparks pushed the cart down the corridor. Percy opened his box and unfolded a hand-written note.

Captain, this afternoon, when you go out to exercise, stay in the northeast corner. There's a blind spot in the way the cameras are set up. We've loosened a seam in the chain link. Crawl through the storm drain. We'll meet you by the flood control channel, **signed Sparks.**

Percy read the note several times, put the paper in his mouth and swallowed. He jumped as he heard a guard's footsteps, leaned against the door of his cell, *Focus now. You can do this.* He pushed away from the opening and filled a bag with his few possessions.

The guard's keys clanked against the lock. "Captain, it's time for your exercise period."

The Federal officer surveyed the small room that had been home for the past seven months. *How long will it take to get back to Emily? How long to make our nation whole again?*

The guard pointed to the sack in Percy's hand. "What's that for? You never take anything with you during your exercise period."

The prisoner opened the bag. "Just my family's picture, a deck of cards, and a few energy bars."

Apparently suspicious even though Percy sounded nonchalant, the guard grabbed the plastic sack and dumped its contents on a table. "Just why are you bringing this?"

Percy smiled. "I met a fellow prisoner I haven't seen in years. I wanted to show him a picture of my family. When we were in War College together we used to play cribbage. Yesterday I challenged him to a game, at a penny a point of course. I've been saving the energy bars for a rainy day. Today seemed like a good occasion."

The jailer frowned, "I don't buy it for a moment. But I've got a schedule to keep." He pushed his charge toward the hallway, and said gruffly. "Get moving. You're putting me behind."

As the sun started to set, Percy strutted his usual fast walk around the perimeter of the yard. *I'll take my usual three laps, and then slip out.* He finished the first and caught up with a fellow prisoner. "General," he whispered, "follow me, do exactly as I do."

When the former Chief, Joint Chiefs of Staff turned his head to look around, Percy put a hand on his shoulder. "Don't draw attention to us. We're to take our normal stroll. I've been contacted by one of my former crewmembers. He's planning a breakout. He told me I was the last one to leave; they don't have any more room. But, I decided that you have to get out. The USA needs you more than me. If they don't have room for both of us, I'll stay behind and cause a diversion." He firmly glanced at his former superior, "Got it? Sir?"

The General winked and they continued in silence, a silence broken only by the scrunch of their boots on the gravel walk.

They reached the far corner, Percy dove into the opening and crept on his hands and knees "follow me." He screamed in pain as a strand of chain link scratched his back. "Ahhhh!"

His fellow prisoner, right behind, scurried through the storm drain and stumbled into the flood control channel. The two of them rolled in the muck until they reached the bottom.

Before they could stand to their full height several hands were on them. "Sparks frowned at his commander. "Sir, I told you we don't have room for anyone else. You've endangered the entire escape by bringing your friend with you."

Percy brushed mud and debris from his clothing. "I heard you. But we have an opportunity to free the General. We must get him to Washington."

They all jumped when they heard sirens on the hill above them.

Another escapee rushed up behind Sparks. "I told you officers would foul this up! They're onto us earlier than we expected. We have a vehicle that will hold four. Now we're five. That'll be conspicuous enough as we drive along."

Percy grabbed the enlisted soldier and sailor by an arm. He motioned with his head toward an escapee sitting in the driver's seat of an old Honda Civic. Through his clenched teeth he said, "Play the hand you're dealt with. Let's get moving. We'll get another vehicle later on. How long did you expect to remain undetected anyway?"

Resigned to the fact they had no choice, the enlisted escapees hurried toward the small car. Sparks pointed to the open hatchback. "General, you're the smallest, and you weren't invited. You get the way back." He looked at the older man's face. "Don't try to pull rank. It's not going to work here. You're the smallest and lightest. None of us will fit. If you don't like it, you can stay."

Reluctantly, the four-star crawled in. Sparks covered him with a blanket. "Need I remind you that no matter what happens, be quiet? Got it?" As he spoke he pushed the man's head inside and slammed the lid, ran to the front of the car, jumped into the shotgun seat, and shouted, "STEP ON IT." He rolled the passenger window down and searched the sky for helicopters.

The dingy red car slowly started under its excess weight and headed toward the highway.

SIERRA– Gun Control
(December)

Bobby slammed the phone into its cradle. "I don't believe it. That new commander I assigned to Alpha Troop broke a leg jumping off a tank. Of all the rotten luck." He turned to Grimes. "General, get me a replacement. I'll take almost anybody. The mission must go off as planned." *Lord why was that guy so stupid? What am I gonna do now? If we don't find anybody I have to take the mission myself. As if I don't have enough on my plate.*

Grimes pulled his cell out of its carrier, and punched a few numbers as he walked into another room. A few minutes later he came back. "Mr. Lee, the only officer who's familiar with your battle plan is a woman. She doesn't have any combat experience. As a matter of fact, the only experience she has is ROTC."

"What? A woman, leading this mission? On short notice? I . . ."

Grimes interrupted. "The priority is a strong leader who's familiar with the plan. When she gets here you can reject her if you wish. Unless you want to postpone the mission, or assume command yourself, she's your only choice. And you as our Secretary of Defense have more important things to do. At least talk to her and give her a chance. You may like her."

"Arrgh!" Bobby punched the intercom button. "Reiner, go to my quarters and bring back my battle uniform."

Immediately, a voice came back over the speaker. "Yes, Sir. Right away, Sir." A few minutes later they heard a truck start up outside Bobby's office window.

An hour later, while Bobby laced up his boots, Catherine walked in wearing her combat uniform. She stopped in front of Bobby and saluted. "Rebel Lieutenant Jobe reporting as ordered. Sir."

Bobby stared at his wife. "What are you doing here? You were supposed to leave on your tour two hours ago."

She smiled at her husband and shook her head. I heard about the accident. I called Grimes and volunteered before you even knew about it. From what he told me, you don't have anyone else." She snapped her fingers. "Wait a minute," She said sarcastically. "I've been around the entire time you've been planning this mission. I even helped with figuring out the logistics. You can't go. You have too much to do. I'm briefed. I understand what needs to be done." She leaned forward and whispered into his ear, "If you expect to get lucky before this war's over, you better change your attitude." Then she glanced over at Grimes. "General, can you think of any other options?"

Laughing, Grimes smiled. "Sir, I think she has you over a barrel."

Two hours later Catherine walked onto the drill floor where her new unit was waiting for orders to move out. Several soldiers were in exceptionally high spirits.

One black man, six-foot five, and two-hundred-eighty-five pounds bragged about what he was going to do after the battle was over. "My family suffered from that criminal Sherman's March. His soldiers raped my ancestors." He winked at a friend and leered. "Now it's my turn to return the favor. I promise you any soldier in my platoon who kills more of them Federals than I do, can have their choice of any woman." He lowered his voice to a whisper, "or more if he can handle it."

Catherine calmly walked up behind the Platoon Sergeant, took out her pistol and fired it into the weapons clearing barrel next to him. Everyone jumped and looked at the newcomer amongst them.

"Gentlemen, I'm your new commander. If you have a problem with that let me know. I'll explain it to you in detail." She stood in front of the ashen-faced, towering giant and looked up. "I consider any rape or mistreatment of any civilian or prisoner as a war crime and will take the necessary and appropriate action. It was wrong for Sherman to lose control of his men back 'In The War Of Northern Aggression,' and it will be wrong if you can't follow my guidance. If I can't trust you, I'll leave you behind." She stood back and surveyed the soldiers in her new command. "Got it?"

The big burly man spoke for everyone. "Yes, Ma'am. We get it."

"Good, see that you keep that in mind. You know who I am. Don't push me." She glanced at her clipboard. "All right, First Platoon." She handed a piece of paper to the burly soldier, "This is the list of shops I want you to visit. Second and Third Platoons here's your list." She handed out several lists to the remaining Platoon Sergeants. "These are houses the federal data base we hacked into says we should have as a priority. Your First Sergeant informs me you've trained for this mission the past few weeks. Let's get going and get the job done."

Several long, loud, Rebel yells screeched and echoed off the walls. Every soldier ran to the motor pool and jumped onto their tank or troop carrier. As soon as the last soldier was in a vehicle they started to move. The whine of engines and the smell of jet fuel filled the air.

#####

Catherine's tank stopped in front of a brick home on a quiet country road. The turret traversed over until it pointed at a large bay window. She spoke into her microphone. "Sergeant, go knock on the door. Maybe he'll come easy." *I hope so. We have many homes to search.*

A soldier exited a fighting vehicle, ran to the front door, and knocked. The forty-year-old man's eyes bulged out when he opened his door and saw an Abrams tank parked in his driveway.

The soldier pointed to a list on his clipboard. "Is this your name?"

"Yes."

"Our records show you have these weapons registered to you. Do you want to turn them over to us voluntarily, or do you need some persuasion?"

At that moment, Catherine's gunner lowered her tank's gun tube a few feet.

The man looked down at his children clutching his pant legs, and felt his wife standing behind him. He gulped, looked back at his frightened wife, and then. "There won't be a problem."

Four stops later, Cat's gunner traversed the turret toward a brick warehouse. She raised her bull horn to her mouth. "Mr. Johnson, we know you're in there. You have five minutes to come out."

In two minutes a young man in an old ragged army uniform came out a side door, approached the tank and stood looking up at Cat. "Hey, Lady, what you want?"

With a hand on her holstered pistol the thin woman leaned forward. "I need to talk with your father or uncle. Are they home?"

"Don't see how that's any of your concern. We're just minding our own business. We don't support the USA, or care about the ROA. Just go away."

Cat shook her head. "Don't think that's going to happen. We can't allow a weapons cache the size of yours to exist. What if it fell into the wrong hands?"

The young man stroked his scraggly beard. "I guess we don't have anything to talk about. I'll get back to my chores. My Dad'll kill me if I don't finish them before he comes home."

"So you're home alone?"

"Yes Ma'am."

She nodded her head and a squad of Rebels surrounded him. *This child should be easy.* "Take him away."

He struggled until a Corporal pulled a knife and held it at his throat. "Do you want to come easily? Or would you prefer we cart you off in pieces?"

At that moment he ceased to struggle and the men took him over to a nearby cargo truck.

Cat opened a binder to the correct page. "Sergeant!"

Her Platoon Sergeant ran over, climbed up onto the tank, and said, "Yes, Ma'am?"

She tore a page out and handed it to him. "Here's a list of weapons registered to this building. Remove as much as you can. We're a little ahead of schedule, so take extra time if you find more than is listed. When I blow my whistle start setting the C-4 charges. I want this place leveled when we leave."

His white teeth gleamed as he smiled. "Yes, Ma'am. I understand." Then he jumped down and ran off, calling out to his men. "Second Squad, over here."

As his men surrounded him, he pointed where he wanted them to position themselves. They ran off as directed. When they were in place, a soldier grabbed his battering ram and shattered the warehouse door. Four other soldiers ran in and searched the building.

The Platoon Sergeant positioned himself so he had a good view of the warehouse, and the long sloping driveway. Cat, in the turret of her tank, kept an eye on the tree line a hundred yards away. Out of the corner of her eye she spied a glint of metal. She pulled her binos out and focused on the closest tree.

Keeping the glasses trained on the foliage, she called to her gunner. "Hand me a rifle."

"Yes, Ma'am," he said, and immediately the muzzle of a loaded M-4 with a scope appeared at her waist.

The binos dropped to the end of their lanyard and clanked on the turret as she reached down and grabbed the firearm. "Thanks."

In the split second before she fired, a bullet wheezed by the Platoon Sergeant's helmet.

At that moment, she thought, *All right, easy now, you can do this.* She steadied an elbow in front of her, aimed, and squeezed a round off.

The young prisoner watched the entire scene from the back of the truck where he was being kept. "Papa!"

It was too late, his father fell head first from his perch in the tree. At the crack of the sniper's rifle shot, the Platoon Sergeant dropped flat on the ground, his pistol searching for a target. "Thanks, Ma'am. Good shooting."

Wow, what a rush. I can take more of this combat stuff.

Twenty minutes later, as the cargo truck pulled away, the black Sergeant ran over to Cat's vehicle. "Thanks again for saving my life. The prisoner told me that was his father; he'd been out hunting when we showed up." Then he checked his wristwatch and shouted over the tank's turbine engine. "Okay, Ma'am, 5, 4, 3, 2, 1."

BOOM. Then the brick walls imploded, and dust billowed out, up, and over, the crashing building.

#####

Cat came into the conference room dragging her pack. Bobby, Grimes, and Ayers jumped when they saw her. As he rushed to her side, Bobby tossed her gear aside. "Sweetie! You look terrible, are you alright?" *Dreadful would be a better word. But I'll never tell her that.*

Grimes pulled a chair over. Ayers handed her a large glass of water and reached over and moved a pitcher close to the exhausted woman.

She wiped her forehead with a forearm. In between breaths she spoke. "Boy, what a rush. I never knew combat would be so invigorating. No wonder you guys try to hog all the fun."

Relieved that his wife seemed to be in good shape, he got off his knees and sat next to her. "Take it easy. You can brief us all about it when you're ready. We've had reports from several other units in your sector. We've had good results so far. Your report will fill in what we didn't get from them."

Ten minutes later she came from the washroom, drying her face on a towel. "Boy, splashing cold water on my face made a difference. I feel like I could eat a horse. Can you get me something to eat?"

Ayers nodded. "Sure." He picked up a phone and punched a few buttons. "Mess hall?" He didn't wait for a response. "Get me a porterhouse steak, medium, baked potato with all the trimmings, a dinner salad with ranch, coffee, and a coke. I want it ten minutes ago." He hung the phone up and tilted his head toward Cat. "I think I remembered your favorites.

She took a deep breath, pulled a tablet from her cargo pocket, opened it and said, "I'm feeling better, let's get going."

"We destroyed every house whose owners didn't cooperate." She tore a page from her notebook and slid it over to her husband.

Bobby, ran a finger down the list of weapons and ammo her unit had collected, or destroyed, and winked at her. "Very good Lieutenant. How many put up a fight? How many of our soldiers were injured?"

"We had two casualties. About a third of the Federals put up a fight. We destroyed seventy-five homes, sixty-five Federal civilians died, one-hundred-forty were wounded, and we took five-hundred-sixty-seven prisoners."

Fifteen minutes later a steward brought in her meal. She continued talking as she cut her steak. "Where was I?" She set the knife aside and ran a finger down a page and spoke with her mouth full. "Oh, let me back up and start at the beginning. When we arrived I divided the town into three parts. I assigned a section to each Platoon. I went with the First Platoon."

She paused to smother a piece of steak with barbeque sauce. "I had First Sergeant sort through the Federal Gun Registry. I sent a Tank or Bradley to every house that had a large quantity of weapons on the list. I sent three soldiers to those homes which only had one or two guns registered. Headquarters Platoon was my Quick Reaction Force. They blocked off the entire town."

Cat stopped, took a swig of her coke. "I haven't been this famished in years. I don't think I've eaten in over sixteen hours." She pushed her plate away, picked up her pen and scratched off several items she'd already briefed.

The entire time she talked the men sat, took notes, and sipped their water or coffee.

"I went to one house on Elm Street," she paused, flipped a page, "here it is, 1394 Elm. I called out over my bull horn for the man to come out. I noticed a drapery flutter, then glass shattered from that window and the muzzle of an old Light Anti-Tank Weapon popped out. As soon as I saw it I called for a high explosive round to take out the house. We left it in flames and moved on to the next address."

Cat stood, walked over to the fridge. "Still have ice cream bars in here? I sure could use one." She opened the freezer drawer grabbed a chocolate bar and tore the wrapper. "Now, about the other platoons. . ."

The next morning Bobby met Lieutenant Reiner, and Generals Grimes and Ayers for their regular meeting.

Cat stuck her head in the door. "Gentlemen, I'd like to have a word with you if I may." She entered before they could respond. "Thank you, I have a request."

Surprised, Grimes and Ayers made room for her to sit next to her husband.

Bobby shook his head. "Watch it gentlemen. When she uses that tone of voice she wants something she knows you don't want her to have." *Whatever she wants I have to say no. She probably wants to keep command of the unit she went out with yesterday. No way! She's too valuable to me.*

She sat next to Bobby and smiled at the Generals and said in the sweetest southern accent she could muster. "Why Bobby dear, I don't have any ulterior motive." She glanced at the three men before she continued as she stroked his cheek. "I do have one small request."

Grimes leaned back in his chair and tapped Ayers on his forearm. "Here it comes, watch it now."

Cat stroked Bobby's arm as she resumed talking. "You realize that my unit performed better than any of the others assigned to the mission. With that in mind, I think I should continue in command." She held a hand up and stopped Bobby from interrupting. "Don't give me the women can't be in combat routine. I think I handled myself quite well, especially on short notice." She tapped the table in front of them. "And don't try to get me to stay on the island mission that Bobby's going on. You're short of company commanders. You need me in my unit."

"Get a load of this," Grimes chuckled. "One successful mission and she's an indispensable combat veteran. Why. . ."

At that moment Cat jumped up, ran to the washroom. For several minutes they heard her retching her guts out into the toilet.

While she was out of the room, Ayers winked at Grimes, and then Bobby. With a smirk on his face he said, "I wonder, if she might have more than the flu."

Bobby leaned forward, shook his head, and whispered. "Oh no you don't. Don't even think it's possible. We've used protection every time."

Ayers, peered over his glasses. "Son, I learned a long time ago, no birth control is guaranteed to work one-hundred percent of the time. I know, three of my five children were accidents. You have to let God be God."

They heard the tap running and then she came back into the conference room. "Sorry, I don't know what came over me. All of a sudden I felt nauseous."

An awkward pause hung in the air.

Ayers coughed, and then winked at Grimes. "We'll consider your request. Right now, I suggest you go to the infirmary and see if they can find out what's causing your nausea."

TANGO – The Viewing and Memorial Service
(The Next Day)

Linda McClellan guided her granddaughter Missy through the baggage claim area. "Sweetie, Mommy and Daddy are getting the car for us. You need to help me get our bags. Can you be a big helper?" As she talked, she put a credit card into a slot and jerked a handle as she tried to retrieve a stuck baggage cart from the rack. It came loose, and she stumbled backward until she regained her balance.

"Yes, gamma. I'm a big girl now. I'm four-years old!" Missey smiled and ran over to the baggage carousel. She ran in between the legs of adults waiting for their luggage.

"Missy, stay near grandma." The toddler scampered back to Linda's side. "That's a good girl." While Linda scoured the carousel, the little girl held the cart handle with both hands, and stepped on the bottom rung. Out of the corner of her eye Linda saw the toddler's curly blonde hair falling back toward the terrazzo floor in slow motion. *Oh no! I should've been paying more attention to her.*

Then she saw the sleeve of an army uniform reach out and grab the toddler. A deep voice called out softly. "Watch it little girl. You have to be more careful."

As the soldier stood Missy on her feet, he smoothed out her clothing. "You're just my little girl's size. I bet you're at least five years old."

The tot put her hands on her hips and frowned. "I'm not five! I'm four. I'm a big girl now!"

The soldier winked at Linda. "My mistake. You look so big. I really thought you were older tha . . ."

Linda interrupted, thank you Captain. I'm glad you happened to be passing by.

The young thirty-year old man smiled. "No, Mrs. McClellan, I'm one of the escorts for your husband at the Memorial Service."

Startled, Linda shook her head. "But, I've never met you."

He talked as he grabbed her bags from her hand, and loaded her baggage cart. "I served under General McClellan for many years. First as an enlisted soldier, and then as a company commander. I remembered you from the picture on his desk. I must say, it didn't do you justice."

Embarrassed, Linda took Missy with one hand, and pushed the cart with the other.

The soldier took the cart from her and deftly pushed both carts through the crowd, through the sliding doors, and onto the sidewalk. He shouted over the cacophony of horns, screeching brakes, and buses. "My family lives in the area, they're picking me up. I'll push this out to the curb."

#####

The next morning, Missy and her parents entered the viewing room. The young girl skipped along, carrying a storybook in her arm. She ran up to Linda. "Gamma, gamma, can I read my story to gampa? Can I huh?"

Linda crouched down on one knee and took the book from the little girl. "Sweetie, he can't hear you now. It won't do any good to read it to him."

Missy's lip quivered. "B . . . B . . . But he always read this story to me when I was sick. It was his favorite. I want t. . ."

Maria knelt next to her mother and daughter. "Honey, gampa went to heaven to be with Jesus. He can't hear you."

Confused, Missy looked between the two older women. "Jesus is in Missy's heart, right mama?"

"Yes, Honey, he is."

"Jesus is in heaven, isn't he?"

"Yes, Honey, he is."

"An gampa had Jesus in his heart. Well, if Jesus is in heaven and I can pray to him, and if gampa is in heaven with Jesus, why can't I read my story to gampa?"

Maria sighed and shook her head. "Okay, Honey, let me get you a chair to sit in."

"No, I want to see gampa when I read to him."

Seeing that they were going to have to humor the child, Linda took a chair from a corner, and put it next to the head of Garfield's coffin. Missy put her book under her arm, climbed onto the folding chair, and stood. She peered at her grandfather, and then turned her head and said matter-of-factly. "Mama, he's not dead. He's just sleeping."

She rested her book on the side of the coffin and started, "The Little Engine That Could, by Mary C. Jacobs." She turned her head and glanced at her grandmother. "Gamma, why are you crying?"

Linda and Maria dabbed their eyes with a tissue. "Sweetie, you are so wonderful to read to your grandfather. He really liked this book. He told me he enjoyed reading it to you."

Missy smiled, turned and started to read again. "The Little Engine That Could, by . . ." Ten minutes later she closed the book and put it on her grandfather's chest. "Here gampa, you can read this to Jesus now."

Then she turned and hopped off the chair.

A line of mourners had queued up for the viewing. Everyone stood speechless and teary-eyed as they watched Missy take her mother's hand and walk away.

#####

The next morning at 1100 hours the Fort Chapel was filled with mourners. Linda and the rest of Garfield's family sat in the first pew. President Barnes, William Carter, and Lyle sat right behind. Many lower-ranking soldiers stood in the side aisles. As the organist played softly in the background, a soft murmur filled the sanctuary.

Chaplain Charlie stood, and motioned for everyone to rise. "The family would like to thank you for coming today. They appreciate that some of you have made quite an effort to attend."

"Please turn to hymn number 372," he nodded and the band started to play, 'I Come to the Garden Alone.'

As the notes of the last stanza faded, Chaplain motioned for everyone to be seated. "Ladies and Gentlemen, at this time we have some distinguished guests who would like to say a few words."

President Barnes stood, and made his way to the pulpit. "I first met Garfield last April. I was . . ." Ten minutes later, he moved to the left of the podium. "So, if I had the time, I could tell you stories I've heard in just the past day that attest to the fact that since Omar Bradley, there hasn't been an officer who cared more for the common soldier. Thank You."

As the President moved back to his seat, Ski approached the front of the chapel. He turned in front of the pulpit and glanced at the family. "Being a Jew, I've rarely attended a Protestant Service. But in Garfield's case I knew that I had to be here. He was the best mentor I could have . . ." Fifteen minutes later Ski stood back from the pulpit and stretched an open hand at Garfield's casket.

Fighting back tears he was barely able to be heard over the sound system. "Here lies a great friend, great father, and husband, most of all a great man. I only hope to be half the soldier he was."

As Ski stepped from the altar, Chaplain Charlie came alongside, put an arm around the general's shoulder. He whispered, "Garfield knew how much he meant to you. He told me often what a great man you are."

Ski wiped a tear off his cheek with the back of his hand. "Thanks," he sniffled.

At the end of the service, the Chaplain rose, and faced the congregation. "There will be a celebration of General McClellan's life in the fellowship hall, next to the chapel." He raised his hands and bowed his head as he gave the benediction: "May the God of Life, the Creator of all things, give you peace and grace. May you understand the richness of fellowship with your Lord and Savior, Jesus Christ, Amen."

#####

Twenty minutes later as mourners paid their respects and made for the buffet line, Barnes, Bill, and Lyle sat at a corner table away from the crowd.

Bill filled his water glass from a pitcher. "Mr. President, you can't fire General Prewkowski just because he wants you to consider a truce." He glanced over at Lyle for support. "What's happened to you? You've never wanted yes men around you before. Ski definitely will support whatever decision you make.

But you have to let him express his feelings." He raised his head and tilted it toward the far door. "Here he comes. Sir, you don't have generals sitting on the bench waiting to take his place. He knows McClellan's plans inside out. Anyone else you assign will have to start from scratch."

UNIFORM – West Virginia
(Late December)

Brigadier General Donald Rodgers checked the perimeter of the room as he entered. Aggravated at what he saw, he called out, "Sergeant!"

"Yes, Sir?"

The big Catawba Indian glared at the short female soldier. "I'm giving a briefing in this room. Why isn't it ready?"

"Sir, the location was changed. You were enroute, and didn't answer your cell." As she talked, she gestured with a hand at a door on the far end of the room. "If you'll follow me?"

This new headquarters commander they assigned me leaves something to be desired. This shouldn't have happened. "Sergeant, where is your Commander? I want to see her right away."

As she reached the connecting door, the young woman turned her head, "She's in here, along with everyone else." When the door opened he stepped through.

As he entered someone called out, "ATTENTION." Everyone stood.

Rodgers walked briskly to the front. "Carry on. We'll get started in a few minutes." He walked up to the Headquarters Commander and a man who stood near the podium.
"Would either of you care to tell me what's going on? Why wasn't I informed about this change? I'm in charge, or at least I was when I left on my tour of the battlefront."

Both officers stood erect when he approached. The female Major, being senior, spoke up. "Sir, General Ayers informed me, that Intelligence believes the Federals have compromised our cell phones. General Jobe ordered all phones at your level disconnected. After this briefing I'll give you a new phone. Also, General Ayers changed the focus of our mission. His helicopter should've landed ten minutes ago."

The Captain standing next to her tapped her on the shoulder. "There he is now."

From across the room Ayers and Rodgers made eye contact. Ayers tilted his head toward the front. Rodgers nodded, turned to his two staff members and said tersely, "I want to see both of you after this meeting is over." He rushed off to meet his fellow Catawba.

They reached the steps leading to the stage at the same time. Rodgers paused to let Ayers go ahead of him. When Ayers reached the top, he waited for the bigger man to catch up.

Ayers led him to a corner and through a curtain. "Don, we have a change of plans."

Steady now, just because we've spent the past week planning for one mission, doesn't mean we can't shift our focus. "I understand. How big a change is it?"

Ayers handed a large envelope to his friend. "All the details are in here. The reports in this packet will give you the broad outline of what we expect. I can't stay. I could've sent this by courier, but I have a special announcement to make." He moved the curtain with one hand, and motioned for Rodgers to go ahead.

When they reached center stage, everyone turned toward them. With a gleam in his eye, Ayers adjusted the microphone to his height. Rodgers moved where his boss directed. "President Gressette and the rest of our command team have been impressed with the performance of Brigadier General Rodgers. It's with great pleasure that I announce the ROA Senate has approved his promotion to Major General." He reached into a pocket, and pulled out Rodgers' new rank insignia. As he replaced the old with the new, he slapped Rodgers on the shoulder. "There, that's well deserved. I have to leave for Richmond. I'll let you prepare for your new mission." He nodded at Rodgers.

The newly-promoted General waited for his friend to exit before he moved close to the microphone. He held up the envelope for all to see. "I have new orders. I haven't had time to review them. Rather than our planned briefing, I want each of you to give me a down and dirty assessment of what your current capabilities are. Don't give me any embellishments. My staff will get you an operations order by the end of the week." He looked around the room and pointed to a Colonel seated in the middle of the back row. "You go first."

He jumped from the stage, and said, "After you've briefed and I've asked my questions, you and any of your staff are dismissed." He nodded to the officer working his way toward the front. "I'm ready when you are."

Two weeks later, Rodgers paced the floor in front of the large twelve-foot monitor. He kept glancing at the map, and then his watch. *Did I miss something? Will they perform as planned? Will the Yankees get lucky?*

His aide approached and stood by silently. When the General reached the end of the room, he turned and noticed the young lieutenant. "Why didn't you tell me you were here?"

"You seemed deep in thought."

"I know the Bible says to be anxious for nothing, but boy am I apprehensive this morning."

The aide approached and handed him a clipboard. "Sir, its two hours till the battle kicks off. The latest intelligence report says we expect complete surprise."

Rodgers scanned the reports in front of him. "Hmm, it says here our advance teams have reached the West Virginia National Guard Headquarters. I see Second Brigade's approaching Camp Dawson outside of Kingwood, West Virginia. So far it's quiet." He checked the clock on the wall. "In ten minutes that'll change."

#####

Captain Horning peered through his binos at the choppers overhead and then back to the building ahead of him. *Good, right on schedule.* He called out. "Gunner, what kind of round do you have in the tube?" He steadied his arm as the Abrams tank jumped a curb.

"Sabot."

"Well, it's like hitting a fly with a sledge hammer." *A sabot is meant for a hardened target, I don't need a shell with a penetrating probe for this building.* He rubbed the stubble on his chin, and clicked the microphone. "When we pull up by the entrance, aim for the front door. The attack helicopters will back us up."

"Yes, Sir. If you want, I have time to change it out."

"Let it be. I don't want to chance having an empty tube if we need it beforehand." He clicked the switch on his helmet and spoke into the mic. "Listen up, First Platoon; we're coming up to our target. My gunner'll put a round through the front door, Bradley one-four and two-three, be ready to move in before the dust settles and the guards recover from the shock. Bradley two-two, are you ready?" The whine of the Abrams jet turbine engine filled the air.

Static came over Horning's earphones. "Say again, two-two, you broke up. I can tell you keyed your mike. Nothing came through."

The static cleared, ". . . we're ready. I'll be in the Physical Security Office two minutes after you beat down the door."

"Listen up, everyone. This is the Headquarters for the West Virginia National Guard. At this time of day they have a minimal number of guards on duty. We don't want any unnecessary bloodshed. But if anyone gives you a fight, take 'em out. We have to get the combinations for every vault, in every Armory, that the West Virginia National Guard still has control of. Got it?"

Within moments all radio operators had checked in.

At exactly 0410 Horning yelled, "FIRE."

The muzzle of his gun flashed as the round left the tube. In seconds, the front entrance was strewn with glass and twisted metal. As directed, before the dust settled, two Bradley Fighting Vehicles raced in from the right and left of Horning's tank.

When they came within twenty feet of the gaping hole, both vehicles turned ninety degrees, slid into position, and opened their back hatch. Soldiers from both ran down their ramp, rifles at the ready. In seconds the front entrance was secured.

Horning twisted his torso so he could look at the activity around him. He keyed his mic, "Good job. The front entrance is secure. Two-two get going."

Before he finished his sentence, another Bradley roared up and discharged two soldiers.

First Sergeant, carrying a tool sack, ran as hard as he could through the debris.

As they covered the short distance to the foyer, the Corporal running next to him kept moving his rifle as he checked for the enemy. "First Sergeant, this is a big building to search for all those combinations. Why'd they just send the two of us?"

The two men slowed to a walk as they stepped over dead Federals. "Son, until last week we had a spy working in this Headquarters. He told me which office we need to pay a visit to. I'm a locksmith in civilian life." He tapped his tool bag at his side. "If we don't find the combination to the master safe, I have the tools to drill the dial off."

They picked up speed and started to run down a hall to a flight of stairs. As they took the steps two at a time, Riley pulled a piece of paper from his chest pocket.

He grabbed it with his teeth and opened a door with a free hand. "Here, Corporal, down this hallway, second door on the right. As the younger Rebel stood guard, Riley pulled out his wallet and grabbed an ID card. "Our spy gave me a stolen ID badge. He knew they'd deactivate his once they found out he was a spy."

As the senior sergeant opened the door, the Corporal put a hand on Riley's shoulder. "I hear someone coming. Get in quick. I'll take care of him."

"Right." He slipped through the open door, closed it behind him, and pulled a flashlight from his belt.

The Corporal, placed his rifle on the ground, pulled a knife from his boot, and moved to the corner next to the elevators.

Radio static reverberated off the walls. The Federal guard called out, "Guard Post 1, come in. What's happened? I'm coming down stairway one. I'll be there in two minutes. Out."

The Rebel wiped his forehead with the back of his hand. *I can hear his footsteps. Seems he expects trouble.* As soon as the guard passed him and headed toward the stairs, the Corporal grabbed the

Federal's arm, twisted it behind him and spoke into his ear. "Don't put up a fight, or I'll have to kill you."

The Federal guard, a full foot taller than the Rebel, used his height to his advantage, reversed the young Rebel's hold and slammed his enemy to the ground.

The Corporal's knife slid across the floor.

Riley, his mission completed, had entered the hall and sized up the situation. He picked up the knife as it touched his boot. He grabbed it and jammed it into big man's side, then twisted the sawtooth blade and pulled it up.

As the Federal slumped on top of the Corporal, Riley pushed him off. "Let's go, got what we needed."

#####

Meanwhile at Camp Dawson, Second Brigade pulled up to a brand-new security gate.

Rodgers shouted into the phone receiver, "I don't care if it's not safe. Whatever gave you the idea that war is a safe occupation? Your objective is to secure the Camp. He slammed the phone into its cradle, and said to no one in particular "Imagine, thinking that because a building might be booby trapped that he should go around it and leave it for another unit." He took a swig of his water bottle and tossed it into a wastebasket. "Sergeant?"

#####

At 9:00 am, President Gressette entered the conference room and rushed to the podium. He stroked his beard as he glanced around the room. "Ladies and gentlemen, I have a statement to make. After which I have time for two questions." Ignoring the teleprompter, he moved to the side of the podium, and leaned on the edge of the carved lectern.

Smiling broadly, the ROA President started to speak. "In 1861 President Lincoln decided that while it was illegal for our forefathers to secede from the USA, it was legal for him to have an illegal election in what became the State of West Virginia. The winners of that election were sent to the Senate and House of Representatives as the Virginian Delegation. Their first action was to request that their portion of Virginia be admitted to the Union as a separate state."

He paused to take a sip of water. "To me, the duplicity of Mr. Lincoln's actions was unconscionable. Today, we're rectifying the situation. At 0410 this morning, ROA forces, led by Major General Rodgers, entered the former State of West Virginia."

He pounded the top of the stand in front of him. "As of today, West Virginia has been re-annexed with the Commonwealth of Virginia. I can see that some of you are surprised. I'll take two questions, and then I need to be off. Marc LeBlanc, your hand was up first."

Marc stood. "Sir, how can you justify today's action? After all, it's been over one-hundred-fifty years since West Virginia joined the Union. Isn't it a little late to be raising the issue?"

Perfect, that's the question I need to start with. "Marc, that's a good question. There's no precedent for this. If the USA has the might, they can take it back. Mr. Lincoln's actions were illegal back then. We've just righted the wrong."

Marc took his seat. Gressette surveyed the hands that jumped into the air. He pointed to a red-headed woman in the back row. "Yes, Ma'am. What's your question?"

The woman frowned as she ran a finger down her note pad. "Mr. President, why haven't you, or someone from the South raised this issue before?"

Good follow-up question. I couldn't have planned it better. "If we'd politely asked President Barnes does anyone really think he would've willingly complied? Does anyone really think it would've been wise to let the Federal government know we were a viable foe?" He lowered his voice. "I think not."

VICTOR – Rigging The Election
(Late December)

Two days later Grimes, Ayers, Cat, and Bobby were seated in the mess hall. While the men ate fried chicken and dumplings, Cat played with a bowl of soda crackers.

Grimes smiled at her. "Mrs. Lee, I'm sure you would've made a great infantry commander. And in the future, you will be one. We'll have to wait until your baby's born. At that time we'll see what we have available."

Bobby smiled and replied, "She would've been a distinguished infantry commander. On her first mission her unit out-performed every company in the Brigade. I don't know which I'm more proud of, her first combat mission, or that she's pregnant." *It's a toss-up. At least now we don't have to use a condom.*

Cat frowned at them. "Would both of you please quit talking about me in the third person?" She nibbled on a cracker. "Since a combat mission's out of the question, I guess we go back to the island mission, right?"

All three men shook their heads. Bobby spoke up. "It's too risky, you're pregnant."

Cat scowled. "I'm pregnant, not disabled, not an invalid. I'm not even half-way through the first trimester. This is a cake walk. No combat, no danger. You need a better reason."

Grimes put a hand on Bobby's shoulder. "Wait a minute, let's think about this. We could use this to our advantage." He turned to Cat. "Would you agree to stop your activities when you reach the fourth month?"

She stroked Bobby's neck. "Sweetie, I wouldn't do anything to jeopardize our baby. I've been in on planning this operation. I'm familiar with the software. And you don't have time to get anyone else up to speed, and if the software doesn't work, we'll be found out, and the entire operation will fail."

At that moment Ayer's cell rang. He pulled it out of its holder, and checked the caller ID. "I gotta get this. Be right back."

After the older man left, Grimes pulled a file from his briefcase. "Cat, if you're willing to stop all activities when you get farther along, I think we can work this out." He turned to Bobby. "Will you agree to a compromise?"

Talk about being backed into a corner. We've gotta get moving on this or we'll lose too much. He kissed Cat on the cheek and patted her stomach. "Okay, we can't be too careful with our little boy."

Appearing aggravated with both men, she removed Bobby's hand from her stomach and glared.

Grimes put a hand on her shoulder. "Son, you need to treat this lady right. If you don't you won't live to fight another battle."

What'd I do now? I guess I should apologize anyway, even if I don't know what's wrong. "Cat, I'm sorry. I was insensitive." He looked at his watch. "We need to get going if we're to be ready for our flights."

Cat shot a quick glance at Bobby. "Flights? Wouldn't it be more convenient for all of us to fly in the same plane?"

Grimes pulled several folders out of his briefcase. "Here are your undercover passports. General Jobe's people had them updated as if we've been traveling under our aliases." Then he slid a packet to Bobby and Cat. "Especially in a war, it's too risky if we have the four senior members of our defense department in the same aircraft. Something could go wrong. The plane could malfunction. Or worse yet, shot down by a lucky. . ."

Ayers returned and sat next to his old partner.

When he saw the look on his friend's face, Grimes asked, "What happened? Bad news?"

Visibly shaken, Ayers steadied himself by holding the table top firmly with both hands. "That was Dr. McCall. I haven't felt well lately. He ran tests. It's terminal. I feel like my world's turned upside down. Doc says I waited too long to see him. The cancer's in my prostrate, liver, and right kidney. I could go at any time."

Cat gasped, dropped her coffee cup. "No! That can't be." Hot liquid and shards of glass flowed toward Grimes' elbow.

The old Indian shook his head. "He offered to start chemo, but I told him no. I saw my wife go through that. It's not worth it. If it's my time," his voice trailed off, "it's my time."

The old black man stared at the table top, then reached over and hugged the Catawba. As he pulled away he noticed the coffee had soiled his papers.

Grimes grabbed several napkins and sopped up the mess.

Bobby shook his head. "We'll get another opinion. We'll run more tests. We gotta beat this. We need you, especially now. You leave next week to negotiate with the Shoshone, we need Nevada."

Cat and Grimes scowled at Bobby for being insensitive.

Bobby reached across the table, pulled the folder from the stack in front of the black man, as he smoothed out the soggy mess. He sympathetically said to Ayers, "Sir, I know you must be in pain. I've seen others suffer, and you don't deserve to go through this. I know Dr. McCall will do everything he can." Then, as if to imply, *satisfied,* his eyes flitted between his wife and Grimes. "Now, we need to find a replacement for you on this mission and for the upcoming Shoshone trip. Who do you recommend?"

For some reason, now that the secret of his illness was out, Ayers seemed no longer able to hide the pain. He visibly shook as he laid out his plan. . .

Twenty minutes later he sighed. "I really thought I could make it on this trip." He said haltingly. "I haven't thought of anyone. I'm sorry, but, you three will have to take up the slack for my abs. . ." At that point a heavy coughing spell took over and Ayers grabbed a stack of napkins.

Startled, Cat reached for her phone to call a medic. Ayers covered his mouth with one hand and waved with the other. As he tossed the bloody napkins aside, he wiped his forehead. "I'll be all right." He wheezed. "I want General Rogers to take my place on the Shoshone mission. He did extremely well in West Virginia. After me, he's the highest ranking American Indian we have. They'll respect him. If only based on his reputation and especially after they meet him face-to-face."

Two days later, Bobby, alias Lee E. Robertson cleared customs at the Luis Munoz-Marin International Airport. He grabbed his carry-on case and headed for the first taxi in line at the curb.

The driver ran over, and opened the door. "Where to señor ?

Bobby tossed his bag in the back seat. "Hampton Inn, *por favor.*" Then he laid his head back and closed his eyes. *Okay, we have our first meetings tonight. Why did Cat have to come? I have a bad feeling about this.*

Later that evening they met in Bobby's room. Cat arrived last.

When she walked in, Bobby jumped up and took her suitcase out of her hand.

"Honey, that was exciting. How did you guys make out?" She picked up a plate from the room service tray, and filled it to over-flowing with guacamole and chips.

"I guess we don't have a problem with morning sickness?"

Cat nodded, as she licked her fingers from the guacamole overflow. "It passed a couple of hours ago. I talked to my mother about it. She said the women in our family only suffer for a few days." She set her plate next to Bobby and went back for tea. "So, my contacts are willing to meet with us tomorrow. I set it up for 0900. How'd you guys make out?"

Bobby took out a pen and scribbled on his organizer. "Okay, media, 0900." He looked at Grimes over his glasses. "General, what about local politicians?"

Grimes cut into his porterhouse steak. "1400 hours, they were open to our proposal." He took another bite, and pointed his fork at Bobby. "Had a brainstorm on the way down here. I surfed the Internet and found several blog sites for each of the factions we want to influence. I scheduled individual meetings with each faction." He pulled a piece of paper from his shirt pocket. "Here are the times."

"Good idea." Bobby ran a finger down the list. "It's doable. You left enough time for us to make it work." The young Secretary of Defense wrote Grimes' schedule under Cat's meeting time. "Now all we need is Fendemere's times. He sh. . ."

There was a *rap* at the door, Grimes, moved to open it. He called out to Bobby and Cat. "That's him now." He opened the door and two men and a woman walked in behind Fendemere.

The diplomat waited for his guests to enter and Grimes shut the door. "Governor Jorge Gonzales, Lieutenant Governor Diego Garcia, and Speaker Maria Sanchez, I'd like to introduce you to Mr. J. Hampton Lee, Mrs. Catherine Lee, and General Robert Grimes."

He turned to the Rebel leaders "Gentlemen and Lady, I'd like to introduce you to the Governor, Lieutenant Governor, and Speaker of the House for Puerto Rico."

Grimes, apparently aggravated, motioned for the ROA Secretary of State to come out to the balcony.

As everyone shook hands, the diplomat followed the old officer.

Grimes shut the sliding glass door, and pointed a finger inside the hotel suite. "Just what are you doing? You don't bring people directly to us without clearing it in advance! Whatever got into you? Just because you're the President of the Knights of the Golden Circle doesn't give you the right to go rogue and blindside us."

Fendemere leaned against the balcony rail and listened to Grimes vent. "General how long have we been working together? You recruited me thirty-five years ago. You were my mentor for the longest time. Do you think I'd do this without a reason?"

Grimes folded his arms tightly in front of his chest as he listened to his former protégé. "Go ahead."

The diplomat pointed a hand at the closed door. "When I met with the Governor this afternoon, he was reluctant to even consider our proposal. He's scheduled to fly to Washington tomorrow. He won't be back for two weeks. This is the only chance we have to get him to listen to us. We can't afford to wait for him to come back and then get him to consider our plan." He put his hands on his hips. "Give me credit. I've gone head-to-head and toe-to-toe with Kings, Presidents, and diplomats all over the world. If I had a choice, we'd have met him tomorrow as planned." He moved away from the end of the balcony and opened the door. "Now, let's get to work."

Bobby and Cat turned as the sliding door opened. Grimes entered first, walked over to the Governor, and gestured to the sitting room. "Shall we sit while we talk?" He turned to Bobby, "Did you call room service to send something up?"

Bobby nodded as he crossed the room and stood next to their guests.

Cat moved over to Maria. "Señora, follow me."

There was a knock at the door. "Room Service Señor."

A trio of bell boys pushed in their food-laden carts. Bobby pulled a wad of money from his pocket and tipped each of the young lads.

When he returned to the sitting room everyone was standing around the food carts. Grimes started the conversation.

"Governor," he began, "I'm really glad you were able to visit with us today. I understand you leave for Washington tomorrow."

"True General."

Grimes held a chaffing lid so the politician could serve himself, and then continued. "Can we rely on your discretion, not to tell anyone about our proposals?"

The Governor whispered to the black man, "Senor, we will use the epitome of discretion."

After everyone was seated, Bobby leaned forward in front of Cat, "My wife will brief you on our proposal." He turned his head in Cat's direction and nodded.

Cat stood, and passed out a report to the three Puerto Rican politicians. "We're proposing to fund an election to be held when you think it's most advisable. We'd like it in two months, but we'll let you decide. At that time we propose that the electorate be given five options.

1. Remain a Commonwealth of the USA.
2. Become a Commonwealth of the ROA.
3. Become a State in the USA.
4. Become a State in the ROA.
5. Become an independent nation.

Governor Gonzales shook his head. "My people will not like it if they feel an outsider's trying to buy them out or influence them to do something. How are you going to keep them from believing that?"

Grimes leaned forward. "Sir, if I may interrupt," then he stood, "we'd like you to make the announcement. Feel free to mention that we are proposing and paying for the election. That we aren't going to return to the island until, and if, Puerto Rico chooses to become part of the ROA." He sat down and tapped a finger on the arm of his chair. "We want a fair election. We'll even pay for international observers of your choice, at every precinct. Can it be any fairer than that?"

Two hours later the politicians stood, and everyone shook hands. Jorge started toward the door. He smiled, as he let Maria leave first. "It's agreed then. I'll make the announcement when I return from Washington. You may stay on my island for one week. During that time you may talk to any faction you can get to listen to you. But after that, you aren't to have any contact or interference with our politics. If we decide to join you, then you may come back."

(One Week Later)

Captain James Mac Connell and a new Ensign watched the bow of the Federal nuclear attack submarine New Orleans slice through the calm Atlantic waters. Their torsos swayed with the slight movement as the boat moved through the Caribbean on patrol.

"Sir, can you tell me what happened that day?"

J. Mac frowned as he recalled unpleasant memories. "Sure son. What a six months. I still can't believe what happened. I considered him my best friend. I heard a scuffle as I walked past the wardroom. When I opened the door, I saw XO wrestling with the Diving Officer. 'What's going on here?' I asked."

I rushed in and tried to break up the brawl. As soon as I put a hand on XO's shoulder the two men turned. XO stepped aside, and the six foot, two-hundred-twenty pound Dive Officer belted me in the stomach. I bent over, XO pushed me aside. As I lay on the deck, I heard him say, "Tie him up. I'll pass the word to the rest of our guys."

Then the burly man pulled a handful of plastic ties from a pocket and started to secure my limp limbs." J. Mac instinctively rubbed his wrists as if he could still feel the restraints.

"Later I found out the XO had rushed onto the Conning tower, and picked up the microphone. Back in the wardroom I was lying on the floor, when I heard his voice over the PA system, "Attention on the Boat. We are a go. The condition is green."

All over my boat men turned on their shipmates. After a few minutes my Yeoman came in and as he cut my bonds he whispered, "Sir, XO's trying to take over the boat. Several of us are fighting back. Here's a Taser." He looked at his watch. "In five minutes torpedo room guys are going to retake the Conn."

J. Mac shifted his stance and poured a fresh cup of coffee from a thermos.

The Ensign replied in admiration, "I heard if you hadn't moved fast, the Rebels would've had another boat in their fleet."

J. Mac slowly, nodded. "I don't doubt that in the least. Most of my crew was loyal. Without their help, nothing I could've done would've worked. When I left the wardroom and peeked around the corner, I saw XO standing with his back to me. He was next to the periscope. It looked like he was ready to make tick marks on his roster as department after department called in that they'd been successful. I heard his calm voice from across the room. "Department heads rep. . ."

Before he could finish I dropped him to his knees, I leaned over, ripped the microphone from his hand and kicked him in the side. 'I'll have you hang for this.' I clicked the button on the side of the mike, and hurriedly spoke. "Attention on the Boat, Attention on the Boat. XO and an unknown number of crew members have attempted mutiny. Short of deadly force, all loyal members are to restrain the mutineers by any means necessary. Loyal Department Heads, report by messenger." J. Mac chuckled. "The whole event was over in less than ten minutes."

He put a hand on the young man's shoulder. "Our crew's proud of what we did. The Admiral told us we were the only sub the Rebels tried to get, but didn't. Now with the other subs they never captured, we're hoping to regain the advantage."

J. Mac picked up his thermos and started toward the hatch. "Secure this watch in thirty minutes. We'll submerge on schedule."

"Aye, Aye, Sir."

#####

Cat booted up her computer and prepared for their late-night conference.

Bobby pulled two tables together and asked, "You want any of this left-over food?" *I can't eat another thing. I'd hate to see all this go to waste.*

Cat ran over. "Let me at that guacamole, it's awesome. I can't get enough of it."

Fendemere and Grimes stopped and grazed over the buffet. Cat turned the monitor so all four of them could see. "Our projections show we'll win with 84.4% of the vote."

Grimes pulled his head back in surprise. "What? I don't want to set our expectations too high."

Cat winked at Bobby, turned to Grimes and smiled. "Don't misunderstand me. All the polls we've projected show we'd lose with 22.8%."

Fendemere glanced at the paper Cat had given him. "So you're projecting we'll win in spite of what the polls say?"

"Yes, Sir. Would you like to know how?"

All three men said, "Yes."

Cat, appeared to be pleased. "Recently, through intermediaries, we acquired controlling stock in a software company. Last year, before General Lee resumed 'Mr. Lincoln's War,' this company, located in Chicago, Illinois, had been awarded the contract to provide every Voter Registrar on Puerto Rico with computerized voting software. Our people have imbedded a worm into the program. This will kick in after they run their simulation tests. No one on the island knows about this. In fact," she smiled broadly, "no one in the company even knows that we own them. Our agent has been an employee for decades. We should be able to add Puerto Rico to our country without firing a shot."

Fendemere started putting papers and files into his briefcase. "Outstanding. Bobby, you married a genius. The casualty estimates for the invasion Grimes and Ayers planned are more than President Gressette and I want to risk." He put a hand on Cat's shoulder, "The lives you'll save with this election will make everything worthwhile. I foresee great things coming from you two."

Twenty minutes later, Cat and Bobby were getting ready for bed. "Honey," he asked," what time's your flight? Mine's at noon, the day after tomorrow."

Cat rinsed her mouth after brushing her teeth. She wiped her mouth, opened her purse and pulled her boarding pass out. She winked at him standing in front of her with a towel wrapped around his waist. "8 am. I changed my mind. I don't think I'm going to get much sleep. It's not worth going to bed for two hours."

Bobby smiled, crossed the room and took her in his arms. "Anything you say."

#####

J. Mac peered through the periscope. "All clear, Diving Officer, bring her to course zero-five-zero." *Gotta keep alert, never know when an opportunity will come up.*

"Zero-five-zero, aye."

The Radar Operator called out. "Sir, you need to see this."

J. Mac moved behind the sailor. "What is it?"

"Sir, at 0800 a flight took off from the San Juan Airport. For some reason it has two transponders. I only saw it for a second. It's like they had one on, turned it off, and then turned the second one on. It was only a milli-second but our computer caught it. That seems odd."

Sparks called out from his station. "Sir, I know what it is. I read a security bulletin from COMSUBLANT that some of the Rebels would fake their travel routes, have phony passports stamped to look as if they'd really been traveling where they hadn't been. Then they'd fly in civilian aircraft disguised as American airliners. At the right time, they'd have their aircraft switch transponders so they could fly back to the ROA. I bet that's what this is. We just happened to notice the change on the screen when they switched over."

The Captain rushed to the intercom. "Missile room. Ready one."

"Aye, Sir. Ready one."

J. Mac called out, "Sparks, you earned your pay on this one. I've two reasons for wanting to even the score with those bastards. One is their attempted mutiny. The other is my older brother is the Captain of the Seattle. I can't get back at him, for his attack on the Lexington, but I can strike a blow against his cause."

Static came over the intercom speaker. "Sir, Missile Room. One's ready."

He didn't even hesitate. "Fire one."

J. Mac and several members of the conning tower crew watched the blips on the radar screen. The two images headed toward each other until they merged and went blank.

#####

Bobby woke with a start. He flopped on the bed. Put his forearm over his eyes. *Wow! What a night. She really knows how to say good-bye.* Dixie ran through his mind. It was a few moments before he realized it was Grime's ringtone chiming on his cell. *Where's Cat? Oh, that's right she's on her flight.* When he reached his pants and pulled the phone out, he stared at the screen.

Missed call – Grimes - 0815.

He jumped when someone pounded on the door of his suite. He peered through the peep hole in the door, then hurriedly put on his robe and opened it.

The normally composed, Grimes rushed in. "I'm sorry to have to tell you this, but a Federal sub just shot Cat's plane down. Don't know anything else. Get dressed, we gotta sort things out."

Stunned, Bobby dropped to his knees, cried out, "NO, LORD, IT CAN'T BE."

Both men were startled, when for the first time, they heard the shower running and a woman's voice singing at the top of her lungs.

Bobby ran across the room and shouted, "Cat! You're here!" Then he peeked into the bathroom. The young woman jumped, slipped, and then caught the handicap bar with one hand and the shower curtain with the other. "Don't you ever do that again! I almost fell. What's wrong?" She steadied herself, took the bathrobe her husband offered, and wrapped it around her slender body.

From inside the suite Grimes shouted, "Cat? Is that you?"

Apparently agitated, she called out as she dried off, "Well who else would it be? My double better not take a shower in my husband's suite." She stormed into the sitting room.

"And General, I don't care who you are! I won't have you barging into my room unannounced! I demand privacy." Her eyes flared at the humiliated black man. If he hadn't been so dark-skinned he would've turned beet red in embarrassment.

Bobby stammered, "Y-Y-You were supposed to be on the 0800 flight."

Still not aware of the seriousness of the situation, Cat waved a hand at the men. "Hummph, I decided we needed a honeymoon. Since we're done with the mission, I felt we deserve some free time. I thought that after a wonderful night together, that we might take in some sights. I switched flights with Sandra, my double. Her flight leaves tomorrow at 1100. I'll take her place," She winked at her husband, "I have plans for tonight."

She stroked Bobby's back as she cooed. "I hope you enjoyed my surprise."

Grimes clicked the remote for the entertainment center and waited for the TV to boot up. "Cat, thirty minutes ago a Federal sub shot your plane down. I'm ecstatic you're alive, but we have work to do."

Cat shook her head. "No, that can't be!"

A news reporter's image pixelated onto the screen. ". . .riquez here for Channel 3 News." The camera panned from the reporter's face to show an airport terminal.

#####

Late that afternoon, Cat and Bobby sat on a sofa in the Presidential Suite. "Listen, Sweetie, I'm tired of being cooped up by the Watchers. I'm upset about Sandra getting killed, but we deserve a night out." She glared at the young Indian sitting across the room, "without the Catawba observing our every move."

As she talked, Bobby shook his head. He stroked her cheek with a finger. "Honeybunch, we have to be careful. After all, we're in enemy territory. " *Another day, another time would be alright. But not now.*

She smirked. "Listen, Scaredy Cat. We need time alone, even if it's in a crowded restaurant. I've done everything for the cause. I even went to combat for you. I've done everything you wanted. Now it's time for you to do something I want." She nuzzled his cheek and whispered, "There's one Watcher on duty now. His partner will be back in ten minutes. Now's the time. Meet me in the lobby in fifteen minutes. Alone."

Looks like I don't have a choice. 'She, who must be obeyed, has spoken.' "Honeybunch, we're outta ice. I'll fill the bucket."

With a wink at her husband, she rose right behind him. "I need to go to the gift shop. I need some tampons." She turned to the Watcher sitting at the desk. "You gonna come with?"

Reaching for his jacket the young man headed toward the door. "Yes Ma'am." He tapped his side and felt for his pistol. Apparently satisfied, he glanced over at Bobby. "Sir, my partner will be back soon. Please wait until one of us comes back."

Bobby hugged Cat, "Sure, Son, no problem."

Cat and her security guard walked down the hall. Searching for signs of danger, his eyes flitted around. When they reached the bank of elevators, he pushed the call button. In seconds the car came and the door opened. He ensured it was empty and held the door open while she entered. He glanced over his shoulder for one last check of the corridor, and saw Bobby opening the stairway door. "Hey, Sir! Wait for your Watcher."

While he hesitated, the door started to shut. Cat pushed her guard away, the door closed, and she escaped.

Ten minutes later, giggling like a school girl, Cat ran down the alley. "Come on Bobby, we did it. We gave our Watchers the slip. We'll get at least one night with some privacy."

Laughing as he caught up with his wife in her red satin pant suit, Bobby sniffed her neck as he took her in his arms and nuzzled her. "Is that the new perfume I gave you yesterday?"

She smiled, and kissed her husband. "Um, hmm. Sure is. I just love it. I love every present you've given me this past week."

They strolled, arms around each other's waist, down the alley to a taxi stand. *Maybe this won't be so bad. We've had a good run of luck.*

The driver of the first cab opened the rear door. As Cat slid across the seat, Bobby said, "Where do you want to go?"

The driver started the engine and pulled into traffic. Cat tapped the driver on the shoulder. In perfect Spanish she said, "Señor, nos llevan a de Guillermo en el viejo San Juan."

The driver shook his head. "Señora, no. You don't want to go there in the daytime. And no gringo goes there after dark. Too many gangs, too many bad men."

Bobby picked up her hand and squeezed it. "He's right. I've heard stories about that section of town."

Cat scowled. "I told you before, I'm tired of living in a fish bowl. I want to live. I want to take chances. It's our last night in San Juan." She whispered in his ear, "I've given you everything you wanted. I want to spend time with you. Share emotions with you. Be seen with you. I want to be alone with you in the middle of a crowded room. Give me this, and when we get back to the hotel I'll let you do whatever you want."

His eyes got big. "You mean, ev. . ."

Cat licked her lips and put a finger on his mouth. "Um, hmmm." Then she kissed him.

Two hours later, they emerged from the restaurant. Bobby patted his stomach. "That was wonderful. I must admit this was a fantastic evening." As they walked toward a lone taxi that had dropped someone off in front of the restaurant, he nibbled on her ear.

"Stop it." She laughed. "Not in public. Don't start until we get back to our room."

The cab pulled away before they reached the back bumper. Bobby waved an arm and shouted, "TAXI."

He started to guide his wife toward the long line of cabs fifty yards away. Before he could hail the first one in line, a muscular hand twisted his arm behind his back. Another assailant put a bag over Cat's head and secured her hands with plastic ties. Bobby reacted immediately, pulled out his revolver with his free hand, and fired at one of the men attacking his wife. The man was dead before he hit the ground.

CRACK! Another gunshot echoed down the street. Searing pain racked Bobby's shoulder. *Lord, God! I've been shot. This is worse than when I hurt my knee.* He dropped his weapon, grabbed his shoulder and attempted to stop the bleeding.

"BOB. . ." Her scream for her husband was stifled by a tattooed hand and arm.

The first attacker threw Bobby to the ground, taped his mouth shut with duct tape, and slid a trash bag over his head. Tires screeched next to them. In seconds both Rebels were in the trunk of two different Mercedes sedans.

#####

In a panic, the young Catawba Watcher darted five feet toward the door Bobby had passed through, then back to the elevator that carried Cat to freedom. "What am I gonna do now? I'm a dead man." He looked at his watch, reached for his cell, and twirled around as he tried to decide on the best course of action.

He punched numbers into his cell. *Bad news is like dirty laundry. It doesn't get better with age.* The picture solidified on his video phone. "Chief, uh, uh, I have some bad news Sir."

Seeming to sense the panic in the young man, the senior watcher on duty tried to calm the lad down. "Don't worry son, nothing's so bad that we can't fix it. Slow down and tell me from the beginning. No, wait a minute. Are you in a hallway?"

The lad sniffled. "Y-Yes S-Sir."

"Take the northern stairway; come to room 1642 right now."

"I'm on my way, Sir."

"Good, now keep me on the line and talk to me while you…" The old Catawba hit his head. "Wait a minute! You traded shifts didn't you?"

"Yes, Sir."

"Then you were watching Bobby and Cat. You better hope nothing bad has happened. I'm coming up there right now. Don't move I'll be there in two minutes."

In thirty seconds the far stairwell door opened and a barrel-chested full-blooded Catawba rushed to his subordinate's side. He grabbed his arm and moved him to The Presidential Suite. He opened the door with his pass key and looked around. Sensing there was a serious problem, he turned to face the quivering security agent.

"All right, what happened?"

Ten minutes later, he spoke, "You idiot! A pregnant woman doesn't need tampons. It was a ruse to get away from you." He turned to a horrified Grimes. "Sir, I immediately called our man, in the San Juan Police Department, . . ." he flipped through his clipboard, "here it is, a Detective Sergeant Emilio Delannoy. He'll be discrete. He'll keep all of our names out of the press. He's going to meet us at the hotel security . . ."

There was a knock at the door. The Chief rushed over, peeked through the peephole and opened it. "Here he is now."

Delannoy, a muscular man with a thin-grey mustache, entered, set his attaché case down and started to sweep the room for electronic bugs. "Chief, I decided to come here. There are things I don't even want my team to know about our operation." After he made a complete circle of the suite, he returned. He stopped in front of Grimes.

"Sir, it's so good to finally meet you. I wish it could've been under better circumstances." He turned to the Chief, "I see you checking the time. I have my team reviewing all security footage in this district. I assure you everyone who will be present in the room with us, is on our payroll. . ." Minutes later, he motioned toward the door, "Sir, if we leave now we'll all arrive as they finish their initial sweep of the security cameras."

Grimes sat in a chair.

"Are you coming, Sir?"

The tired black man slowly shook his head. "No, you need someone who can keep up. I'll only slow you down."

The Catawba Security Chief stopped in front of the old Rebel. "I'll keep you posted." Then he ran to catch up with the detective.

As he rushed to the freight elevator he took a deep breath. "Chief, I have the best equipment in this monitoring center. Hotel management thinks it's theirs. Sure they paid for it, but I recommended everything I thought we would need. They even pay for the upgrades every year or so. And their staff has been on our payroll for years."

When the elevator car reached sub-basement "E" the policeman placed his hand on an apparently non-descript panel. Immediately the door swung open, they rushed over to video monitors along a side wall.

"All right, anybody want to tell me what's going on?"

A young woman, in her mid-twenties, rose from her seat. "Sirs, we found footage of the two of them entering a cab on fourth street." She punched a few buttons and the upper left monitor immediately displayed Bobby and Cat walking arm-in-arm up to a taxi. "Now, this next clip will show up over there," she pointed to the screen below the first one. "We found this of them coming out of a restaurant. Why they were foolish enough to go there, of all places?"

She shook her head, and pointed to a third picture. "This one shows them being kidnapped, and watch this. I knew your Bobby was fearless, but wow!"

By this time every staff member stood around watching the video. They gasped as Bobby fell to the ground and they saw them thrown into the trunk of the two Mercedes.

She continued, "That was the last video clip we have. However. . ." She paused and led everyone over to a computer operator who was busily pounding on a keyboard. "My sister here was able to ping Cat's cell." She took a laser pointer from a pocket and focused it on a map that was hanging on a wall. "For the past ten minutes it's been stationary here. I alerted SWAT. They're enroute."

#####

Cat felt the vehicle slow, turn, and come to a stop. She cocked her head in the darkness. *That's a rollup door. Sounds heavy. Must be a warehouse.* As she struggled with her binds, the car backed up, pulled forward, and then came to a stop. When the trunk opened, two pair of hands pulled her to her feet. As they stood her up, one of the kidnappers groped her body.

The bag on her head slipped off and fell to the asphalt. She glared at a swarthy man who licked his lips and leered. "I hope you enjoyed that Señor, because that will be the last time you ever feel pleasure."

The swarthy man laughed. "Jefe, we have a feisty one here. Can I have her when you're done with her?"

The leader exited the car with Bobby in the trunk, and admired Cat from head to toe. "No mi amigo, she's mine." He rushed over, grabbed her by the shoulders, and whistled. He pointed at a man getting out of the first car. "Cut her loose." He pointed to a door at the end of a loading dock. "Take her into my office. Her husband goes in there. Make sure he can see the monitors. I want him to see what I do to her."

He grabbed her elbow as he reached his office, and said, "This way my dear."

Her eyes flashed in anger. "Don't *my dear* me." *Okay, I can do this. I've given enough self-defense classes. Now's the time to do it for real.*

He laughed and pushed her through the door. She stumbled over the threshold and caught herself before she fell onto the carpet.

Jefe reached out and steadied her.

She shrugged off his hand. "Don't touch me, you slime ball."

He pushed her onto a couch and started to take his shirt off.

Cat's head bounced off the sofa's arm. *Focus now, you've taught other women what to do if this happened to them. Focus, focus.* Before he could start to take off his pants Cat jumped up. "Señor, we got off on the wrong foot. I know what you want. I don't want to get hurt. I know it'll be easier on me if I cooperate. Before you go any farther, will you listen to me?"

Suspicious, Jefe jerked his head around to see if anyone else had come into the room. He testily said, "What do you have in mind?"

Be coy. Focus on his eyes. He has to believe you really want him. She sat back on the couch and ran her hands on her thighs. "My idea is simple. I can tell you are an experienced man. If you can make me squeal with delight, I will let as many of your men have me as you want. I won't resist. In return, you release my husband. He needs to see a doctor. He's all I care about."

Surprised at such a proposal, Jefe shook his head. "I don't know if I can trust you." His pants slid to the floor exposing his genitals. What guarantee will you give me?"

She slid off the furniture, unbuttoned her blouse, and moved closer to the forty-year-old
gang leader. "Oh come on, Jefe." She cooed, "I can see you want me." She pulled her blouse up and exposed her navel. "You want to see more? Are you man enough to satisfy me? Or are you afraid? Why do you need a guarantee? I can take all of you, and whatever your men have to offer."

Licking his lips in anticipation he let his guard down.

In an instant Cat pulled a knife from her thigh, grabbed the man's testicles with one hand, and stuck the knife against his neck. "Now, I'll give you a guarantee. I'll remove your manhood with my bare hand as I slit your throat. I see you have security cameras.

I hope they're on so your so-called men can see how brave you really are."

She squeezed her hand around his private parts.

BOOM, BOOM, echoed off the walls.

He jumped, her hands instinctively squeezed, he screamed, and fell back onto the carpet.

SWAT quickly moved in and captured the kidnappers.

Two EMTs rushed stretchers over to both Bobby and Cat. In twenty minutes Delannoy had the recalcitrant couple back in The Presidential Suite.

As a team of doctors worked on Bobby's flesh wound, Grimes sat next to Cat. "Young lady that was a foolish stunt the two of you pulled. You put our entire mission in jeopardy. Just what were you guys thinking?"

Still shaking from her ordeal, Cat started to speak, "General. . ."

A nurse came over and stood next to her. "Sir, I need to take her into the other room and examine her." She frowned at Grimes. "Don't give me that look. I know who you are. I don't care about your politics. My sole purpose in life is to heal. And if you don't mind my saying so, the last person she needs to talk to right now is a man."

That said, she bent down, helped Cat to stand. "General, I don't care who you are. Where my patient's concerned, I outrank you."

On election night Bobby, Cat, and Grimes sat in their suite at the La Verne Weber Conference Center. Cat, now obviously pregnant, slid her backside off a couch and stood. "What did I tell you General? Did we call it right or what?"

"Young lady, you just took all the suspense out of the operation. This election was so anti-climactic it makes me sick."

Bobby looked up from the stack of reports he was reviewing. "Grimes, need I remind you that you yourself thought the casualty estimates for our invasion of Puerto Rico were unacceptable. So what if we stole the election? If they knew what we've done, mothers on both sides would sing your praises." He pulled all his files together and swept them into a box.

"Have either of you heard from Fendemere? He should've been here thirty minutes ago. I need him to brief us on how we're going to control Mexico.

WHISKEY – Fulfilling A Promise
(End of November)

Secretary of State Fendemere ushered everyone into President Gressette's office. "Mr. President, we're here."

Gressette peered through his glasses as he swept files aside. He rose and gestured toward the far corner of the room. "Let's sit over there."

Fendemere frowned. "Sir, I asked for this meeting as President of 'The Knights Of The Golden Circle.'" He glowered at Bobby and Cat sitting on the settee. "General Lee put us in a bind when he took it upon himself to offer five acres of excess Federal land to those with slave ancestry. He compounded his error when he made the same offer to anyone who served in our military." He vigorously shook his head. "I think the entire idea was just a ploy to get public support for our cause. We need to come up with a reason. . ."

Bobby interrupted, "Now wait a minute. My grandfather thought this through." He turned to Gressette. "Mr. President, think of the credibility issues we'll have if we go back on our pledge."

Gressette sat and puffed on his pipe as he listened to the debate. After twenty minutes of conversation he held a hand up. "Enough!" He leaned forward and poked a finger on the table in front of them. "The General and I worked together on putting this plan together. I agreed with it then." He jabbed a finger at Fendemere, "And I don't see any reason to change my mind now."

He turned to Bobby and Cat. "As for you two, don't you have enough on your plate? And you want to add something as complex as this? Let's wait for the war to be over."

236

Bobby shook his head. "No, Sir, I'm not looking to add anything to my plate. We promised that after the cessation of hostilities we would address the issue. All we want to do is start the process. We'll tell the public that we're going to begin setting up the 'Transition Boards.' We need to appoint members of regional and national panels. That will take time and at least tell the world we're serious about our apology." *It's not like I'm going to have to work full-time on this. I'll delegate everything to capable staffers. I think he wants to control everything. He really wants to strengthen his chances to become our President. Not if I can help it.*

Fendemere vigorously shook his head as the young man talked.

Bobby shook a finger at the older man. "This won't take up a lot of my time. We'll set up a shell to begin with. Over the next few years we'll flesh it out."

The Secretary of State scowled as he sat with his arms crossed. "Mr. President, I must protest. If you insist we follow this foolish course of action, it'll mean the end of our Republic. We should at least wait until the self-imposed deadline that General Lee committed us to. We need things to calm down."

Cat's eyes shot daggers at Fendemere. "Mr. President this man isn't a true southerner. He has no business discussing the issue of slavery, reparations, or an apology. Why. . ."

Ayers, Bobby, and Grimes jumped as Fendemere slammed a fist on the table top. "How dare you question my loyalty? It's a question of being realistic. We made a commitment to our citizens that shouldn't have been made. If we honor it our movement could fail!" He sat back in his chair and sighed, "And might even blow up in our face."

The tension rose as everyone regained their composure.

Fendemere glared at the three people sitting across from him. "I've been loyal to 'The Cause' my entire life. You have no right to make such an accusation."

"Humph!" Cat threw her pen on the table. It skidded, bounced off a book sitting in front of her, and landed on the floor next to her husband.

Bobby picked it up and handed it to her. "Thanks."

She pointed it at the diplomat. "You were born in Wisconsin. Your family has always resided in the north. True, you did attend Southern colleges. But that doesn't make you a southerner any more than my sitting in a garage makes me a car." Out of breath from her outburst she sank back in her hair and rubbed her belly. She continued, "You Sir are a true member of 'The Knights of the Golden Circle." The original members were northerners who sympathized with us. They never fought in any battles. They funded money and supplies to our troops. I don't deny that your help these past few months have been invaluable, but you don't have any business discussing slavery or any of the ramifications of that abhorred policy of our ancestors."

Fendemere fumed as he listened to her. "Let me tell you, I'm just as much of a citizen of our country as you. I'm entitled to speak on any issue that affects the outcome of our conflict. And I for one don't see any need for us to apologize for slavery in any way until the sea captains, northern banking interests, and the like apologize before us. We didn't dream up the idea of slavery. It was given to us by outsiders who bear every much the blame as we do." He sat back into his seat so hard that his chair slammed against the wall and made a dent in the plaster.

Coming to the defense of his wife, Bobby pointed a finger at the man sitting across the table. "You sir are out of line talking to her in that tone of voice! To begin with, your argument is like an alcoholic blaming the distillery, truck driver, and liquor store owner for his alcoholism. I see no problem with, and I see a lot of benefit from our being the first to offer reparations. It's starting a dialogue that should've happened centuries ago. It's not our fault, but it's to our credit that we're addressing the issue."

It took several moments for Fendemere to calm down. He eyed everyone in the room and then said, "We have to find a legitimate way to not give them what they were promised.

Grimes pursed his lips and leaned forward to make his point. "Mr. President, I was involved in the discussions that led to the promise. His intent was to get support from as many as possible. The resultant response was overwhelming and, in my opinion has been very instrumental in the success of our cause."

Bobby put a hand on his mentor's arm. "Sir, there's more to it than you think."

The older men turned and looked down at the young man.

Glad I listened to my Professor. If I hadn't done that extra credit project I wouldn't know what I know now. Bobby, ignoring them, continued, "Sirs I did a paper on this in college." He stood and faced them. "As you know, many Southerners, slave owners included, were Christians. As Christians we're in the same situation. In 1861 our leaders ignored what God wanted them to do and he ignored them. It's my belief that if they had found a way to free the slaves before the conflict started, that The Lord would've given them success." He rose to his full height. "If we don't right the wrong we'll have no more success than our ancestors. Even if grandfather's intent was misguided, at least he was trying to make amends for our past sins."

Gressette trembled as Bobby presented his information. After calming down he said, "To free the slaves at that time would've devastated our economy. It was unrealistic to expect our society to bear that burden. No. . ."

Bobby interrupted. "Excuse me Sir; our economy was devastated by four years of brutal fighting. Not to mention reconstruction. Do you really think The Lord was going to side with a society which supported an evil such as slavery?"

"Humph." Gressette frowned. "I'm not defending the institution. But it's easy for you to apply modern day values and mores to antebellum society."

Bobby tapped the table top in front of them. "Sir, morally slavery was wrong. Even General Lee knew that. Why he freed his slaves prior to the start of 'Mr. Lincoln's War."

Fendemere nodded, "I'll grant you that, and I've heard that President-elect Grant finally freed his slaves just before he ran for election. His excuse was that his wife wouldn't free them because good help was hard to find."

Gressette leaned forward in his chair and spoke firmly. "We need to take advantage of recent events. General Lee's timeline was tentative." H turned to Bobby and Cat. "Here's what we need to do. . ."

At 0900 the next morning, Mary Rochard stepped into President Gressette's office. *I wonder what this could be about. They can't have a clue about my activities.*

Grimes looked up from the papers in his hand. "Rochard thanks for coming so quickly" He nodded to the President, "We've been impressed with your work and would like you to consider taking a position with us.

How could I get so lucky? When I put my name in for a media position I had no idea it would get to this level.

Gressette moved from behind his desk and motioned for Grimes that they were to sit on the far side of the room. "Shall we sit over here? If you're going to be working for us I want to get to know you better."

An hour later he rose and winked. "I'm sure you'll do fine. Grimes and Fendemere will get you up to speed on what we want. My secretary will review your salary and benefits with you before you leave. Do you have any questions?"

"Uh, uh, no Sir! You've just fulfilled one of my life-long dreams. I just hope I can meet your standards."

The President and the old black soldier smiled. Grimes put a hand on her arm. "Young lady, you're just the person we need in this job. You've been committed to our cause for over twenty years. It's time your talents were recognized."

As she shook Gressette's hand she stammered, "Ye, yes S, Sir." Watch it now, don't give anything away. She opened her portfolio and sat poised to write. "Sir, how soon do you want me to have my first press conference?"

Grimes reached behind him and picked a folder up off a table. Gressette nodded and he handed it to his new Press Secretary. "We know you're familiar with the reparations and five acre issue. Review this file and announce this tomorrow. You coordinate the time and handle everything yourself. Your predecessor had just hired a staff before his heart attack. If you want you can hire your own staff or keep his." As he spoke he ushered the new staff member out of the room.

Rochard entered the conference room and stood in front of the podium. "May I have your attention please?"

The room became quiet. *It sure is different being on this side of the fence. If I fail maybe I can get my old job back at XYZ. But I can't help my new boss if I go back there.* She held the sides of lectern and smiled.

"Our President would like to fulfill a commitment General Lee made last year."

She waited a few seconds, and then tapped the microphone. "Ladies and Gentlemen, please let me finish, this may be my first press conference, but give me a chance to present my information."

241

She said firmly.

Strains of "Sorry," and "Okay, Boss." Carried throughout the auditorium.

She took her glasses off and pointed them at the front row. "I have a prepared statement, and then I'll take a few questions." She put her glasses back on and read.

President Gressette has announced that he's going to start filling positions on our 'Reparations Board." We're announcing this earlier than promised because we want everything to be open and above board. At the end of this conflict, The Republic Of America will honor the commitment General Lee made last April. We will accept applications for compensation one year after hostilities have ceased. Between now and the final peace, we will organize our boards and panels, setup procedures, and most of all make a list of what property belonging to the old Federal government will be made available. Each individual, who has at least one-quarter slave ancestry, is a citizen of the ROA, or if they honorable served in our military, will be entitled to their five acres."

She slid her spectacles off and smiled. *Well, so far so good.* "I'll take the first question from a guest from the North, the Washington Post."

An elderly bald man stood up in the front row. "Ms Rochard, isn't this just a smokescreen? After all, we all know that slavery was the real reason for the 'Civil War.'"

Shouts and cat calls came from all around the northerner.

She raised a hand for quiet. "Listen up! The man's entitled to his opinion, even if he's wrong." She faced him directly and laughed. "I bet you believe all the crap you've been taught in your politically correct northern school. If you're right, why did Mister Lincoln wait so long to free the slaves? Wait because he didn't want Delaware and other Northern slaveholding states to secede

242

and join the Confederacy?" She frowned, leaned forward toward the Federal reporter. "If you're going to ask a question like that, at least get your facts straight. " She glanced around the crowd. "Now, does anyone have an intelligent question?"

A young woman rose, "Ma'am, I'm with the Los Angeles Times. What about the slaves who joined the North in fighting for their freedom. Doesn't that prove anything?"

Rochard laughed out loud. "It's true some slaves joined the Union Army. However, a vast majority supported the south." She paused in her answer. "Don't give me that you've got to be kidding me look. If the slaves were so eager to fight for their freedom, why didn't a majority of them flee as soon as Union troops arrived in their area? Who wait that stayed on the plantation and worked in the fields? Who was it that transported the supplies to the southern armies? I'll tell you, it was the slaves. The same slaves you're trying to get me to believe wanted their freedom. It's true many would've gladly accepted their freedom if it had been offered. Actually most slaves considered themselves southerners."

She surveyed the room and pointed to a middle row. "You there, Marc Le Blanc, what question do you have?"

Marc rose and nodded to his former producer. "Ms Rochard, how are you going to divide up all this land? And how sure are you there will be enough land?"

"Excellent question Marc. That brings up my last point. Like I said a short time ago, between now and one year after hostilities cease, we'll setup regional and national boards. Each board will survey all the Federal land in their area. This land will be divided into four categories ranging from undeveloped in a rural area to a skyscraper downtown in a major city. Each classification will be weighted epending on how technologically advanced it is, or if it contains valuable natural resources. For example, a section of wilderness will not be rated the same as a twenty story skyscraper in Dallas."

She paused, took a sip of water from a bottle. "In answer to your last question, it's possible we might run out of land. That's why we're bringing this up now. We want public discussion about this. Nothing's going to be done in secret. One option we're considering is putting a dollar figure on five acres. We might, from the beginning, offer a cash payment rather than land. But that's all to be determined." She paused and glanced around at a section of Northern reporters, "If we do run out of land, as some of the Union media contend, we can at least honor our commitment."

She closed her portfolio and stepped away from the podium. "That's all for now. Thank you for coming."

She walked to the rear curtain and hurried to a corner. After furtively glancing around she punched numbers into her cell. When the ringing stopped she spoke, "Don't say anything. I received the package. I will send my first shipment tonight."

She heard footsteps as she pocketed her phone. She pulled a compact out of her purse and pretended to adjust her makeup.

X-RAY – Going for Silver
(January)

Major General Rodgers walked through the Reno Sky Harbor airport and headed toward the rental car counter. *Man, I've never seen so many Chinese in an airport. What gives with that?* Later, as he turned his head to scan the parking lot for his car, he bumped into someone coming the other way.

The short man stumbled and dropped his luggage. "Excuse me sir, I should have watched where I was going."

Startled, Rodgers let go of his *Ea*sy Cart and helped a Chinaman retrieve his belongings. "Sir, that's all right, it was as much my fault as yours."

The diminutive man stood with his heals together and bowed. "You are too kind sir. Thank you for your help. I must go." Then he grabbed his luggage, and before the Rebel could say another word he hurried off.

Rodgers watched him walk away as he turned his head and continued to search for his rental car. "Wonder what that's about?"

An hour later he walked up to the receptionist at the Shoshone Tribal Headquarters. "Ma'am, my name is Donald Rodgers. I have an 11:00 am appointment with Chief Grey Wolf."

The young woman didn't even raise her head. "Chief Wolf isn't in charge anymore." She punched a button on her phone. "Chief Grey Wolf's eleven o'clock is here. Should I send him in?"

A dulcet voice came over the speaker, "No, the new Chief doesn't want guests wandering the halls un-chaperoned. I'll be right down. "The receptionist pointed to a seat along the wall. "Wait there, she'll be down in a minute."

After ten minutes, he sat, drumming his fingers on his briefcase. Rodgers surveyed the room, stood and admired the Shoshone artifacts displayed on the wall and in display cases. He did a double-take when he happened to glance out the window. "Uh, Miss? Why is Chief Grey Wolf being led away in handcuffs?"

She shook her head. "I wouldn't know Sir. Today is my first day."

He turned his head when he heard footsteps coming down the marble hallway. They stopped outside the open door and he saw the same Chinese man he'd bumped into earlier. He held his hand out to the newcomer.

He smiled, "Sir, we were in a rush before and didn't get a chance to introduce ourselves. I'm Don Rodgers. And you are?"

"My name is Mr. Lee." He said curtly, then turned and walked past the receptionist. He winked at her as he went past. "I'll only be a minute."

"Oh yes Sir, go right in. I know he'd like to see you."

Not used to being treated in such a manner, Rodgers leaned forward and said, "Miss, I would like some answers. Is there someone I could talk to?"

She smiled. "Yes sir. My Supervisor's on the way down. She'll be here shortly."

Frustrated, he sat and checked his e-mail on his cell phone for the tenth time. *What's going on here? They've never treated us this way.*

Ten minutes later he heard high heels coming toward him. He raised his head, stood and saw a middle-aged Shoshone woman standing in the far doorway. He walked over to her and shook her hand.

"General Rodgers, sorry to keep you waiting. Chief Walking Deer had an important visitor. Please follow me."

Important visitor, my rear end. I've never been treated in such a manner. Especially by a Chief. The Shoshone don't act this way without a reason. "I appreciate the Chief seeing me."

Her pace slowed and she opened a door. "This way, Sir." She moved inside the massive office. Chief Deer sat at his desk. Mr. Lee sat in a corner and started.

When Rodgers reached the front of his desk, the old man rose and extended his hand. "Welcome General. So good of you to come." He gestured toward the other man in the room, "I hear you already have met my good friend Mr. Lee."

"Yes, we were both in a hurry. Maybe we'll have time to get acquainted later."

Lee, apparently not interested in socializing, rose, shook the General's hand and tersely said, "We'll see."

Chief pointed to a small conference table. A woman entered with a tray of tea and pastries. He walked around his desk. "Shall we?"

Rodgers sat where he was directed. *What's going on here? Ayers told me I was coming to finalize the Shoshone joining the ROA.*

The old Shoshone man poured tea for each of his guests. Rodgers accepted his cup. "Thank you Chief."

Mr. Lee reached for the sugar, "Yes, thank you Chief."

Rodgers pulled a file folder from his attaché case. "Chief, President Gressette sends his greetings. Lieutenant General Ayers regrets his health has kept him from meeting with you."

Chief Deer smiled. "General, I appreciate the effort President Gressette and General Ayers have made on this matter." He shifted in his seat. "A year ago, my son and his cohorts over-stepped their authority when they initiated contact with your people. . ."

Rodgers' mind wandered, *the tone of his voice tells me we're not going to be signing anything today.* "Chief is there a problem with the agreement my President prepared?"

The Shoshone leader took a breath. "No, not really a problem with the document. But circumstances have changed. You see, the older generation is back in charge." He paused and nodded toward Mr. Lee. "Our friends in China have provided us with more than you can offer." He smiled an insincere smile. "We have decided that it's in our best interest to work with Washington and the Chinese." He stood, and extended his hand. "I'm sorry you made such a long trip. But I felt it was important enough to tell you in person. Good day."

Five minutes later Rodgers stood in the parking lot. *What just happened? I thought we had this wired.*

Almost three-thousand miles away, President Barnes glared at the Chinese Ambassador, then over at Lyle and then Bill. "Sir, I think I misunderstood you. What is the justification for your infringing on our sovereignty?"

The Ambassador smiled. "Mr. President, we're not violating the autonomy of your country. You have to realize the amount of money my people have invested in the USA is enormous. Our advisors are only going to protect our investment."

Barnes slammed a fist on the arm of the chair. "I won't stand for this! You will not implement this plan. You will contact your government and tell them we don't need any assistance."

Lyle and Bill nodded in agreement as their boss continued his tirade.

248

The Ambassador sat impassively and listened. When the President finished and sat back in his seat the foreigner leaned slightly forward.

"Sir, calm down. You have every right to turn down our offer. Please consider our point of view. We have invested trillions of dollars in U.S. Treasury bonds. We have invested trillions of dollars in every major company listed on Wall Street. You can't control your cities. Your military is spread thinner than watered down won ton soup. You need to willingly accept our help now; or. . ." he paused and peered over his glasses at the three men sitting across from him, "We'll have to send in hundreds of thousands of troops to control your cities."

The Secretary of State shook his head. "This is totally unacceptable. Mr. President, you must stand your ground.

The oriental diplomat rested his hands on the table in front of him. "At this point we have ninety-five thousand advisors ready to offer their assistance. We've positioned them in every major city. I make one phone call and in six hours they will be in position. If you fight us on this, I will order our troops into every city with a population of more than twenty-thousand."

YANKEE – Time For A Decision
(January)

Visibly shaken, Lyle handed the one-page document to Barnes. "I don't like to admit it, but we have to give in. We can't supply our troops in the field, and the remaining states in the Union can't support the Federal government. At least the Rebels will assist us in rebuilding."

There was a light rap at the Oval Office door, a woman entered; her hands visibly shook as she handed a file to Lyle. He speed read it before he passed it on to Barnes. He peered at Carter and then at his boss. "Sir we've just been informed the State Of California has declared itself to be an independent nation." Then he set the paper in front of Barnes.

Barnes laid it next to the surrender document and held both in place as if he expected a gust of wind to tear them from his hands. "What they're demanding is 'Reconstruction' in reverse. I can't let that happen."

Bill leaned over, put a hand on the President, "We have to accept this. If we don't then in two weeks they'll have control over what's left of the USA." After squeezing his boss's shoulder he said, let's face it, with more states threatening to join the Rebels, for survival, not because they support them, we're getting weaker by the day." He let out an exasperated sigh, "California's action only makes it worse."

Barnes moved across the room. *Why won't this headache go away? Focus now; try to keep from blacking out.* "I won't give in. I believe The Lord will provide a miracle. That traitor, Fendemere will be here soon. I need to be strong."

Bill rose and walked over to a window. "No matter how you look at it, this is the best we could do. They're offering billions of dollars in aid. We'll be able to start from scratch. I don't like it. But we're between the proverbial rock and a hard place."

Barnes gritted his teeth. "This is total defeat. I can't do it."

The intercom buzzed, and the President nodded. Lyle picked up the receiver. "Yes?" A secretary's voice was heard throughout the room. "Security informed me that Secretary of State Fendemere has entered the building. I'll bring him in when he arrives at my office." Bill gathered his papers and slid them into a drawer. President Barnes moved behind his desk. "Boeing only needs two months to produce their new weapon."

Lyle shook his head. "No, Sir. In two months we'll have nothing. The military is finished. Many have died a valiant death. Many more will die needlessly if we continue."

Barnes pounded a fist on his desk top, "My minds made up. We won't surrender. We'll. . ."

There was a brief knock, and then the secretary escorted Fendemere into the room. She stood erect. "Mr. President, Secretary of State Fendemere. . ." She choked and recovered her composure. "Of The Republic Of America." She immediately turned and left.

The Rebel Diplomat smiled as he approached Barnes. "Sir, it's good to finally meet you."

Barnes frowned, "I can't say I'm pleased to see you," he said curtly. "However, we do need to discuss the document your courier delivered."

Fendemere shrugged. "We can discuss it if you wish. But we will not make any changes."

Barnes sat up. "What right do you have to demand that? Our forces are still viable, our economy is strong."

The Rebel scowled. "Doesn't that depend on which side of the fence you're sitting? You've declared martial law in all major cities. Black markets are creating shortages in many commodities all across your country." He said, "Mr. President, it's your choice. But if this isn't signed today, our forces will move." He glanced at his Rolex, "On all fronts at 0500 hours. That's six hours from now. This will cause more death and destruction."

The Chief Executive stood, and pointed a finger at his adversary. "But why should we accept what you call 'ADVISORS?'"

Fendemere confidently leaned back and crossed his legs. "Simple, we have compassion for the American people. We've never had any animosity toward them, just the Federal government they elected. The same government that Mr. Lincoln led to destroy the South in 1865, before the North occupied our country for over one-hundred-fifty years. We're willing to help the common man who didn't have a say in the actions perpetrated by their elected officials."

Lyle slammed a fist on the table in front of him. "Poppycock! Mr. Lincoln was an honorable man. He strove to preserve the Union. In the end he gave his life for what he believed."

The southern gentleman smiled. "You're entitled to your opinion. We don't have time to debate this. If you reject our offer, the Chinese will be right behind. I've heard their claims of having over ninety-thousand advisors ready to come out of hiding. Our sources tell us that's an inflated number. You run the risk of having a permanent Chinese presence in the USA. If you accept our offer, you will only have advisors for five years or until the state involved becomes stable enough to maintain viability."

He stared at Barnes, glanced down at his watch. "We're running out of time, Sir. I need to leave in ten minutes. You can contact me at any time and I'll take your word that the signed document is enroute to President Gressette."

He rose, straightened his tie and extended his hand to Barnes. "We'll also honor that if you change your mind after hostilities resume. We want the lowest number of casualties as possible."

When the President didn't reciprocate, he reached for his briefcase and left.

Barnes sat back down into a chair by the window. He seemed to come out of a fog and looked around the room. "What? What happened to Fendemere? Did he leave? I wanted to negotiate with him. We've got to resolve this."

Bill winked at Lyle. "Yes, he did Sir. He had to leave." He pulled out and checked his phone. "Sir, can I get back to you? I need to check on something." He turned to Lyle and whispered, "I need your help. Follow me."

#####

After they left the President, Lyle rushed Bill into his office. *I feel like a traitor, but I don't follow through with what has to be done, the USA is finished.* "Last week I didn't think you were right when you thought he was having PTSD issues. I checked with some friends of mine at Walter Reed. They don't know I'm concerned about him. They think I asked about my cousin."

He led the Secretary of State to a sofa, and they sat. "When I saw how he reacted to Fendemere, I decided you're right. Barnes's told me about a few instances when he was in combat. It could be the reason he's been acting strange. He seems to be having more frequent flashbacks. I think when he gets that look in his eyes he's having them. He tries to hide it. He's afraid of what might happen."

Bill pulled out his organizer. "I've been keeping track. He keeps on talking about nightmares. I've noticed when we get combat reports he gets real tense, his breathing becomes rapid, and he starts to sweat. You're his Chief of Staff. What do you think we should do?"

Lyle reached for his phone. "I'm calling the White House Doctor. We need an evaluation to see if he's fit." He pulled his shirt sleeve up and checked his watch. *I'm glad Doc's a patriot. Sure hope he agrees with us.*

"That's a big step. Last week you wouldn't even consider he had a problem. Now you're questioning his mental ability. Does the Vice President know about your concerns?"

Lyle wiped a tear from a cheek. "The realization of how serious his condition is has been creeping up on me. You and I both know he hates Fendemere. But we also know he would never be rude to anyone. He's not himself. Like it or not, we have to sign that paper. I'm sure the VP will agree."

"Okay, we need to go slow with this, but we need to get the paper signed. You get the Doctor to evaluate him. I'll prepare a report for Vice President Underwood and Congress." He looked at the moon setting outside the window and back at his friend. "Many lives depend on us."

Lyle rose and moved behind his desk. "Bill, I'll get the Cabinet on board with everything. I sure hope he doesn't fight this."

#####

Everyone stood as President Underwood entered the Cabinet Room. A short woman, her head was barely visible over the heads of her seated Cabinet members as she walked along the side wall. "Thank you for being here." Her dark brown eyes swept the room. "Lyle, did you get that report to everyone?" She moved toward her seat and sat.

"Yes, Ma'am."

"Good." She studied the faces of her advisors. "Can I assume everyone's reviewed this?"

When no one responded, she turned her tablet on, and her wallpaper appeared on the screen over her shoulder. Her fingers whisked over the device and a chalkboard program appeared.

"Here are our options: 1) To continue fighting and hope Boeing comes through with another miracle. 2) Sign the damned paper and accept defeat. And 3) Accept assistance from the Chinese."

There was complete silence.

She raised her head, "We don't have all day. Gentlemen and Gentlewomen. If you want to keep your job, I expect you to participate in my meetings."

Sitting at the far end of the room, the Secretary of Defense spoke up. "Ma'am, most of our people just want to put food on their table and enjoy their family. I don't see it getting any better for us if you continue to hold out for some miracle."

The room came alive as everyone clamored to speak. Later, after everyone had expressed their point of view, Lyle reached over and punched a few buttons on a panel. A map of the USA slid onto the monitor. He pointed his laser pen at the screen. "Madam President, in my opinion, we don't have any choice but to surrender. We've exhausted every option. If we don't, either the Chinese will have a permanent foothold in the USA, or the Rebels will continue until they reach the Canadian Border. Either is completely unacceptable."

Lyle slid the surrender document across the table. Mary surveyed the room, picked up a pen, quickly signed it and shoved it back to her Chief of Staff. "The deed is done. Get that damned thing outta here."

ZULU – A Final Good-bye
(Late January)

Donald Rodgers sat next to Ayers' hospital bed. "Jacob, it's been many years hasn't it?"

Ayers' head lay on the satin pillow. He turned, and nodded. "It sure has We're almost there, the circle's nearly complete. Doesn't look like I'll make it."

Rodgers swallowed, picked up his organizer, and sat poised to take notes. "Yes, that's what the Doctor told me. He said you want me to help plan your memorial service."

With his eyes closed, Jacob sighed. "I don't want to put it off any longer. I want a service that will get our message out. I want a traditional service. Bishop Rockford died last week. He was going to take care of everything. You're the only other member of the faith who knows me well enough to get my message across, the only one I'd want to help send me off. Find his notes. I don't have the energy to go over it again."

Ayers sat up, sipped water from a glass and continued. "Basically, I want a simple service, only two testimonials, a talk about our faith, and a celebration of my going to glory. Since I don't have any family left, could you escort me down the aisle for the last time?"

Rodgers leaned back in the over-stuffed chair and sighed. "Of course I will. I'll make sure your service befits our faith and your stature. Of all the Catawba who've served the South the past three-hundred years or so, you've done more to further the cause than any member of our tribe. Chief Klegg's already talking about erecting a statue."

Ayers waved a hand. "No, I don't want any of that falderal. My life and faith are the only testimony I want."

Rodgers closed his day book and stood. "As you wish my friend. I'll get Bishop Rockford's notes. I'll come back tomorrow. You can decide on the final draft for the order of service. I spoke with the new Bishop; he said he'll work with whatever you want."

Ayers mumbled as Rodgers leaned over the bed rail.

He tried not to stare at his friend's haggard face. "Say that again?"

"Good-bye, my friend."

"No, don't say that. I need your advice so much."

The old Catawba shook his head. His voice wheezed as he struggled to talk. "The time has come for you to take my place. My stint is over." Then his head fell back onto his pillow.

Two days later Bobby, Cat and Grimes sat in the third pew waiting for the service to begin. The young man leaned to his right and whispered to his grandfather's aide, "Ever been to a non-Baptist funeral?"

Grimes glanced around the sanctuary, and said, "No, can't say as I have. This should be interesting."

Before Bobby could respond, the organist started to play Amazing Grace. *Lord, I don't want to be disrespectful of the dead. But he really wasn't a believer.* He glanced around the sanctuary, *sure hope this doesn't take forever.*

The first cord was struck, Rodgers, dressed in an immaculate Rebel Dress Uniform, followed the casket as it entered. As he passed each row of pews, the audience sat.

The pallbearers positioned the casket in the cent. Rodgers moved to the podium and spoke into the microphone. "Ladies and

Gentlemen, we're here today to honor a man who served his Nation, Tribe, family, and most of all The Lord." He paused and nodded to a man seated in the first row. The man rose, and walked to the front.

Three hours later, Bobby and cat walked toward the back of the sanctuary. He whispered into his wife's ear. "I can't believe they actually tried to convert us during the service. I knew they'd push some of their faith, but I didn't expect them to dump the entire truck load on us."

Cat stopped as the crowd thinned out. She leaned over and whispered, "It's no different than hearing the plan of salvation at a Baptist funeral. Give them a break."

As he made their way through the crowd, Bobby shook his head. "Oh come on. No Baptist service ever had almost three hours of hard sell."

The crowd thinned out even more as they walked into the fellowship hall. The young couple made their way to a table where Grimes and Fendemere were seated.

The two elder Rebels stood, shook Bobby's hand and slightly bowed to Cat. After everyone had taken their seats, Grimes smiled. "My Dear, how did you keep him in line? I could see him fuming the entire service."

She winked at them and then turned to Bobby. "Dear, don't be so embarrassed. I saw several non-Believers who were as antsy as you were."

Ignoring his wife, he lightly tapped the table in front of him. "Can we take advantage of this time and conduct some business?" *At least this trip won't be a total waste.*

Fendemere said, "As long as you realize, just because we're among friends, "he surreptitiously looked around the room, "doesn't mean we can talk openly."

Bobby followed his glance as his eyes covered the room. "Of

course, Mr. Secretary. All I want to know if you expect to close the circle on time?"

Indignantly, Fendemere pointed a finger at Bobby. "I resent the tone of your voice. Just because you were born under a lucky star and inherited a position of power, doesn't mean you can question me in that manner."

A few months ago I'd have let you get away with that remark. Not today. Bobby cleared his throat, Sir, it's my responsibility to ensure the timetable is met."

"Mr. Lee, do I have to remind you that we're three months ahead of your grandfather's timetable?"

"No reminder necessary. However, it appears you forget. You wouldn't be ahead of schedule if it hadn't been for my wife and me risking our lives and bringing Puerto Rico into the circle."

Grimes intervened. "Gentlemen, gentlemen, please. This is not the occasion for this."

Both men stared each other down.

A few nearby guests glanced their way when they heard the commotion.

Cat reached over, picked up Bobby's hand, "Sweetie, let's go through the receiving line. It's shorter now."

Scowling at the diplomat, Bobby followed his wife. "I don't like that man. I'll never understand why Grandfather selected him for the position."

"Bobby, you really should give him a break. You know he's done an excellent job of getting diplomatic support for us. He's quite capable. You don't have to like him, but you do have to show him some respect."

"Ahh," he sneered "You might be right, but I still don't trust that conniving bastard" *Especially the way he's leered at Cat.*

Later, after everyone at their table had finished their meal, Bobby interrupted Grimes's and Fendemere's conversation. "Excuse me Sirs." Then he turned toward Fendemere, "Mr. Secretary, I owe you an apology. I've been broken up about the General's death. I should've ben kinder to you earlier." Then he sat back and smiled.

Fendemere returned the gesture and shook his head. "Don't worry son. I understand. Jacob was a friend of mine too." He reached into his coat pocket and pulled out a tablet. "Let's see," he ran his finger over a few pages. "Here we are. Next week I meet with several politicians. It's not going to be easy."

Grimes pushed his plate away. "Easy or not, we are ahead of schedule. President Gressette expects results." He slid a desert plate in front of him, picked up a fork, and dug in. In between mouthfuls he said, "The timetable says we should complete the circle five years after hostilities cease." He frowned at Bobby, "Son, three months doesn't count. It's getting the job done that does. In the next few years we'll be ahead or behind schedule many times."

The Rebel diplomat nodded. "General, I can't worry about timetables. The political climate will determine when we're ready to make our move. I guarantee you we'll be ready. I believe it'll be within the five-year estimate, if we're lucky, we'll beat it. However, I guarantee the circle will be complete before President Gressette's term expires."

BAM, BAM, BAM.

The Press Secretary woke with a start and glanced at the alarm clock. *2:30 am! Who would be coming to my door at this time of the morning?* "I'm coming, keep your shirt on." She fumbled with the security chain and the dead bolt as she rubbed sleep from her eyes. She looked up and saw a lanky man standing in front of a squad of burly men in black. A black woman in a suit stood in the rear.

"What can I do for you?"

Sherwood pulled a picture from a shirt pocket. "Yes it looks like you. I assume you're Mary Rochard, Press Secretary to our President?"

Aggravated, she started to close the door. "If that's all you need to ask you could've waited until morning."

He pushed her aside and made room for his team to enter. "Secure all electronic devices." He turned to a short man who'd just run up. "You're late, go through all filing cabinets and secure anything you think is pertinent."

Shocked, she started to interrupt. "No wait a. . ."

Sherwood put a hand over her mouth. When I want you to speak, I'll tell you what to say." He peaked over his shoulder. "You, in the back, pack a bag for her." Then he turned back to Mary. Ms. Rochard you're being arrested as a Federal Spy. This arrest is being videotaped and recorded. Anything you say will be used at your trial."

"A SPY? Me! I've been loyal to the cause for many years. Just what right and evidence do you have to accuse me of being a spy?"

Through a light rain, Sherwood led Mary to a waiting sedan. "All in due time Ma'am. All in due time, right now," he paused as he slipped her hands into the cuffs, "you just sit tight. You'll have plenty of time to explain your actions."

"Do the President and General Grimes know about this? I guarantee you they'll have your head."

He smirked, "When the computer nerds checked your laptop last week they found you've been sending classified files to a Federal website." He put a hand on her head and used the other hand to guide her into the back seat.

After he shut the car door an officer approached Sherwood from behind. "Sir, you need to see this. I think that clinches it don't you?"

Sherwood skimmed through the file on Mary's i-Pad. "Yes, it does. Let me see what they say." He pulled out his cell. As he walked away he punched a few numbers. Five minutes later he returned and motioned for the officer to remove Mary from the car. "Bring her into the garage."

Their shadows moved as they passed several street lights and into the parking structure. When they arrived at an empty corner Sherwood turned and showed the screen to his prisoner. "Would you care to explain this document on your device? Why did you send it to the Feds?"

I've been a Christian my whole life. When I've been in a bind I've always told the truth. Why change now? She looked straight into her captor's eyes. "Sir when I first joined the cause I didn't have a clue what we were fighting for. I was a Southerner and working for my elders who told me it was what I needed to do. After General Lee's interview last year, I finally came to realize that even though I'm a southern girl and that I believe in state's rights, that I think it's in the best interest for the south to remain part of the Union. If we don't then in ten years there won't be a USA or ROA."

"I appreciate your honesty. So you intentionally worked with the Federals?"

"Yes, Sir I did."

Sherwood checked to see if there were any civilians around, pulled a pistol from his holster,. "The penalty for being a spy is death. There's no trial. Just immediate execution, if you have any prayers you'd like to say, now's the time to say them."

"Sir, I've been praying ever since you came to my door. If you feel that's what you must do. I pray for you and your soul."

The lanky man chuckled, aimed his weapon at her head and fired. Then he turned to the man standing next to him, "Clean up my mess."

The whine of the whisper jet engine hummed in the background. Fendemere slept soundly in his reclined seat.

The steward approached. "Mr. Secretary, Sir? You wanted me to tell you when we were on approach."

Waking out of a deep sleep, he jumped. "Huh? Oh, yes, that's right. Thank you."

After Fendemere moved to the front of the aircraft, the steward returned the reclined bed to the upright position. "Sir, breakfast will be served by the time you finish shaving."

"Thank you. Have the pilot see me as soon as we pull up to the terminal."

The steward paused, turned his head, "Yes, Sir."

Fendemere sat in the foremost seat, opened an attaché case with one hand, and pulled his cell out with the other. After spreading out several folders, he punched numbers into the phone.

The steward brought his meal, poured coffee, and left. Fendemere pushed the speaker button, set the phone down, and buttered his toast as he waited for his call to be answered.

On the second ring, a thick accented voice came on the line. "Señor Fendemere, so good of you to call."

"I just arrived at the airport. My driver will have me there in an hour. Will your President be available for our discussion?"

"Sí, lo he hecho consciente de nuestras discusiones anteriores. Él está muy interesado."

The Rebel put his papers back in order and returned them to the proper place. "Thank you, I too am looking forward to our meeting. I'll see you soon my friend."

"Adios, mi amigo."

#####

Three hours later, Fendemere pushed his plate back. "Senor Presidente, you have out-done yourself. This has been the best meal I've been served in all my visits to your country. We appreciate your hospitality."

Presidente Juarez frowned at the Rebel. "Can you assure me the treaty you've negotiated with the Cubans is not more favorable to them than us?"

Fendemere moved his plate and silverware aside, and placed his attaché on the table. He removed two folders and handed them to the Mexican officials. "Sirs, please review this before you submit our agreement to your legislature. If you notice any differences, I'll be happy to make adjustments."

The Mexican President stood, lifted his wine glass to make a toast. "To our endeavor. May the union of 'The Republic Of America' and 'Los Estados Unidos de Mexico' be strong and fruitful."

Fendemere and the Mexican President's Chief of Staff rose and answered the tribute.

The President nodded and everyone moved toward the door. "Gentlemen, I must leave you. The main details have been agreed upon by your Presidente and me. You must have the final draft completed by this coming Friday. Understood?"

Both men continued walking on either side of the Mexican leader. Fendemere smiled and accepted the offered handshake. "Sir, that will be done. Both of you will have the final treaty on-time. My President has assured me the ROA Senate is eager to review our document."

I wonder if he realizes all the ramifications? Now the real negotiations begin. "Senor, I'm ready. Shall we meet on the terrace?"

"Yes, by all means. I'll have refreshments brought out." He clapped, and a servant appeared. "Bring refreshments on the veranda."

"Sí, señor, el cocinero tiene todo listo."

The Rebel patted his stomach as he sat. "I'm looking forward to eating some of his food again. That man really knows his way around a kitchen."

Two hours later, Fendemere put his fountain pen down. "Well, let's review what we've agreed to."

"Yes, that would be a good idea." The Mexican Chief of Staff picked up his tablet, and drew a line down the page. Let's see, numero uno, each Mexican State has the option of becoming a full-fledged state in the Republic Of America; dos, each Mexican State will remain part of a confederation of Mexican States; tres, every Mexican National will automatically become a citizen of the ROA, and cuatro, the armed forces of both countries will merge."

The Mexican gentleman put his paper down. "My friend, this is still a problem for us. You don't expect to do this overnight do you?"

The Rebel smiled, and puffed on his cigar. "No, Sir. Our suggestion is that every Mexican military unit will have a ROA unit of equal size attached. If you want, your Generals may select any of your units to be stationed in the ROA. Is that acceptable?"

"Sir, I don't really think our people are going to approve having your troops on Mexican soil."

Fendemere pointed his cigar at his friend. "This won't happen right away. Only when your people and government feel comfortable with this condition will we start the consolidation of our forces. We don't want to rush anything."

Both men stood and walked toward the front of the hacienda. Fendemere vigorously shook his friend's hand. "Deseo verte otra vez."

"Good-bye, I'm looking forward to seeing you again too."

#####

The next day, Fendemere arrived at Gressette's Rock Hill office. He nodded to Bobby, Cat, and Grimes. Then stood in front of his President. He pulled a rolled map from under his shoulder. As he laid it out in front of everyone, he said, "Sir, as your Secretary of State, as the President of The Knights of The Golden Circle, and as a true Southerner, I present to you the completed Golden Circle.

ABOUT THE AUTHOR

Jim was born on Staten Island, NY, and was raised in Southern California. While in junior high he started writing stories, but it wasn't until he joined the High Desert Chapter, California Writer's Club that he really started to focus on his work.

Jim recently retired from active duty with the California Army National Guard which completed a twenty-eight year career, which included a three-year enlistment in the U.S. Marines.

Currently Jim lives in Tigard, OR. And is working on a series of four mystery novels, and has written several short stories.

33314006R00154

Made in the USA
Columbia, SC
23 November 2018